Samantha Mackintosh

EGMONT

EGMONT

We bring stories to life

Kisses for Lula
First published 2010
by Egmont UK Limited
239 Kensington High Street
London W8 6SA

Text copyright © 2010 Samantha Mackintosh

The moral rights of the author and cover illustrator have been asserted

ISBN 978 1 4052 4962 1

1 3 5 7 9 10 8 6 4 2

www.egmont.co.uk

A CIP catalogue record for this title is available from the British Library

Printed and bound in Great Britain by the CPI Group

For my father

Chapter One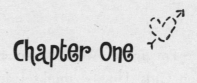

Sunday night, my bedroom, in despair

'Girls! I got an article published! In the *Herald*!' Alex stopped shrieking and shaking the newspaper to do a Christina Aguilera bump and jive in the doorway. 'Me, me, me! Famous at last!'

'Hardly,' drawled Carrie. 'Alex, get in here and focus on our friend. We three depart in' – she stopped to consult her watch, her head flopping back on my bed – 'twenty minutes, leaving Tallulah thoroughly in the dwang.'

'Up the stormy creek,' murmured Tam, checking for split ends in her long brown hair.

'Without a paddle,' ended Alex, no longer jubilant. She dropped her arms and folded the *Hambledon Herald* carefully before kicking my bedroom door shut. 'Okay, so what do we have?'

What we have is me, Tallulah Bird (aka Lula, Lu, Tatty, T-Bird (yes, like the car, *groan*), sometimes even Tatty Lula) in a frikking *desperate* state. I'm fifteen years and 360 days old.

AND
UNKISSED.

Why?

Because I'm jinxed. Well, everyone at my school – Hambledon Girls' High – thinks I am. Which means everyone at Hambledon Boys' High too, and that's the *real* problem.

Proof?

1. Bliddy Stan Pavorovich, my year-eight dance partner, getting rushed to A&E with food poisoning. Even before the dancing began! We'd just walked in the door!
2. Dr McCabe being called out when Robert Blugle zipped his bits into his jeans after an afternoon of innocent sunbathing with me at the uni pool.
3. Simon Smethy getting gum in his hair at the cinema on our first date. That bubblegum stuck so deep his whole head had to be shaved. It took him six months to convince the girls of Hambledon High that he wasn't a total thug.

So. Just a few incidents . . . Not worth a mention in my opinion, but with a witchy grandma . . . well, people jump to conclusions they shouldn't.

I focused on the now. My three best friends were staring at me with kindly pity in their eyes: Alex with her long dark hair, matching eyes and restless energy. Carrie with all the calm in the world, her brown eyes and elegantly cut chestnut hair. Tam with long tawny tresses, hazel eyes and a skin so porcelain it seemed she'd never seen the light of day, which pretty much summed up her other-worldliness.

'How did it *get* to this?' I wailed.

'Definitely Simon Smethy and the gum incident,' replied Alex promptly. 'He started the jinx rumour for real.'

'You're forgetting Cam Sharp-Jones getting that weird migraine every time he saw you. That was the clincher,' said Tam, giving me an understanding little pat on the arm.

'Stop!' I pleaded.

'Yeah, but the real nail in the coffin was Gianni Caruso ice skating at the pond over half term,' said Alex, throwing a handful of peanuts in her mouth. 'Mwhanuthin thinth,' she finished.

Tam stared at me. 'Gianni Caruso was with *you* that day?'

'Come on, Tam,' said Carrie. 'You know this.'

'I do not know this! He was what, like, your *date*?'

I flared my nostrils and narrowed my eyes ever so slightly. 'All these,' I said in a low voice, 'are coincidences. *Coincidences*, people.'

I saw my friends exchange glances and felt a sense of unease prickle up in goosebumps all over my body.

'Look, Lula,' said Tam gently, breaking the awkward silence, 'even if there is no jinx you've got to kiss someone to *prove* there isn't. You need a List of Candidates. Without a kiss before your birthday this Saturday, you're doomed. You'd have to go looking for strangers. And even then they wouldn't necessarily help, because a stranger is not going to spread the word that you're a safe smoocher – that's if they *survived* the experience . . .' She trailed off after fierce squinty glances from Alex and Carrie, but she'd said enough.

'Today is gone – that means Saturday is five days away. Frikly *frik*,' I groaned, dropping my head back in my hands. 'Frikking frikly FRIK!'

'It sucks,' agreed Alex, 'but . . .' She went a little blank, and her eyes glazed while she hunted for a bright side. A silver lining. A possibility that a normal teenage life for her friend was not totally down the toilet. Her eyes lit up. 'Tam is an *excellent* list-maker!'

'I am!' said Tam with fake confidence. She began writing really fast in her lyrics book. 'We'll help you beat this jinx, Lula.'

I shook my head sadly. 'The jinx, the rumour – whatever – has got too big.' I suddenly felt bad-mood lines creasing my forehead. My eyes narrowed. 'Simon Smethy and his big mouth . . .'

'Don't go thinking revenge, Tatty Lula,' warned Alex, wagging a finger at me and trying to get a look at Tam's list. 'There's no time for that. You need to be remembering my flirting tips, stocking up on breath mints, raiding Darcy's cupboard for cool clothes in preparation. Focus, girl.'

'But it's the holidays! Everyone's left Hambledon,' I bleated. (This is what comes of living in a town consisting of a university and a bunch of boarding schools.) 'There's no one left to kiss!'

'There will be, but don't lower your standards,' warned Carrie, her dark eyes serious. 'There's got to be a gorgeous local we've all overlooked.'

I spotted Alex giving Carrie that blank *are you out of your mind?* look.

'What?' said Carrie.

'Our friend is about to be sweet sixteen and never been kissed,' hissed Alex. '*There are no standards!*'

'Here's The List,' said Tam, hastily tearing a page from her lyrics book. 'These guys all live here. All aged twelve to twenty.'

'Twelve?' I squeaked. '*Twelve?*'

'Let me edit that,' said Carrie. She snatched The List from Tam, who whipped it back and shoved it in my face.

'Carrie,' said Tam sternly. (Tam is never stern.) 'If Tallulah Bird does not bag a man by the seventeenth of April it'll totally validate the jinx rumour and she'll be' – she blinked rapidly – '*alooone*. Till the end of her days.'

Chapter Two

Monday 12 April, too long till lunchtime. The girls have gone and left me 'working' at my holiday job

So here I am, a day later, sitting on the icy library floor puzzling over a very short list of who I could assault in a non-commital French-kissing kind of way.

LULA'S LAST CHANCES (*thanks, Tam*)
1. **Fat Angus** (*says it all*)
2. **Billy Diggle** (*ah, the twelve-year-old*)
3. **Bludgeon** (*Fat Angus's brother, not much better*)
4. **Gianni Caruso** (*victim of the ice-skating incident. What was Tam thinking? Was he likely to forget that two months ago I sliced his fingers off with my skates?*)
5. **Vadin Shariff** (*tends only to speak to girls in burkas*)
6. **Olaf Söderberg** (*no way he is younger than twenty! The guy has a GREY goatee!*)
7. **Arnold Trenchard** (*the best option, surely? And, let's face it, convenient cos he works at the library with me. Does he make my heart pound? He does not.*)

Splat splat splat.

Footsteps. Big feet in flip flops, by the sound of it. Wouldn't do to be caught skiving. Calling on my extensive special-forces training (i.e. watching more boxed sets of *24* and *The Wire* with Mum than was good for a healthy mind), I sat up soundlessly and peered through the book stacks.

Arnold Trenchard. Man of the moment.

Here he comes.

You can see him now, can't you? Just by me saying his name you've got the right picture of him in your head. Masses of curly red hair, glasses, tall but all slouched over. Bad clothes. *Such* bad clothes. Way too cold for flip flops.

Arnold was at the very bottom of Tam's list. For alphabetical reasons, but still.

The bottom.

'Tallulah? Where are you?'

I slumped down again. Sigh. 'Here, Arns. In the six hundreds.'

Shuffle, shuffle. He appeared round a book stack, but still couldn't see me.

Sigh again. 'Down here, Arnold.'

'Oh. What are you doing on the floor?'

'Contemplating my navel.'

'Oh. Hn. Have you seen Sophie Wenger anywhere? Mike wants her to go to the archives room for him.'

'Sophie Wenger? That crazy goth girl? What, she's

working here now? That's just *great*.' My mood grew dark. Sophie was as goody a two shoes as you could get with all those tattoos. She would rat me out for navel-gazing for sure. My leisure time during work hours could well be a thing of the past.

'She may have a pierced tongue, but she's unexpectedly normal,' said Arns, leaning against a book stack and flexing his toes.

'Don't be fooled,' I said ominously.

'Well, she's keeping out of our way, working for Mike. He's back from lunch, by the way. Wants to know if you've finished the photocopying.'

'Bliddy Stinky Mike. No, I have *not* finished the frikking photocopying!'

'Geez. Take a chill pill!' Arnold looked a little afraid. I could tell by the way his feet were suddenly motionless. Hmm. Nice feet, actually.

I glanced at The List then back up at Arnold, thinking, before shoving the paper into my jeans pocket and smiling sweetly.

'What do you want?' asked Arnold suspiciously.

Uh-oh, I thought.

'Would you help me, Arnold?' I batted my eyelashes, just once – for subtlety. 'With the photocopying?'

He shook his head sadly and said, 'You're out of your mind,' before shambling off again.

All things considered, I like Arnold. He is so uncool that popular people see him as kind of edgy in his individuality. Personally, I liked the way he didn't take crap from anyone. Including me. And he had hairless toes. Huh. It could be that Arnold *was* a good candidate for a kiss. He was my age, for one, and scientifically nerdy enough to pooh-pooh curses . . .

Curses!

Fffff!

Just five days till the dreaded birthday, all of them working at the library – that *had* to be enough time to seduce Arnold Trenchard. And enough time to forget about the boy I'd been in love with since I was six years old.

My mind beginning to tick, I hauled myself to my feet and tried not to breathe too deeply. These ageing books are full of microbes. Lung-damaging little mites that keep my mum coughing till the wee hours. As head honcho of the historical research section of this university library, it's lucky she loves her job. Like, she gets excited about local farmers who die and leave all their diaries to the library . . .

'Elias Brownfield kept a diary for sixty years!' she squeaked, when I found her in the back office a little later. 'Noted the rainfall every day! What an amazing meteorological record! Hmm? Isn't that incredible?'

I gave her a slow blink. Her small, round body seemed ready to bounce off the walls.

'Ye-es, Mum,' I said in calming tones. 'Have you seen the photocopy card?'

Mum frowned. 'Is it this one?'

'Yep.' I plucked it from her outstretched fingers. 'Thanks.'

'You left it in the machine. Mabel complained.'

I made a face, not a very nice one.

Mum sighed. 'Mike's looking for you.'

'Ew.'

'Tallulah Bird,' said Mum in her stern voice. 'Mike is a lovely man and the best chief librarian we've ever had. I wish you'd give him a break!' She put down the farmer's journals and made a tortured sound in the back of her throat. 'At least the copy card's all you've lost today. I can't find that bundle of documents on Coven's Quarter. I photocopied it last thing Friday night and now the copies *and* the originals have disappeared. You seen anything anywhere?'

'Mum,' I said in a stressy voice, 'no pressure, but those documents are Coven's Quarter's only hope of not getting bulldozed. Even then nobody's sure the council will be persuaded.' Mum ignored me, but her desk rummaging moved up a notch. 'And Alex got her first ever article published on it in the *Herald* so it's a hot topic. She wrote that we're all counting on your historical evidence. You want me to help you look?' Mum snorted and started going through the filing cabinet, slamming the drawers really hard.

I was suddenly just as stressed as she was, the seduction of Arnold Trenchard instantly insignificant.

Coven's Quarter is this weird collection of enormous rocks in the middle of the woods to the west of our town. It's known as a spot where druids, witches, that kind of crowd, have met since time began. My Grandma Bird was reputed to be the witchiest of them all and Coven's Quarter was her special place. She'd gather up there with her cronies at least once a year, always trying to get me to go along with her. We had some kind of special thing, Grandma and I; we clicked. 'Cos you're witchy, just like me,' she'd say with a wink, but nuh uh, no way. I did not need more craziness in my life. Why couldn't she pick my older sister, Darcy?

'Darcy doesn't have it,' Grandma Bird would say sadly. 'But it sizzles out of Tallulah.'

And over the years, somehow, that's how the rest of the town saw me too. Not a problem if they're looking for a cure for warts, but what boy wants a weirdy witch girlfriend? Exactly. Big problem – even though Grandma died a year ago, and I've never, ever cured a wart.

But I don't hold anything against Grandma Bird. It still hurt to think of her not being here and no way was some hairy-butt developer going to move in and mow down the place she loved most in all the world.

I bit my lip so hard I tasted iron, my eyes starting to scan piles of paper everywhere. I noticed Mum had stopped her frantic search and was looking at me hard. 'Hey,' she said gently. 'Go get a hot drink, you muggins. Those documents are here somewhere. Harrow Construction will never build townhouses on Grandma Bird's place, okay?'

'Okay, Mum,' I said, swallowing the lump in my throat.

I hurried out of her office and bumped into Stinky Mike. Literally.

Eugh.

I don't know what he smells of, but *oh* it's horrible. When I call the man Stinky Mike it's because that's what he *is* – it's not just me being mean. Maybe I'd be nicer to him if he were nicer to me. Maybe the man just has some kind of glandular problem. Maybe he's lovely, deep down inside . . .

'Tallulah,' said Stinky Mike in his whispery voice, his little baldy head nodding violently. 'Watch where you're going.'

See that? That there? Would a nice person say that?

'Miiichael!' came another whispery voice from behind him.

A strange smile chased across his lips. 'Mabel,' he said fondly, taking off his glasses.

Mabel, the library's deputy chief and the closest living thing to a praying mantis that isn't actually green, scuttled to his side. 'Michael, I wanted to show you these records on the north-west property you asked about,' she simpered.

12

I tried to ignore them, crossing quickly to the casual-staff desk, which is unfortunately next to Mabel's. I wanted to check emails. As I clicked into Gmail I heard Stinky Mike laugh. It was high-pitched and unpleasant to hear. Mabel was laughing too, but in a gaspy way, and I could tell she didn't really know what was so amusing.

Though she weirds me out, I feel sorry for Mabel. Every bone of her angular frame sticks out, making knobs and lines against the thin nylon of the 1940s dresses she wears when she's not in tweed. And she has a vast range of nervous twitches, mostly to do with adjusting the gold-rimmed spectacles that slide up and down a long hooky nose. She was fiddling with them now, her rheumy pale-blue eyes flitting restlessly behind the crescent lenses.

'This is just what I was after, Mabel.' Stinky Mike smiled slowly and lifted a fat hand to her shoulder. He squeezed gently.

Ik!

Revolted, I hastily blanked the images of Stinky Mike and Tweedy Mabel from my mind and scarpered downstairs to blind myself with the copier for the rest of the afternoon. There was a desperate seduction to plan. I checked my watch.

No!

Yeech!

Twelve o'clock already!

I was down to four and a half days!

Where was Arnold Trenchard? Hurrying across the library, the memory of that one and only first love, the delectable Ben Latter, intruded for a moment, but I blocked it out. No chance of that, jinx or no jinx.

Chapter Three

Tuesday 13 April, sooo early, like, *dawn* maybe

I woke with a start.

Someone in the room above me was yodelling with an intensity piercing enough to shatter a wine glass, let alone the eggshell fragility of my skull.

I pulled a pillow over my head and the noise stopped.

But no.

My little sister Blue had only paused to catch her breath.

'Lula? Are you ready to go?' Mum's voice trailed up the passage to my bedroom door.

Frik! Forgot I had a library shift. Bum bum bum. 'Just got to finish up!' I shouted back, with a twinge at such a bare-faced lie.

Scuffle scuffle up the hall. I could hear numerous plastic bags being gathered together. 'Shall I start walking?' she said loudly outside my door, amidst hurried rustling.

'Yes!' Throwing back the duvet. 'Which way're you going?'

'Past St Alban's.'

The elite boys' school. Plodding this route with Mum would ordinarily be a trauma, but in the holidays the place is a graveyard.

''Kay! I'll catch up!' I rolled out of bed and assessed the crumpled clothing tossed on the floor from yesterday.

Big sigh.

No one to impress.

Pulling on my jeans, something rustled in my pocket. The List. *Frik*. What was I thinking? Just four poxy days till my birthday!

Arnold!

Seduction!

Of course someone to impress!

I had to look fanfabulouslytastic!

Yesterday afternoon had been a total washout because Arnold had been put to work in the library's rare-documents room deep underground and I hadn't laid eyes on him for the rest of the day. I paused in front of my near-empty cupboard, wracked with indecision. If I were late again, Stinky Mike would fire me for sure. I weighed it up: job . . . or . . . lifetime curse. Hmm.

If I didn't have money for chocolate, I was doomed anyway.

I'll wow Arnold tomorrow, I vowed, pulling on my T-shirt faster than Blue can shove a pea up her nose, and was out the door without brushing my teeth or my hair. The apple I snatched sorted out the gnashers and my hair was all scrunched up high on my head in that, um, *I've just got out of bed* look that I do a little too often.

By the time I leapt up the garden steps to the front gate, Mum had already disappeared from sight. I sprinted down the road and caught sight of her cruising down the hill into town. I grinned despite myself. Watching my mother from a distance always makes me smile. She wears enormous caftans, and her short white hair stands up in a shock all around her head. You'd never think she once raced Harleys and drank beer out of other people's helmets. I caught her as she rounded the last corner of the block.

'Good morning, Dr Bird!' I said, like a centimetre from her ear.

'*Eeeee!*' Mum leapt away like a flying tree frog and I fell about laughing till I could barely breathe. 'Cripes, Lula! Will you not creep up like that! In today's world! You could have been a mugger! You're lucky I didn't brain you with my bag!'

'Bags!' I gasped.

'What?'

I stood up slowly. 'Bags. Plural.' And took a deep breath. 'What's with the Third World's quota of plastic?'

Mum's fingers were turning blue round the handles of a gazillion shopping bags, all stuffed with –

'HEY! Mum! Where are you taking Golly? And Bubbles! *Geez!*'

'Lula!' Mum whisked the bags round to the other side of herself and started beetling off briskly again. 'You're too old for these things. I'm taking it all to Oxfam.'

'Noooo!' I wailed. 'Nooooo!'

She yelped as I grabbed the bag with Golly and Bubbles. 'Tallulah, give that back immediately. Golly is no longer politically acceptable, for a start.'

'Muuuum! Please!' I'm embarrassed to admit this, but my eyes filled with tears. I pulled Golly and Bubbles from the bag and clutched them to my chest.

'Tallulah. No nonsense. There's absolutely no room in the house for all this stuff!'

'Mum, we have a huge house! And if you let me live in the annexe, you wouldn't need to bother about storage!'

'Don't start with that again. You've already taken over all of the cellar with your motor mechanics.'

I started to babble about how no one used the cellar anyway, but Mum fixed me with a rare steely gaze. 'Lu, don't you think it's a little unfair if we let you stay in the annexe and your sister has to stay in the main house?'

I sniffed and rummaged in Mum's handbag for a tissue. 'I'm the oldest at home now. Pen will get a chance when I move out. And Blue when she moves out.'

'Ohhh, *you*! Blue is *four*,' growled Mum. 'Let's talk about it later. Come on, we're going to be late. I've got a meeting with Security this morning. No sign of the Coven's Quarter documents yesterday. Somebody must have taken them.' Mum looked genuinely worried. 'Don't say anything to anyone about this, Lu.'

As we began hurrying towards the university campus, I decided to try another tack: 'Mum, this annexe thing . . . How about –'

'Oh look,' exclaimed Mum. 'There are still some boys in St Alban's!'

How I kept walking I. Do. Not. Know.

Dear. God.

Let. Me. Die.

Now.

Let's set the scene for you here, lovely reader. Me red-eyed, in yesterday's clothes, clutching unattractive childhood doll and politically incorrect Golly. With Mum in flowing caftan and hand-hewn hair. And 'some boys' from St Alban's. It's just unspeakable on all counts. Could it get any worse?

Hoooo, yes.

First of all, not *some* boys. An entire row. Lined up on the boundary wall, legs hanging over on to the pavement. Grinning like apes at us scurrying along. I couldn't look. Just turned my face away, praying Mum would increase the pace along with me.

Second of all, my mother is a law unto herself. She is mostly hermit-like. Every decade or so she has a flash of sociability. I should have been vigilant.

Vigilant.

'Hello!' she now chirped to the mob at large. 'Are you boys not on holiday?'

'Hi, Mrs Bird,' replied the biggest and the blondest. (They know her from library visits.) 'We're doing extra graft for the Science Fair. Which we'd like kept quiet,' he added with undue emphasis, looking at me pointedly.

I nodded obediently, snatched another look at him and ducked my head in horror.

Oh no! Frikfrikkery frikly frik! It's him! It's Ben Latter! My first and only real crush. I squeezed my eyes shut so tightly that black dots speckled my vision. But even with eyes closed, even with black dots, I could still see Ben Latter's blue, blue eyes, lips that gave me shivers, his perfect sun-kissed hair, that highly charged body taut with tonedness that you only get from hours of, you know, sailing or polo or . . .

I felt myself get hot all over and might have made a small strangled sound. *Eemph*, maybe, or *arrark*. Something unattractive.

I felt painfully, agonisingly aware of my crumpled clothes, my scrunched hair, my furry teeth. The skanky plastic bags in my hands. And then, still staring at my grungy trainers, I caught a glimpse of movement. Suddenly Ben Latter's shoes were facing mine.

'Do I know you?' he asked.

Fffff!

I couldn't breathe. I couldn't look up. I couldn't do anything at all.

Someone said, 'What's the bet she's been Ben Flattered.' There were titters behind me and I distinctly heard 'Is that a baby *doll*?' from the ranks.

I felt Mum look at me, very quickly, and she stepped closer to stand right beside me. 'Of course you know me, young man,' she tweeted to Ben. 'I distinctly remember your last class visit. Such *energetic* boys, aren't you all? Well! Science, hmm? Good luck!'

And we were off. In silence. Mum to her lovely wooden-panelled office and me to crumple next to the photocopier with a vacant stare.

There was no way a person could undergo such humiliation and still be breathing.

Oh, who had I been kidding all this time? Ben Latter didn't even *know* me. And thank frik for that.

I tried not to think about how just one look at him made me feel like a pile of mushy peas. *Maybe I am jinxed,* I thought to myself. *Maybe some of Grandma Bird's crazy magic* has *messed me up somehow.*

Alex's voice came into my head.

Focus, girl.

Okay. Maybe, just maybe, if I could somehow land my first kiss, then everything else would fall into place. I'd be normal. I'd be amazing. *If I could get Arnold Trenchard to oblige.* Uh-oh. What if that went all wolly winkas too? Who else was there?

With a dry mouth I pulled The List out and was soon muttering quietly to myself, assessing all the options, trying not to think of blue, blue eyes, that strong body . . .

'Tatty?'

'Nyhee!' I gasped, crumpling The List in my hand and resisting the urge to chew it up and swallow it. 'Sophie! Geez, you gave me a fright.'

'What are you doing here? Shouldn't you be working?'

See what I mean? How can someone with multiple piercings have this solid a work ethic?

'I *am* working,' I said tetchily. 'Just planning how I'm going to do all of Mike's photocopying.'

'Have you seen my access card?'

'No. How'd you get in without it?'

'Security let me in, but I need to find it today or file it as lost. It's been gone since last Friday maybe.'

'Right,' I said. I mean, like I care about Sophie's security card in the grand scheme of my seriously sucky life. Suddenly two things occurred to me: 'Hey, you could check with Mabel. She found my copy card. Obviously got an eye for finding lost cards.'

'Right,' echoed Sophie, looking at me oddly. I know, my suggestion was lame, but I needed to *sound* like I cared so I could broach my second idea.

'Um, don't you have a brother, Sophie?' I smiled at her encouragingly.

Sophie smirked. 'Don't even think about it, witch girl. He likes his fingers.'

Well, what do you say in reply to that, hm? Exactly. Not much. As Sophie left, I sank back down with The List. It was quiet. My stomach rumbled peacefully. My dark thoughts began to float away.

Then:

'Dude.' Arnold loomed above me.

I jumped. Frik. Arns was not supposed to see me today, looking like this.

I shoved The List into my back pocket and considered options. Maybe I should let Arns see my vulnerable side.

Yes!

That could work! He might want to cheer me up with a kiss! A French one!

'Don't speak to me, Arns,' I said in a quiet desperate-maiden voice. 'I am the laughing stock of all St Alban's and may infect you with social unacceptableness.'

'Too late, my friend.' (Oh no! The F word . . . not good.) Arnold slumped beside me. 'Tallulah, I'm starting to think carefully about a makeover.' Turning to look at me, he bit his lip anxiously. 'I've got a pash.'

My heart sank. *Nooo!* After sixteen years Arnold was choosing NOW to be interested in the opposite sex? Couldn't he have waited a few minutes for me to make my move *before* he decided to fancy someone else?

I gritted my teeth. Still the brutality crept out:

'Arnold. The cool speak. It's not working for you.'

'Neither are the clothes,' he agreed.

'No. The clothes do nothing.'

'Is there anything to work with?' His eyes were pleading and wide. A little too wide.

'The desperation is also not a good look.'

'Duh, of course I'm desperate!' he cried. 'Did you know the Science Fair lot from PSG are here?'

'The girls as well as the boys?' I could feel my forehead crease in distress. Pamponia School for Girls was the neighbouring school to St Alban's. More competition for scant boys. This was not good news.

'So you know about St Alban's.' Arnold sighed. 'Wish you'd given me a little warning. The walk over here was . . . not comfortable.'

'Were they all on the wall?'

'Like buzzards on a wire.'

'The horror.'

'Tell me about it.'

'So who are you in luuurve with?' I couldn't help it. I was feeling perkier. Despite heading for the black world of a lifetime jinx I could be happy for others. Yes. Yes, I could, dammit.

'Mona de Souza.'

(Mona de Souza! We're talking The Hottest Girl in

Hambledon here.)

'Yowzer. I'm pleased to see you aim high, Arnold.'

He sighed. 'Look, Tallulah, just help me. Without any of your silly sarcasm.'

I swallowed my pride. 'I'm hardly the ideal candidate. You're viewing snog-free city here, Arns.'

'Oh . . . yes. The curse. Pffteehee.' How could he *laugh*? He flapped his hand dismissively. 'Surely, though, it's more because everyone knows you're in love with Ben Latter. And have been since Year Two.'

'Year One.'

'Whatever. And you're so bad at flirting. I'm not coming to you for that. It's just that *you know how to look good*.'

I found the superficial compliment oddly comforting in this dark, dark time. 'Thank you,' I said.

'Please, Tatty. Help me look good,' begged Arnold.

I gazed at him and sighed. He was clearly desperate for Mona. He was clearly lost to me. I pulled The List from my back pocket and grabbed a pen from the top of the copier.

'What are you doing?' asked Arns as I crossed his name out.

I should start at the top. Fat Angus. Nooo. I had a feeling my sister was up to something there. I shuddered. Better her than me. Next: Billy Diggle. Working at the DVD rental place must mean he's really mature, right? Responsible. Wise way beyond his few, few years.

Oh, please. I wasn't even fooling myself.

Next up: Bludgeon. Gulp. Next? Gianni Caruso. Oh, yep. I could see *that* happening.

'Tallulah!' yelled Arns.

I jumped in fright and hit my head on the copier's A3 photo-paper tray.

Yeech! 'What's *with* you, Arnold?'

'The Science Fair is Monday next week. It's already Tuesday. I have three and a half working days before Mona de Souza is in wall-to-wall calculus seminars and I'm back at school! There are no men in Hambledon right now except me – my time is now! *Now!*'

'You're forgetting the St Alban's guys,' I said. 'Those bliddy buzzards on a wire.'

And then it hit me!

Of course! St Alban's boys! Forget The List! I jumped to my feet in wild excitement, but Arnold was already taking up my air time:

'Mona doesn't like public schoolboys,' Arnold was saying. 'Everyone knows that.'

'But I might!' I squeaked, doing a little dance. 'They don't know about the jinx! And Mona could help!' Thanks to this morning Ben My First Love was definitely a lost cause, but there were plenty of others!

Arnold didn't bat an eye. 'You get me Mona; I'll get you a man,' he promised.

'Makeover at yours? Eight p.m.?' I said blithely.

'Done.' We high-fived (I know. I wouldn't do it in public. Just humouring Arns) and went our separate ways. Well, Arnold went back to the stacks and I got flirty with the photocopier.

I felt a shiver run down my spine.

Mona de Souza, Hambledon It Girl, just *had* to know a guy over twelve with all his fingers . . .

Chapter Four

Tuesday, late afternoon

I tramped home alone. Mum was working late – Security had suggested someone who might have 'borrowed' the documents, and Mum had to make a few discreet calls. I had a flash of guilt. Alex would expect me to be helping with something – she'd made me promise that I'd keep sending snippets to the *Hambledon Herald* to keep her storyline on Coven's Quarter alive, but for now there was nothing I could do, and definitely no articles to write. My mother did not need that kind of publicity: a MISSING DOCUMENTS headline would not help her cause.

I hefted my bag higher on my shoulder and took a right up the final hill home. The pointed rooves and turrets of the Setting Sun, the old-age home across the street from our house, were visible now. It was a huge rambling mansion, much bigger than our own home, a storey higher, with two more turrets than our lowly one. Both houses were the last on the road, a kind of full stop for the town. From that point our road, Hill Street, became a potholed track, winding up and up into the woods. The wide stretch of tarmac was divided in two by a long green swathe of unruly grass punctuated by a massive tree stump and a flaking fire-hydrant sign opposite the Setting Sun and the Bird residence.

I pushed hard against our small, rusty front gate, hidden in a welter of rambling roses. I was glad I hadn't asked Arnold round here. The house was a complete tip. And then there was the fact that Dad was oft passed out in the front bedroom, snoring loud enough to deafen the OAPs at the Setting Sun. (He drinks. A *lot*.)

When I got in, the house was silent. Grrr. Dad should've been getting dinner ready, and it sure didn't sound like *that* was happening.

I threw my bag down with a crash and cupped my mouth with my hands, face tilted towards the ceiling. 'HI, DAAAD,' I yelled at the top of my lungs. '*I'm hooo-ooome!* WHAT'S FOR SUPPER?'

There was a thud just above me, and a groan. I grinned. Result. *Yesss!* I pounded upstairs, belting out Eminem's latest as I went. I got outside Mum and Dad's bedroom door and paused to yell out the chorus a second time before stopping suddenly as if something had just occurred to me.

Knocking timidly on the door, I called quietly, 'Dad? Are you in there?'

'Spawn of Satan,' came a croaking reply.

I smirked. Abuse I could tolerate. Cooking dinner a third night in a row, after that stunner of a Sunday lunch too, could not be contemplated.

'Can I come in?' I whispered deferentially.

'Ha,' was the rasping response.

I took that as a yes and pushed at the door.

'Whoa!' I moaned, back at full volume and clutching my nose. 'Dad! It *reeks* in here!'

'Have some respect. I'm not well.'

'No, no, Dad. You're not wriggling out of doing supper that easily.'

'I mean it, T-Bird.' He tilted his head slightly to look up at me. 'Please.'

'No way! You've been festering in here since Saturday. That cold's got to be done now. You need fresh air.' Stomping over to the window I could feel my blood starting to simmer. I had stuff to do. Arns + Mona = kiss 4 Lula. Arnold's makeover needed my full attention. It just had to work, because going back to The List with its pre-teens and amputees was not an option.

At the window, I turned to stare Dad down. Now, there was a lot I wanted to say to my father, but he'd been a different person since Grandma Bird died. A bit volatile. He's an English lecturer at the university, but he writes poetry and song lyrics too. And he's worked with a lot of famous musicians. Why I'm telling you this is so you understand that he's got that creative temperament that means he's allowed to be ultra-sensitive and moody. (What a load of rot. If he just stopped drinking ten pints of beer a night, he'd be a different man.)

I'd heard Mum trying to talk sense to him last week . . .

'Spenser, what's going on? It seems to me your life is going downhill.'

. . . but it didn't seem like the talking sense had worked.

I yanked the curtains open and the late afternoon sun shafted straight into the gloom, lighting up the pathetic bundle on the bed. Dad howled. (I'm being kind here. He actually squealed.)

'My eyes! My eyes!'

'Oh, please. Anyone would think you had measles.'

'I probably have!'

I flung the window wide open and leaned out to breathe. Mum was at the front gate. She looked tired and anxious.

'You okay, Lula?' she called.

'Dad's still got man flu,' I answered. Pause. 'You'll have to do dinner.'

Even from my first-storey height I could see Mum's teeth grinding. She shoved at the gate with her right elbow, bags crashing and slithering in her hold. Her mutters grew louder and I was about to offer dinner services to save us all from the fallout – in return for a lift to Arns's later, of course – when the old soak spoke.

'You're letting your mother make dinner? If I didn't feel so terrible,' said Dad, still motionless on the bed, 'I'd get up and tan your hide.'

'Huh,' I said over my shoulder, fumbling with the window latch. 'You think you feel terrible now . . . wait till Mum serves up her chicken-liver stew.' I waved at Mr Kadinski staggering out of the Setting Sun opposite our house. He waved his stick back and started tackling the steps down from the veranda.

I moved away from the window before he could call for help. (I know how that sounds, but I was up to my eyes in everything and Mr K would be better without grumpy me right now.) A low moan came from under the duvet. I sighed. Maybe Dad *was* terribly ill.

'Okay, Dad, I promise to do supper on the condition that you get up and shower and come downstairs.'

'Don't make me, T.'

'Oh! Can you smell chicken livers? I think I can smell chicken livers . . .' I mused.

Dad flung the covers aside with surprising energy for someone on the brink of death. I clamped my nostrils closed and edged towards the door while he unfolded himself from the bed.

Once I was certain he was headed for the shower, I bolted downstairs to the kitchen to stop Mum from cooking up a load of offal.

Dinner was good, not least because everyone in the house actually sat round the table and ate together. Except for my littlest sister, Blue, who was already in bed. Great-aunt Phoebe was clearly feeling pensive. Blue had probably worn her out with an energetic *you be the murderous troll* game. (Aunt Phoebe is in charge of Blue. She's the only one who could be.)

'How're you, Aunt Phoebe?' I asked, piling noodles on to everyone's plates.

Her dark eyes glanced up for a second through trendy steel glasses, her chic black hair as immaculate as ever. 'I'm glad you cooked, Tallulah. I needed to refuel.'

'Mm,' said Pen, twirling an astonishing amount of noodles on to her fork and into her mouth, 'ss gmmeud.'

'You owe me favours,' I said ungraciously. 'All of you.'

They nodded humbly.

'And I've been thinking,' I continued, sitting down. 'As principal hovelkeeper, I feel I need a bit of personal space and –'

'The annexe is mine,' hissed Pen.

'Girls,' said Mum warningly.

Dad closed his eyes and whimpered.

Aunt Phoebe pursed her Chanel-red lips.

'It will be, Pen,' I said reasonably. 'I've only got a couple years more of school and then I'm outta here.'

'Oh?' said Mum. 'And what about going to university?'

Dad whimpered again, and shifted so he could slump with his forehead on his hand and still shovel in the stir-fry.

'I am, but Brighton. For art.'

Mum went pink. 'My love. You wouldn't do that to us. The tuition fees. The res fees. We get massive reductions here at Hambledon.'

'I have ambitions,' I persevered, flinging my arms in a wide circle. A shred of green pepper hit the far wall. Dad flinched.

Aunt Phoebe maintained a studious silence.

'But, but –'

'Oh, Mum,' said Pen. 'She's winding you up. This is her decoy. So when she flexes her fingers for the annexe, you see it as the lesser of two evils and say yes. Don't fall for it. *I'm* the worthy candidate. Me with my neatness and efficiency. You'll never have to worry about whether the place is secure if I'm the resident thereof.'

(For The Record: my sister Pen is *the* most slovenly of us all. She looks respectable, but noooo. She could fight every ailment known to man with the selection of penicillin she cultivates under her bed in crusty old dishes. And don't be fooled by the way she talks. She is only fourteen.)

I let my jaw hang open and shook my head slowly in disbelief. '*Resident thereof?* Don't talk like that, Penelope. You are not forty.'

'Forty's not that old,' muttered Dad, running his hand through his thick brown hair.

'Sure,' I said hastily. 'Plus you look good for your age, Dad.'

'You can move into the annexe, T-Bird,' he said, and pushed himself up and away from the table. 'Right now if you like. I'm going back to bed.'

'*Whaaaaaat?*' shrieked Pen.

I laughed long and hard. Even Mum was smiling.

'Give it a rest, Pen, dear,' she said. 'You'll get your chance too.'

'It'll be infested with disease, and pestilence, and mould and sundry funguses, by the time I –'

'Fungi,' I said, and promptly regretted it. I needed to shower anyway before going to Arns's place, but it took forever to get the noodles out of my hair.

Mum agreed I deserved a lift to Arnold's house.

'Be gentle with him, Tallulah,' she said, pulling up outside his gate. 'No tattoos. Call me when you're done. I don't suppose you'll be going anywhere on foot with that.' She nodded over at my ancient sewing machine on the back seat.

'I appreciate the lift, Mum,' I said.

'Better than walking past the St Alban's dining halls after supper,' she replied.

Sometimes I think I underestimate Mum's intuition. Pulling out an enormous backpack, I slammed the passenger door and had begun wrestling with the back door when Arns loped up.

'Hi, Mrs Bird,' he said cheerily to Mum, then stopped dead when he saw me staggering under the weight of my bag.

'Uhhh, you staying the night?' he asked me nervously.

Mum pursed her lips and sucked in her cheeks. I did not grace his query with a reply.

'Help me with the sewing machine, will you?'

'Ohh!' Arns looked relieved and I felt strangely irritated. 'It's all your makeover supplies. Good.' He scurried round and had the sewing machine balanced deftly under his left arm by the time Mum had fired up the Citroën. He slammed the door and waved her off. I'm sure I could hear her cackling all the way to West Street, four roads over, but what are children for if not to provide endless entertainment for their parentals. I sighed and followed Arns in through his front door. He headed straight upstairs. I followed, hard on his heels.

'Um. Shouldn't I say hi to your folks?'

'Mum's out on a case, Dad's dead.'

'Oh, geez. Geez. Sorry, Arns. I'm sure I knew that.'

'Forget it. Let's get makeovering.'

'Coo–' I started to say, but on arrival at his bedroom, Arns flung the door open and it came out as, '–ell!'

'Like it?'

'No.'

'No? I've spent hours doing this!'

'You'll have to start again.' I walked into the freshly painted room. The sheer redness of it all made me feel slightly sick. I looked up. 'Thank God you didn't get to the ceiling.'

I heard someone behind me and turned to see Arns's sister, Elsa. 'He said it was the colour of passion,' she said, and that was it. One look at Arns's puzzled face and I dropped my bag, bending over double and shouting with laughter so loudly my throat hurt. She crumpled over too, the only sound an occasional gasp for air.

Arns dumped the sewing machine on his bed with not enough care for my liking.

'Is this humour at my expense?' he asked.

I caught a glimpse of his face looking suddenly vulnerable behind the mock fury, and pulled myself together, wiping my eyes. Elsa mumbled something about getting more paint, and crawled on her hands and knees out of the room, still struggling for breath.

I bent across to lift up the sewing machine from the bed. 'Where can I put this, Arns?'

He gestured numbly to a desk in the corner.

'Perfect,' I said, going over, and put it down carefully.

'I, er . . .' said Arns, taking off his glasses and polishing them on his baggy woolly jumper.

'I knew it!'

Arnold jumped. He saw the look in my eye and took a step back. 'Uh-oh, what now?' he asked.

'You've got a *great* nose. The glasses have got to go.'

'No, no, Lula. Come on now.'

'Have you never tried contacts?'

'They make me feel vulnerable.'

'You don't want to show your face.'

'It's not that.' Though Arnold seemed suddenly unsure. 'I worry they'll fall out, or I'll get infected eyes and not be able to see or – or something,' he ended lamely.

'And you're supposed to be some kind of genius.' I shook my head sadly.

'I wear them sometimes,' was the pathetic defence. 'When I go running.'

'Running. Interesting.'

'Whoa, Tallulah, I'm going to stop telling you stuff. I don't like where things are going. Perhaps this is a bad idea.'

'Three words.'

'Hn?'

'Mona de Souza.'

'Oh. Yes.' Arnold's brow furrowed.

'So, Arns. You got a full-length mirror anywhere?'

His wary eyes never leaving my face, he took a step towards the built-in cupboards and pulled a door open. An enormous mirror glinted red with reflected light.

'Great.' I pulled the chair from the desk in front of it and gestured to the client to sit down. 'Towels?'

'Bathroom. End of the hall.'

'Scissors?'

He jumped straight up off the chair and whacked the bottom of my chin with the top of his head.

'Fffffriiiik! Frik! Frik!' I clutched my face, seeing stars. 'I think there's blood!'

'Blood? Sorry sorry sorry! You okay? Scissors did you say? I'm not very good with scissors – I mean, blood.'

'Did someone say blood?'

'Elsa! I've hit her and she says she's bleeding,' rattled Arns.

'I knew I couldn't leave you alone with her,' cried Elsa from the doorway.

'Hey!' said Arns and I simultaneously.

Dropping a load of heavy stuff on the floor, Elsa came right over. 'No offence, but you two are an accident waiting to happen.' She prised my fingers from my face. 'No blood.' Arns stomped off to the bathroom. I could hear him running water and rummaging in cupboards. 'Are you all right, Tatty?'

I opened my eyes and swallowed carefully. Everything north of my neck hurt. 'I think I bit my tongue in half,' I whispered.

'Open your mouth.'

I obeyed. Elsa was about the same age as Pen, eighteen months younger than me, but two inches taller. She was lithe and strong-looking in a frightening German-aerobics-instructor kind of way. I generally wanted to do what she said.

'It's still in one piece.'

'Thank God,' I slurred.

'Could still be bleeding, but probably just the walls reflecting.'

'Nff?' I was alarmed, and swallowed carefully again before crawling to Arns's mirror and dropping my jaw to investigate damages done. 'Ungrhf.'

'Ouch,' agreed Elsa. 'It *is* bleeding. Good thing you haven't got a boyfriend. Kissing could be a problem. Have a paracetamol.' She rummaged in her jeans pocket, came up with an ancient-looking pack of pills and went off for a glass of water.

Arns returned.

'You cretin!' I slurred. 'I come here to help and now look!' I stuck my tongue out at him. '*Look!*'

'Oh,' said Arnold, slightly distressed. 'I'm really sorry, Tallulah. At least it wasn't your nose. The tongue is the fastest healing organ of the body. You know. Because of the saliva.' He sat down in the chair with the towel draped demurely round his shoulders. 'Sorry,' he said for the umpteenth time. 'I'll be good now.'

'You better be,' I growled, and came up behind him again, staring at his reflection in front of me in the full-length mirror.

Elsa appeared with water and I popped two pills and swallowed with a grimace. It felt like half my tongue flapped open with that gulp of water. Eeenf.

Arns handed me a pair of scissors, and Elsa started rolling out dustsheets and pushing furniture around.

'Let's discuss this before we get going,' said Arns politely.

'Okay,' I agreed amiably. 'Where is your comb, Arnold?'

'You sound angry. How long will you be angry with me? Does your tongue still hurt?'

'Comb?'

'Brush. Top drawer bedside cabinet.'

Elsa, already repainting the walls, began to laugh quietly.

'Wait!' said Arnold.

But it was too late. I'd opened the drawer and was staring at the entire Western world's supply of condoms glittering in shiny foil beneath one of those toddler-sized hairbrushes.

I took out the brush and shut the drawer with a grin. Arnold was forgiven. I love a boy with ambition. 'You dealin'?' I asked in a fake American accent.

'Ha bloody ha.'

'The good boy' – I winked over at Elsa who was trying not to laugh – 'he swears.'

'Just the tip of the iceberg,' promised my client's sister, sweeping away with Bright White interior paint like a woman possessed.

It's hard to cut hair with blunt scissors and a baby-hair brush when you've never done it before, but I have to say the results were pretty incredible.

Arns blinked, swallowed and cleared his throat. His eyes didn't leave his reflection. I took the towel and a sheepful of hair away from his shoulders and he stood up slowly. At last he turned round to face me.

'I think your work here is done,' he said, a slow smile transforming his face. He suddenly bounced out from behind the cupboard door to face his sister. 'Elsa! Look!' He spread his arms wide.

Elsa stood from her crouched position over a skirting board and blinked in surprise.

'Wow, Arns!'

I grinned happily.

She put down the roller and the paintbrush and pushed the hair out of her face with the back of her hand. 'You – you look . . . *amazing*.'

'The walls are looking good too, Elsa,' I noted.

'Yes,' admitted Arns.

'Bro, you owe me big,' Elsa said with narrowed eyes. 'This is going to need another coat tomorrow.'

The comment reminded me of my own indebted family. I checked my watch. 'We've got to hustle. I don't want to call my mum for a lift any later than ten.'

'Arns, you clear up,' commanded Elsa. 'Just leave that paint tray and that roller. I'm going to explain your wardrobe to Tatty.'

'I –' started Arnold. Then he tore his eyes from the reflection in the mirror and looked at the transformation of his room. 'Yes, Elsa,' he said meekly. 'Thank you,' and he started clearing paint tins, brushes and rollers away. Elsa was already talking nineteen to the dozen and opening up the other doors of the built-in cupboards, but I was fascinated by her brother. He currently held the handles of Sahara Sunset, Passion's Flower and African Earth all in his left hand with a dustsheet bundled under his arm, and hanging from his right forearm was a bucket loaded with the rest of the stuff, another dustsheet bunched into his armpit and two paint trays, piled with more brushes, held in his right hand.

Yowzer, I thought. *He's got to be really, really strong.*

'Tatty?' Elsa was behind me, just visible behind a load of grey matter. Not of the cerebral kind, mind. Sweatshirts, tracksuit bottoms, T-shirts.

'What a world of grey,' I said. And got busy with the scissors again.

*

'The room will look great when it's finished,' I called to Elsa above the clatter of the sewing machine.

'Anything to get Arnold out with a girl,' she replied.

'You make it sound like I've got facial warts or something,' said Arnold from the doorway. He looked odd. His head did not match the rest of his body. Old-man sweatshirt and tracksuit bottoms, I realised, had been Arnold's uniform for as long as I'd known him.

'Take off your clothes,' I said to him, pulling out the finished T-shirt.

'Not bloody likely.'

I ignored him, bit off a thread and held up the shirt, side seams taken in by a mile, sleeves lopped narrower, body length still the same. 'Put this on.'

Arnold shuffled closer and took the garment from me gingerly.

'Go on,' said Elsa, remaking the bed.

Arnold stepped behind his cupboard door, blushing furiously. He got into the black T faster than Kate Moss between catwalks, but not before I got a good look at the structure we had to work with.

I was amazed.

This boy's bod was *beautiful*.

I tried to say something. Anything. He was looking at me looking at him and it was all getting uncomfortable even though he had the T-shirt on now. Well, especially now that he had the T-shirt on. It showed off that fine physique like nothing he'd ever worn.

'W-what's with all the baggy gear the whole time?' I stammered in confusion. And then I blushed.

Silence.

It's hard to describe, but there was, like, A Moment.

Then I noticed Elsa looking at Arnold looking at me looking at him.

'Mona de Souza,' said Elsa quietly from the bed.

Arns and I blinked.

'Mona de Souza,' I said quickly, 'is going to, um, be begging you to open the bedside drawer.'

'Brilliant,' said Elsa. 'Even with the old-man trackie bottoms.'

I stood up. 'Give them to me,' I commanded.

Arnold clutched them frantically (as if I was going to rip them from his body. I mean, please) and said, 'Nononono. You step away.'

It's a pity that as I swooped to rip them from his body – tumbling both of us in a heap, bare hairy legs (his) waving desperately around – Sergeant Hilda Trenchard chose that moment to come home. The front door slammed and she yelled, 'Hi, guys, any supper left for me?' up the stairs. I jerked away in shock, pulling the bottoms off Arnold's feet and hitting my head on the desk with a thwack.

'Aargh!' I bleated.

Sergeant T was at the bedroom door in a nanosecond, staring first at her daughter in a nest of tumbled duvet and unbundled pillows, then at her son, naked from the waist down (how was I to know Arnold Trenchard doesn't wear unders?), and then – for the longest time – at the fallen girl with her son's trousers held tightly to her wanton breast.

'What,' said Sergeant T in a dangerously quiet voice, 'is going on here?'

'I ate the last of the Bolognese,' said Elsa blithely, springing from the bed. 'Sorry, Mum.'

Perhaps it was no dinner after a long day that angered her mother. Or maybe the altering of domestic decor without consultation. Possibly, just possibly, the disarray and naked-ness of teens under her law-abiding roof? Dunno. The truth of the matter is that she was Not Pleased. In the slightest.

Elsa turned from plumping the final pillow, saying, 'Ar–' Then: 'Yoooow! Arns! Where are your underpants? I'm *scarred*! I think I can see some bits!'

'Arnold?' added his mother.

Arnold was frozen on the floor, though his hands were now covering himself to some degree. I threw his bottoms back to him and stood up, whirling away to face his mother.

Oh, help, I prayed, and walked over to her with my hand outstretched. She was just as tall as Arns, but built like a big brickhouse, with an enormous head of curly red hair and chunky plastic-rimmed glasses identical to those of her son.

It was vaguely terrifying. I read her name badge and said, 'Hi, Sergeant Trenchard. I'm Tallulah Bird. Elsa and I are just helping Arnold –'

'Get a date,' finished Elsa, grinning happily at her mother.

Sergeant Trenchard looked me squarely in the eye, still clasping my hand, and said, 'With demonstrations of a sexual nature?'

'Mum!' cried Arnold and Elsa, horrified.

I snatched a look at Arns. He'd managed to scramble back into his bottoms.

'Where is your hair?' continued his mother.

'In the bin where it belongs,' said Elsa firmly.

'I just wanted to adjust the tracksuit bottoms,' I said meekly. The eyes swivelled back to mine, then across to Arns again. 'They're a little baggy for this day and age,' I added in polite explanation.

Sergeant T was quiet. We all held our breath.

'Arnie, you don't look anything like me any more,' she said finally in a small, sad voice. She dropped my hand absent-mindedly and stepped over the mountain of cut-up clothes towards him.

He took one look at her mournful face and pulled her into a hug. 'Oh, Mum,' he said. 'I'll always look like you. But it's not good for a teenager to sport the same hairstyle as his mother.'

'No,' agreed his mum mistily. She glanced back at me. 'He looks really great.' She patted his chest. 'About time you showed off the yoga muscles, my love.'

'Mum!' said Arnold, blushing furiously again. Geez, the guy was going to burst a blood vessel at this rate.

'And the white.' She nodded at the walls. 'Much fresher than before.'

'Thanks,' said Elsa, picking up a pillow again.

'Why does the makeover include the bedroom?'

'Uh,' I said hastily, 'we felt the home affects the attitude, the outlook, the, um, feelings of confidence, maybe . . .'

'So you're not planning on bringing a girl back here?'

'Maybe just to listen to music,' pleaded Arnold.

'That's all right, then,' said Sergeant T. She bent her curly head towards me and pushed her glasses up her nose. 'He likes Duran Duran and Wham,' she said in an undertone, nodding at his stereo on the chest of drawers. 'No chance he'll score with an eighties backlash.'

I gulped, startled.

'I'll leave you kids to it,' Sergeant T finished, moving towards the door. 'Elsa, did you at least leave some cheesecake?' we heard as she headed downstairs.

Arns offered to walk me home and Mum was pleased not to have to come out in the fresh night. She probably hoped we'd have a romantic encounter on the way home ha ha ha (bitter laugh). Not likely, thanks to Mona de Souza. I sighed regretfully. What a difference in Arns just with hair, glasses and clothes taken care of. It had been fun.

The front gate yelped at my urgent shove.

'I'd invite you in for coffee, but, um, it's late and . . .' I said to Arnold uncomfortably, thinking of our ramshackle house.

'Tonight's proceedings were exhausting, agony at times,' thought Arns aloud.

'I *have* taken a few blows to the head,' I agreed.

'I was talking about the waxing.'

'Oh. Yes. Well, if you hadn't knocked my hand away at the last minute the strip would never have landed on your um –'

'I'll see you tomorrow,' said Arns quickly.

I yawned and waved him off, wondering at a sudden movement in the Setting Sun's hedge over the road. Arnold noticed it too and shrugged back at me with a grin. Someone spying on us? More likely Mr Kadinski in a wrinkly embrace with Madame Polanikov.

Ew.

Better get to sleep before disturbing thoughts took hold.

Chapter Five

Tuesday night. One down on The List and just three days left to bag a boy

I got in and headed for the kitchen, where I found Mum at the freezer. She offered to share the only tub of Ben&Jerry's. I was impressed.

'So, Lula... Did you have a nice walk home?' she asked, examining the choc chips in her ice cream with feigned interest.

'Mum,' I said firmly. 'Arnold Trenchard and I will never get together.'

'I wasn't –'

'Uh-huh. You were. He's in love with someone else now. That's why he wanted the makeover.'

Mum flung her spoon into her bowl with a clatter and pushed back from the table. She swallowed her mouthful and spluttered: 'No!'

I raised my eyebrows. 'Look, Mum. I didn't really fancy him anyway.'

'Lula, you'll just have to win him back,' she said with surety. 'Who is this hussy with high hopes?'

'Mona de Souza, PSG hot girl,' I said glumly. 'Let's just forget about it, okay?'

Mum muttered something I couldn't hear, and seriously didn't want to know.

I cleared my throat and scraped out the last of the tub into my bowl. 'Dad sleeping better tonight?'

Mum sighed. 'He's not back yet.'

'He went out? Where? I thought he was sick.'

'Just . . . for some fresh air. I think he's recovering slowly. You know, from the flu.'

'Mum, he looks terrible. The sweating, the vomiting . . .' I paused and met her eyes for a second. 'Dad's drinking's got way worse since Grandma Bird died, hasn't it? Is this all just a terrible hangover?' I stopped. This was not easy to talk about and I could tell Mum just wanted me to let it go. I gulped down my ice cream and got up to put my bowl in the dishwasher. 'Do you think he's got, like, a real problem?'

'Don't jump to melodramatic conclusions, Tallulah. Try to be a bit more supportive of your father.'

I ground my teeth and reached over for Mum's empty bowl. It settled into the rack with a crash, as did our spoons. 'What time did he go out?'

'Not sure. Ten maybe? Are you this irritable because you're finding yourself stretched a little thin?'

'I wish I were stretched a little thin,' I moaned, glaring down at my gut. 'I should never have had that ice cream.'

'You know what I mean, Lu. Working at the library, your

coursework for school, the newspaper articles you should be writing . . .'

The horrifically embarrassing implications of being sweet sixteen and never been kissed, I thought bitterly.

'None of that is massively stressful, Mum.' I forced all kissing anxiety to the back of my mind and changed the subject quickly. 'The only thing freaking me out is those missing documents. If Harrow Construction mows down Coven's Quarter, Grandma Bird . . .' I pressed away a sudden ache from my eyes with the heels of my hands. 'She'd . . . Grandma would —'

Mum groaned. 'Oh, Lula, I know. Security said someone from our office came in on Saturday morning. There's a record on the access-card system. Eight a.m.'

I raised my eyebrows. 'Who?'

'Sophie Wenger.'

My jaw dropped. 'No way! What, and they got her on camera too?'

'There are no cameras. Can you believe it?' Mum rubbed her forehead.

'Saturday . . .' I wondered. Then, 'Are you sure she wasn't there for that local history tour you had to go in for?'

'No one in the office knew about that. The main library sprang that on me late Friday afternoon and I forgot to tell everyone to leave their desks tidy. Besides, the tour was at nine. Sophie came in at eight.'

'But you said Stinky Mike was there. I remember you moaning about seeing him in shorts.'

Mum laughed. 'He was most put out by the tour – all those historians staring at his scaly legs! He'd only popped in to get the jacket he'd left behind.'

'So did you see Sophie?'

'There's no record of her leaving. Maybe she slipped out as the historians were signing in. If only she'd come or gone later – Security were in full force with the usual bag searches and she'd never have been able to get anything out.'

'Why would she take the documents? She's only interested in tattoos and scary goth music. It makes no sense.'

'Money,' suggested Mum wearily. 'Wouldn't put anything past that developer Harry Harrow. Bribing an innocent young girl.'

I rolled my eyes. Sophie Wenger? Innocent? Nooo. 'Just get a warrant! Search her house!'

Mum shook her head. 'She says she was never at the library on Saturday – that her card was lost, so she couldn't have got in, even if she'd wanted to.'

'Oh. Yeah. She said that this morning, actually.'

'Though she conveniently found it in her bag this afternoon.' Mum raised her eyes tiredly to mine. 'But forget that, love. Try to relax a little, have some fun, even with your best friends gone.'

'I do miss them,' I admitted, distracted.

'Maybe it was a mistake to stay behind to work at the library.'

'No way – I'll need the spending money next term. And if I'd gone up to the city to stay at Alex's dad's with them I'd have spent what little I do have.'

Mum smiled. 'Sensible. I like it.' Her eyes crinkled at the corners. 'Though I'm sorry they're not going to be here to celebrate your birthday with you. Is it going to be terribly boring, just us and a cake?'

'Depends on the gifts!'

'You cheeky madam!' I laughed, but Mum pursed her lips. 'Actually, Lula, the present we've ordered has been a little delayed –'

'Mum,' I interrupted. 'It's fine. Really. The girls and I are looking forward to a pizza-and-movie night to celebrate when they're back. Okay?'

'Okay,' replied Mum, smiling at me again.

'Or maybe I'll go along to the end-of-holiday party at Frey's.'

'Frey's?' My mother looked horrified.

'Frey's Dam, Mum. Just a few minutes' walk from Coven's Quarter.'

'Oh, of course. I was thinking of nightclubs . . .'

'. . . drugs and alcohol and wanton behaviour,' I finished.

Mum rolled her eyes and stood up from the table.

'Lu, don't worry about Coven's Quarter. Security will get something out of Sophie when her parents come in to see me tomorrow.' She leaned over for a hug and a kiss, then headed out the door. 'See you in the morning.'

'Night,' I said, and unwrapped a dishwasher tablet. My head hurt from thinking. Sophie a criminal? No. It didn't fit. Where was the motive? And then there was Dad to mull over. Dad had been out, in his sweaty state, for nearly two hours. I bunged the tablet into the machine and winced as I pinched my finger in the door when slamming it closed.

'Nya-ha-ha!' I hopped around, sucking the bruised digit, then went to my room. If I had to endure any more pain this evening, I'd pass out.

I pushed my door open just as my computer bleeped in the corner. 'Good timing,' I murmured, and hurried over to hit OPEN.

From: Arnold Trenchard

Subject: Second thoughts

Message: Call me.

Oh, *what*?

After my services rendered was he thinking of asking *me* out instead of Mona?

Chapter Six

Tuesday night, burning midnight oil

I was about to call Arns in my best *I'm the one that you want* voice, but my computer bonged again. Another message from him.

ARNOLD: Lula? Are you there? Please call. I really have changed my mind. Mona is seriously too good for me, and before you pimp me out to show off your makeover you should know I don't want anyone else.

The cheek of the boy! Show off his makeover? What kind of girl did he think I was?

Well, the kind of girl who was trying to pimp *herself* out . . .

Damn. Arnold's second thought was not good news. If it had to be Mona or nothing, then it would have to be Mona – I had a pang of something but swallowed it down – because Mona de Souza had access to lovely boys who had never heard the jinx rumour, and Arns had promised she'd set me up.

This was no time for second thoughts.

I had just three days to kiss a boy.

Time was of the essence. Frik, frik, frik!

I took a deep breath to calm myself and hammered out a message:

TATTY BIRD: You want to have waxed your whatchamacallits for NOTHING? Pull yourself together! Will phone you in a minute to talk strategy.

There. That bought me an hour or so. Time to call in the girls, though it was after midnight. I hit reply to a hello from Carrie.

TATTY BIRD: Whazzup?

CARRIE: Hey! Tam has written the coolest song! She's gonna busk in the morning's rush hour tomorrow.

TATTY BIRD: The suits will love her. I had an Arnold Trenchard makeover tonight to keep me occupied.

CARRIE: YOU STARTED AT THE BOTTOM OF THE LIST?! A makeover was your only in?!

TATTY BIRD: No. He's in love with Mona de Souza and she's in town for the Science Fair. Can't believe none of us knew about that. Well, actually, I can. Anyway, the makeover was the first step. Step two is the encounter. If it works with him and Mona, he's going to get me introduced to the St Alban's boys.

CARRIE: Genius! They don't know about the jinx!

TATTY BIRD: Exactly! But how to get Mona and Arns together? I was thinking a carefully contrived chance encounter.

Carrie: Hey, Lula, Alex here. You mean Mona Lisa de Souza? PSG hot girl?

Tatty Bird: Yep. I know. I can't compete, so Arns has been eliminated from the list, but I thought my Plan B was good.

Carrie: Plan B = brilliant and you're in luck, babyshoes! You ready for this? Mona is my gorgeous Cousin Jack's sister!!!! Erm, my cousin too, though I don't know her like I know Jack.

Ha! How typical that Alex had all the vital info. Though being *related* to the vital info was a bit startling.

So listen to this: Alex is Mona de Souza's second cousin. Probably five times removed. Even though they're the same age they don't have much to do with each other, but Mona's older brother, Jack, is a different story. He's doing first-year journalism at Hambledon University, so he and Alex email and chat every week. Alex says she wants him on her staff when her own glam-mag empire is founded. He's been telling Alex how stressed Mona has been because she's due to debate Einstein's whole theory of relativity bit at the Science Fair opener next week and doesn't understand anything she's supposed to be debating. She didn't want to fess up to her friends down there, and Jack had no clue.

Which is when I had a brainwave. I was getting one step closer to My First Kiss . . .

Alex got distracted then, about Jack's hotness, mainly.

CARRIE: Ooh, so snoggable, T! Dreamy eyes, delicious lips, you know the drill.

TATTY BIRD: Ew, Alex! Blood relative! Blood relative!

CARRIE: Oh. Ik. Hadn't thought of that. What a waste. Hey! He's a perfect kiss candidate for you, Tatty! I've got his number right here! Hang on . . .

TATTY BIRD: No no no! Alex? Alex! Come back!

CARRIE: Right! I've got it!

TATTY BIRD: No no no NO, sirree. First year of university? Two priorities for those students, regardless of gender: doing drugs and having sex. Too scary. I only want a kiss.

CARRIE: Jack's not like that. Actually, now I think of it, he's never even been interested in *me*!

TATTY BIRD: LOL! Yeah, cos he's your *cousin*. Alex, I don't need Jack's number. Your info is more than enough. I've got to rethink the Meeting Mona plan with Arns, STRAIGHT AWAY. Might have an idea for a whole new strategy . . .

I signed off. Taking a deep breath I went into the hall to pick up the portable phone. It was time to call Arns with a very cunning plan.

Arnold was not happy at being woken at one in the morning.

'I was in a deep-sleep cycle,' he complained.

'That's what I wanted to talk to you about,' I said.

'Deep sleep?'

'Cycling. We're going to have to bunk off work tomorrow. Be here by six. You're going to wear my dad's special shirt.'

'Am I going to have to get changed in front of you again? My bike's got a puncture.'

'Doesn't matter, doesn't matter,' I said hurriedly. 'I'm going to be the one on a bike.' I didn't mention Boodle the Poodle, Pen's dog, who is no poodle but rather a Newfoundland of terrifying proportions. Scaring the client at this stage would not be helpful. 'You need to wear trainers and a pair of those long cut-off shorts I made. Be here at oh-six hundred hours and don't be late – the plan won't work if the schedule slips.'

'Wait! Aren't you going to tell me wh–'

'No. Sweet dreams, Arnold.'

I hung up quickly and headed for my cupboard to pull out Dad's too-small Rolling Stones T that I sometimes slept in. Dad always whinged when I wore it – I think some big illogical part of his brain thought he'd fit back into it some day. Mffwwmmff! (Translation: WHAHAHAHA!) It was so old I knew the next time it got snagged on anything it would be irreparable and I didn't want the blame for ruining an antiquity.

I had a twinge of doubt that what I was about to commit

the shirt to would have my father writing me out of his will within an hour.

But I didn't lose sleep over it.

Chapter Seven

Wednesday, definitely dawn

It felt like only minutes since my head hit the pillow when a banging on my window woke me. It was Arnold. And he looked far too spritely for my liking. He laughed at my bed head as I pushed the curtain aside to squint out into the morning light.

'Ffff!' I said, baring my teeth against the window pane, but it didn't scare him.

'Open the door, Tatty Lula. I thought time was of the essence.'

'Gimme a minute.'

Arns rolled his eyes as I dropped the curtain. It didn't take long for me to pull on my running stuff and tie my hair into a bunch somewhere near the top of my fuzzy head.

Strapping my watch on, I caught sight of the date in its tiny window. Oh, man! April was flying by! I took a panicky breath and closed my eyes to give myself a minute, though I could hear Arns getting restless outside. Right. Three days is enough time to meet a boy, make him love me and bag a kiss, isn't it? Yes! Easy! No problem! Frik! Bum, bum, bum. *Stop it, Tallulah! Calm . . . calm . . .*

Sleep rubbed from my eyes, I opened the front door.

The rest of the house was still dead to the world. Arns was lying on the floor of the veranda with two very large, very furry clawed paws on his chest.

'I've met your dog,' he said faintly.

'I'm astonished,' I said, admiration creeping in. 'Boodle the Poodle likes you! And you haven't . . . uh . . . given her reason to . . . uh . . . go all crazy.'

'What, precisely, does that mean? Can you get' – he paused – 'Boodle the Poodle off me?'

'Boodle, inside.' She hopped off Arns and trotted into the house, her plumed tail waving happily. I heard her paws skittering in the kitchen.

Uh-oh.

'Arns,' I said. He was still staring up at the veranda ceiling. 'Inside.'

There was no argument from him either. I hurried the boy straight into my room before he could get a look at the cracks in the walls or the bare light fittings, and snatched up the phone on the way.

'Whoa,' he said, looking around my room. 'Not what I was expecting.'

I jabbed at the keypad on the phone. 'I'm going to phone Stinky Mike at the library to leave my excuses on his voicemail.'

'You need to do that with your mum as boss there? Surely –'

'Protocol,' I interrupted. 'You know what he's like.'

Arnold nodded. 'Elsa wouldn't wake up so I called in myself. Blamed the spag Bol.'

Mike's extension was ringing. I collected my thoughts. Why wasn't it going through to voicemail?

'Hello, Michael Burdon speaking.'

'M-Mike,' I stuttered. 'You're in early.'

Arnold nodded his head knowingly. I punched him in the shoulder.

'Is that Tallulah Bird?' replied Mike disapprovingly.

'In body, but not in spirit.' I laughed, high-pitched and a little hysterical. 'I'm not feeling very well. Been up all night.' No lies there. 'Thought I'd better call to let you know I wouldn't be in today before I passed out again.' I laughed again. Mistake. Stinky Mike had no sense of humour at all.

'Fine.' Mike sounded oddly accepting, almost pleased.

'I'm so sorry,' I said in my *I've just thrown up in a bucket next to my bed* voice.

'No problem, Tallulah. Will you be away all week?'

'No, no,' I said hurriedly, thinking of my depleted chocolate fund in alarm. 'I've stopped being sick now; I think I just need to rest today. Probably be in tomorrow.' I heard a voice in the background. Who was that there with him at this hour? Tweedy Mabel? No. Mum was forever complaining about how Mabel hardly ever got in before ten.

'. . . I've put them in the Duchess of Cornwall's file. Do you want to take it down now before . . .' came the voice. I was sure it was Mabel, but the thought of that stick insect with big greasy Mike, their wrinkles folding together, made me feel as ill as I'd professed to be.

'Er, fine, fine, Tallulah. See you tomorrow, then.' And he hung up.

Feeling ashamed of my barefaced lies, I ducked out of the room to replace the handset in its charger on the hall table and returned red-faced to hunt for my hairbrush. Arns was gazing around, taking everything in. I followed his eyes uneasily. Had I left any underwear lying about . . .?

I spotted my brush. Fantastic! Snatching it up while pulling out my hairband, I brushed vigorously, feeling my scalp tingle, and threw Dad's shirt at him at the same time.

'Put that on.'

He only hesitated a second before shrugging out of a top I must have missed last night and putting on the Stones T-shirt.

'Good.' I nodded, my face flaring at his naked torso, and added hurriedly, 'The shirt's good.'

'So's your room.'

'Thank you. You want some breakfast?'

'No, thanks. You go ahead.'

'Okay, I'll just be a minute.' I turned to the door.

He started to follow me. 'I'll come and get some water.'

'No!'

'Pardon?'

'You – you can stay here. Relax.' I coughed and felt a prickle of sweat on my eyelids. 'It's safe here. Boodle the Poodle might eat you.'

'Boodle the Poodle likes me.'

I stopped and looked him in the eye. 'This house . . .'

'Yes?'

'It takes some getting used to. It's a renovation project. With some way to go. You could be startled. Better you stay here.'

Arns rolled his eyes and followed me regardless.

'I see what you mean,' he said by the time we got to the kitchen and when he said it for some reason it didn't bother me. I nodded and made for the fridge, but paused when I saw that Boodle had managed to lever Pen's special Vogel's bread off the counter and was licking the last of the sunflower seeds off the floor, the wrapper pushed expertly to one side. I stuffed it in the bin to be safe and rubbed at the soft fur behind her ears.

'Good girl,' I crooned.

'Take it you're not a Vogel's fan,' remarked Arns, grabbing an apple from the fruit bowl and twisting its stalk off. 'It's very good for you, you know. No flour enhancers, loads of seeds.'

'I'd love some of that bread – that apple's not been

washed – but Pen buys her own and won't let anyone else have any.'

Arns looked around for the kitchen sink and couldn't find it. 'There's a lot of stuff in this kitchen,' he said, his eyes fixed on the chicken claw hanging from a rafter quite close to his upturned face.

'Uh, yes,' I said. 'My grandmother used to live here with us. She was a . . . er . . . white witch – I'm not sure what she was up to with chicken claws. Mum's too afraid to throw it away, worried about curses and jinxes or something, I guess.'

'As is most of Hambledon Boys' High School,' murmured Arns.

I gave him an evil look before pouring milk into my cereal bowl.

Arns tossed his apple from hand to hand and moved away from the claw. 'So, do you have second sight?'

'Don't you think I'd have bagged my man by now if I had an ounce of witchiness at my fingertips?' I spooned away at my cereal, eating too fast.

'Well, you've got some kind of sight to get me from what I was yesterday to how I am today.' He sat down in a chair opposite me.

I shook my head. 'That doesn't count. Hardly an amazing feat, Arns. If you'd let your sister help, you'd have been trendy from the age of three.'

Arns leaned forward. His hazel eyes were clear and I noticed a ring of dark brown round each iris that made them the first thing you noticed about him now that the huge hair and glasses were gone. 'Any idea how long it took me to put the contacts in this morning?'

'You still got here on time. Remember – no pain, no gain.'

'I –' Arnold began, and I tuned out as I flipped open the dishwasher and began putting stuff away. I tried to be really quick in the cupboards so Arns didn't get to stare too long at the hippo-shaped teapot or the gnome-bum egg cups. I passed by the sink once or twice and surreptitiously hooked out old teabags and stir-fry noodles from the drain, dropping them into the bin with a shudder. Arns was still burbling away happily, tossing that apple back and forth while watching the sun come up through the kitchen window. I snuck off to brush my teeth and came back to discover him at the sink. Before I could warn him he'd turned on the tap, apple held beneath, and all the pipes in the house shook and banged at a terrible, terrible volume.

'Good God!' he cried, and twisted the tap hard in the opposite direction. The banging got so loud it drew a scream from Pen upstairs.

'*Tallulah! Turn that damn hot water OFFF!*'

I ran over and batted Arns's hand away. Hot water in this house was a luxury in more ways than one. You just didn't go there in a sleeping household. I eased the tap open again and then jolted it shut. Silence. Arns and I exhaled together, then widened our eyes at each other as the door to Pen's room slammed and the sound of a stomping run came down the stairs.

'Oh boy,' said Arns.

'Why is Arnold Trenchard in our house?' came the solicitor voice from right behind us. 'And what has Boodlington been eating?'

'*Your* dog,' I said pointedly, 'ate *your* bread.'

Pen pursed her lips and her cheeks puffed out hard. She went a little pink.

'G-good morning,' stammered Arns.

'Don't *good morning* me!' she hissed with venom. 'It's the middle of the night!'

'No,' said Arns stupidly. 'It's time to get up.' I flinched as Pen's eyes narrowed and her fists clenched.

'RUBBISH! I should be asleep – we *all* should be asleep – but you've gone and woken me up! With the taps! What were you thinking? It's *six forty-eight* a.m.! Why are you wearing my father's shirt?'

'Nya! Six forty-eight!' I snatched Arns's apple, crunched out a massive mouthful and handed it back while pulling a half-litre bottle of water out of one of those carrypacks Dad keeps in the store cupboard in case tap water the world over gets poisoned by terrorists. What else did we need?

Grabbing Arnold's forearm, I dragged him out of the back door to help extricate my bike from the shed.

Pen was left speechless, but she kicked the door shut behind us with a rude slam.

'Mwehadmmhrry,' I spluttered.

'Finish the apple first. Nice bike. Bit big for you.'

I swallowed. 'My legs are longer than you think. What's your watch say?'

'Six fifty-five.'

I twisted dials till mine said exactly the same, grabbed an ancient tennis ball and Boodle the Poodle's lead and then explained the cunning Arns + Mona plan as we headed out of the back gate, Boodle waving her tail triumphantly.

'. . . So you see, when Mona knows you're a science whizz, that will be your perfect in! She'll be unable to resist! She's *desperate*, apparently! Oh. Not that a girl would have to be desperate to . . . uh, you know . . . want to go out with you . . .'

I stopped.

Arns was shaking his head. He was pale. 'Tallulah, you're telling me this mad idea *now*? Is it *safe*? I sense personal embarrassment close at hand. We should spend more time preparing.'

'We have inside info, Arns. If we keep to the right timings, there's' – I looked over at Boodle – 'um not much that can go wrong. Just remember that Boodle will drop anything to get to the tennis ball, and don't panic. And if the shirt doesn't give way, you need to help it.'

'No chance. You're crazy.'

'Arnold,' I said warningly, wheeling the bike up the side road round to the front of the house. Mr Kadinski waved from the Setting Sun's front veranda.

'Don't look at the pensioner,' I hissed at Arnold. 'He needs a hand down the steps and we don't have time.'

'But –'

'Run, Arnold, run!'

He set off at a loping pace, a worried look on his face, checking his watch. 'I'm never going to get to the dining hall by seven twenty!' he muttered. 'I should have demanded the details of your plan immediately. What was I thinking? All that idle chitchat in the kitchen! This is never going to work! Never!'

'Get a wiggle on!' I wound Boodle the Poodle's lead round the left handlebar and got on the bike to follow, water bottle clutched in my right hand. It all felt very precarious. Pushing the pedals till we were whizzing along comfortably, we were soon on Arnold's tail. Despite his complaints he was making good progress. I lifted the bottle to my teeth and pulled up the pop top. As we got right behind Arns, I squeezed it hard at him and a perfect triangle of sweat darkened the shirt between his shoulder blades.

'Weergh!' he yelled, and jumped away.

'Watch out for oncoming traffic,' I commented, and came up alongside to squirt at his chest.

'Oh, f-f-f-!' Arnold's lips were a little blue and shivery. 'Is that really necessary, Lula?' he panted.

The shirt clung perfectly. 'Seven eighteen, corner of Stanton and Mason,' I instructed, one final time.

'I know where PSG's dining hall is, Tallulah,' puffed Arnold, too much malevolence in his tone for this early hour.

I pulled away. 'Dunno if that's a good thing, Arns,' was my parting shot before I wheeled into a U-turn. 'And Stanton is the corner *before* the hall – okay?'

Arns flapped his hand at me.

I stood up on the pedals to get some speed going – Boodle the Poodle had to be tuckered out before the planned onslaught up Mason Road. If she didn't play her part properly, the plan would be shot.

Chapter Eight

Early Wednesday, but time running out . . .

Mr Kadinski was still standing despondently at the top of the Sun's steps when I came wheeling back round to head up the hill into the woods. I waved cheerily at him and steeled myself as his plaintive cries carried clearly through the cold morning air. There was no way I could have helped anyway, I told myself, with Boodle on the loose and keen for a run. There would have been a terrible accident. Images of old man, ten-ton hairy dog, sixteen steps and tangles of lead flashed through my head, making me shudder.

'Mr Kadinski,' I muttered, 'it's for the best. Really.'

Despite the pale fingers of sunlight pointing through the trees on to the rough road ahead, it was still cold. The skin on my bare legs pricked up in goosebumps and I wished I'd worn my beanie to cover my burning ears. I kept my hands tightly glued to the handlebars; Boodle was pulling me along, despite my vigorous pedalling, and if we skidded into a pothole I wanted to be prepared. Cycling past PSG with bleeding knees would be too humiliating to contemplate.

'Take it easy, Boodle,' I called.

She showed no sign of slowing down. *Oh, frik*, I thought. *Is there time to take her into the trees? That'll use up some of this energy*. I snatched a look at my watch: 7.02. Boodle suddenly raced after a squirrel and I nearly lost my balance completely. There'd have to be time. I geared down and pumped the pedals even harder.

We climbed up and up the track, every now and again catching glimpses of Hambledon below. Usually I loved coming out here. It felt completely isolated and if you didn't look west, down the slope where the town began, you'd think you were in the middle of nowhere. But there wasn't a moment to lose in day dreaming now.

At the top of the hill the track ended in a wide circle and the trees had been felled here and there so you could see right across to where the sea sparkled on a distant horizon. This morning there was nothing visible in the mist. I let Boodle off the lead for a minute – we could do a little loop through the trees, then back into town after Arnold.

Boodle was ecstatic. She darted back and forth, her feathery tail whacking vigorously to and fro, in search of more squirrels and whatever had made those strange holes at the base of tall beech trees. And then she was gone.

'Boodle!'

Snuffle snuffle, happy bark . . . from far away. 7.06.

Frik!

'*Boodle! Get your hairy butt here right now!*' I shrieked. Dammit. Now we'd have to go through the woods and cut back into the town through the crematorium yard. Thank goodness it was morning. What could be scary about a crematorium yard in the morning? *If there is smoke, I can just tell myself it's mist*, I thought, admiring my courage.

Wrapping the dogless lead into a circle round my shoulder, I rode as fast as I dared through the trees, whistling sharply for Boodle. At last she galloped over, then ran alongside the bike happily.

I followed a small rough path cut deep into dry earth, trying not to waggle the wheel off course. I was no mountain biker. Kids from school loved coming up here to try out the trails and there was a bunch of homemade ramps and jumps in a dell nearby that was a crush of flying bikes on a Saturday afternoon.

I could see the enormous stone chairs of Coven's Quarter up ahead, looming out of the morning mist like something out of *The Lord of the Rings*. Massive slabs of rock just higher than the ground that could seat about three adults side by side, with great boulders on either side for armrests. The backrests were the standing stones, reaching up four or five metres. There were seven chairs in all, placed in a rough circle at the bottom of a vast hollow that the pines and beech trees kept a respectful distance from. I always felt that my chair was the narrowest one with the highest backrest. 'Thronelike,' Tam had commented when I'd declared my spot at a picnic we'd had here last summer.

My stomach twisted at the thought of the development that might take its place. Grandma Bird would never have let it happen. Never. She always said it was one of the few places left where real magic was still possible.

No time to absorb its energy today. I lurched through the undergrowth, Boodle right at my side now, her tongue at last lolling out the side of her mouth, and whisked my hand across the back of my chair as we sailed by.

'Give us luck,' I said softly, and then we were off at a diagonal downhill. I could just make out the tips of the tall peaked rooves of the Setting Sun Retirement Home below, then nothing until the immense chimneys of Cluny's Crematorium. No smoke wisped from the top of them this morning, but Boodle slowed with a whimper anyway. I didn't waste a moment. Throwing down the bike, I clipped the lead back on, rolling it up till it was bunched in my left fist, and took stock of the best way down.

'Ready, Boodle?' I asked. She turned her head and blinked her big brown eyes, tongue still lolling. I grinned and got back on the bike. This could work.

'Let's go!' I whooped, and we were off.

We sped downhill at a million miles an hour till at last the tarmac of North Road appeared through the trees. Skidding to a halt, I checked my watch.

7.13.

Frik, frik. Seven minutes! But the hardest part was over.

Slipping and sliding in haste down the bank, I caught my forearms and shins on a thousand nettles and Boodle had a trail of some green creeper round her neck, like I'd garlanded her specially. No time to address her accessories. We threw ourselves out on to the road and pelted down the hill, wheels a-blur, Boodle's breath starting to gasp faintly. Then left into Stanton. I could see Arns just ahead: he was early, brilliant boy, jogging slowly now on the approach to the corner.

I curved my mouth into a piercing whistle and blasted twice. Arns didn't even look back. From what I could see the fake sweat patches had widened, though he eased effortlessly into one-hundred-metre-sprint pace before I'd even started the second whistle. I slowed the bike and pulled Boodle in hard. The timing had to be perfect. By the time we'd got to the corner, Arns was halfway up the hill and far closer to the dining halls than I'd thought.

Fffff! I gave it everything, which took some doing, because I couldn't adjust the gears while trying to keep Boodle on a tight leash, and balance and steer at the same time. Boodle sensed some kind of urgency and got Arns in her sights. She started to pull ahead.

I glanced up.

Girls had all but exited the dining halls now and hung around in groups under the trees, or sat on the outside walls, just like the St Alban's guys had done yesterday.

You could see the best spot to sit straight away and, being one of the popular ones, Mona had prime seat. I glimpsed her laughing at something a friend was saying before I put more muscle into pedalling.

The approach to the hall on Mason was a killer uphill and I've got no idea how I came abreast of Arns at the critical moment.

He was on the pavement now, coming up to Mona. I made sure I was a little past him, just opposite Mona, before I yelled, 'Hey, Arns! Thanks for helping me with the relativity stuff yesterday. You're a science genius!'

Arns raised his hand in acknowledgement as I braked elegantly and unleashed Boodle.

It was too, too perfect.

Boodle had already twisted round and she leapt towards Arns just as he loped past Mona. Girls scattered in every direction and Mona twisted to drop her legs over the other side of the wall as Arns thumped hard against it, his head sounding on the grey stone with a painful *thwack!*, two furry paws once again firmly on his chest.

He pushed away from the wall with one hand, dazed, the other hand holding the back of his head, and Boodle's paws raked down his chest.

'Nyargh!' yelled Arns as the shirt gave way, two huge rips showing off fabtastic – fab*tastic!* – pectorals to their best advantage.

'Boodle!' I called feebly. 'Get back here now! You okay, Arnold?'

Arns staggered, both hands on his head now, chest totally visible.

Then, to my shame, Boodle jumped again, and ripped that precious Stones shirt from neckline to hem, scratching ribbons of blood across Arns's torso.

I got to him first, bike thrown down on the verge, and tried to haul Boodle off him, but no chance.

'*Bad dog!*' I yelled when she refused to move.

'Blood,' whimpered Arns, and passed out.

I stepped back and pulled the manky tennis ball from my pocket. How could Arns breathe with Pen's hound on his chest? My fingers fumbled. Damn this tiny pocket! I pulled and swore till the ball came loose and then I bounced it once, twice, three times, on the pavement. *Pock, pock, pock.* At the first bounce Boodle was at my feet grovelling for a game of throw and fetch. I pulled back my arm and threw as hard as I could along the pavement.

Boodle the Poodle was off.

Mona, to her credit, had swung back over the wall and now reached out for Arnold's forehead.

'He's very hot,' she said.

Duh, I thought. *Like he hasn't just sprinted up this cliff face of a hill.*

'He certainly is,' tittered a tall blonde specimen.

'He needs medical attention,' I said urgently.

Mona turned to the blondie. 'Hurry, Barbie!' she said. 'Call Nurse Wilton now!' (BARBIE? Seriously?)

Barbie The Useless But Incredibly Beautiful just stood there, but several others set off at a run, their perfectly highlighted hair flying out behind them like the locks in a salon shampoo ad.

'Thanks,' I said to Mona, who was now expertly checking for a pulse.

'Your *dog*!' she said.

'She's usually so good!' I lied. 'I can't believe this happened!' I looked down at Arns's chest. The scratches were mainly welts, not deep at all, and only bleeding here and there. Impressive wounds for the moment, though.

Boodle the Poodle came pelting back in a flurry of hair and slobber. She flopped down beside me, releasing a soggy tennis ball. A long string of drool leaked from her mouth on to Arns's arm. She whined and plonked a massive paw on his head.

Arns's eyes flickered and he groaned.

'Mona,' he mumbled.

'What did he say?' asked Mona querulously. 'Did he say *Mona*?'

'No,' I said firmly. 'He said, "Hold her." Come on, Boodle,' I commanded, pulling on her collar. 'Arns is going to be fine. Here comes the nurse.'

And, yes indeed, the nurse was coming at full pace, with one of those stretcher thingies, which she plonked down alongside Arnold. She got some girls to ease him on to it while firing questions at the rest of us.

'What happened here, girls?'

'Uh, my friend was running and my dog got a bit excited and knocked him into the wall,' I blathered, watching how the lecherous Barbie was lifting Arns by the hips on to the stretcher.

The nurse glanced up at me and then across at Boodle the Poodle, who was standing at full height now, nose in the air, still drooling round teeth and tennis ball. The nurse swallowed.

'Did he bump his head on the wall?'

'Yes,' I said.

'Hard,' said Mona, narrowing her eyes at Boodle.

'Know if he's had a tetanus shot in the last ten years?' asked the nurse with her eyebrows raised, clearly not expecting an answer.

The girls lifted the stretcher on her signal.

'He has,' I said confidently.

'Really,' said the nurse.

'Really. We were just talking about it yesterday. You know, discussing childhood injuries, the whole relativity theory, that kind of thing. The Science Fair has got us all thinking out the box,' I babbled.

Arns moaned again.

'What's his full name?' demanded the nurse, leading the way into the school buildings, past the dining halls.

I cleared my throat. 'Arnold Radbert Trenchard.'

'Do you know how to get hold of his mother or father?'

'Yes.'

'Mona, will you take this young lady to your house-mistress to call them? We'll be in the sanatorium.'

'Yes, Nurse Wilton.'

The little posse of stretcher toters carried on down the avenue and I followed Mona left down another path of dappled shade. Boodle nudged me gently and licked my hand. I swallowed hard.

Mona glanced at me. 'I think he's going to be fine.'

'It's just that' – I coughed – 'he hit his head so *hard*.'

'It sounded painful,' agreed Mona.

'Uh-huh. But Boodle didn't mean it. Did you, Boodle?'

I clipped her lead back on and followed Mona up the steps and into the building, wondering if Pen had woken my parents up yet. Probably not. Mum would be late into work. I hoped I could make more than just one call.

The housemistress was really sweet, and with only a couple of clicks I was put through distressingly quickly to Sergeant Trenchard. Then I had to explain that my sister's dog – no animal of mine – had knocked her son's genius head into a flinty wall.

'H-he may be hurt,' I stammered, 'but I don't think so.' My voice went a little creaky. 'I think he only passed out because of the blood. You know *seeing* it. Not, um, blood *loss*.' A pause. I scrunched my eyes closed, waiting for nuclear fallout, but Sergeant T did not react as expected to my 'blood' observations and sounded more mother and less sergeant when she asked where to find us. I explained to turn left at the abandoned bike and keep going, and she said she was on her way.

Then I phoned home. Mum answered.

'Mum,' I said. 'I just went out for some fresh air cos I wasn't feeling so good and I'll be back soon. I called Mike early this morning to say I wouldn't be at the library today.'

'You okay, Lu? You shouldn't have gone out if you were feeling unwell. Where are you now?'

'You're right. I should have stayed in bed. I'm just having a rest at PSG. Stopped off to let you know.'

'Oh. Do you need me to come and get you? Are you sure you're okay?'

'I'm fine. Just a little tired. I've got my bike and Boodle and we'll be home in half an hour. Okay?'

'Okay, Lu. Call me at the office when you get in, though. I'm leaving now.'

'Really? This early?'

'I've got that meeting, remember?' said Mum, her voice anxious. 'With Sophie, her parents and Security, to talk about the missing documents. Thought it best to get that out of the way before anyone gets in.'

'Mike was at work before six thirty this morning,' I said.

'What?' said Mum.

'Yep, he answered when I phoned to leave my sick message.'

'Gosh. That's early.'

'I've got to go, Mum. I'll see you later.'

'Bye, Lula. Call me if you need me. And get some rest.'

I hung up, rubbed my eyes and turned to Mona and the housemistress. 'Arnold's mum is on her way,' I said, trying not to think about how angry a police sergeant could get with a person.

'Don't worry about your friend,' said Mona as we made our way back to the sanatorium. 'I'm sure there's no permanent neurological damage.' She smiled.

I seized my chance. 'Good – he would never forgive me if he lost his grasp on the theory of relativity.'

Mona laughed. 'Funny you should say that . . .'

'Not funny at all,' I said quickly. 'Arnold is a science genius. He helped me yesterday with a load of project stuff I needed to get done before term started.' I crossed my fingers and hoped I was still red enough from the bike ride to hide my shameful flushes.

Mona blinked rapidly. 'Really? I should know all about

that, but I . . .' she trailed off. 'Here's the san. You'd better leave your dog out here. Will she be, um, okay?'

'She'll behave, if that's what you're asking,' I said. 'Sit, Boodle.' Boodle thankfully sat, and I tied her lead securely to the railing outside.

We went inside. It was cool, though sunlight streamed through high arched windows. I felt sweaty and underdressed compared to the clean crispness of everything, and smoothed my hair down with the flat of my hand.

'He'll be through here,' said Mona, and she pushed open some French doors. We walked into a room of six beds, three down each side. They were all empty but for the last in the far corner under one of the enormous windows. Arnold lay propped up on pillows answering Nurse Wilton's questions. He turned when he heard us come in and I watched his face freeze when he saw Mona.

'Hi,' said Mona at his bedside. 'Does your head hurt?'

'Agony,' said Arns. Then he smiled at her, and my chest suddenly hurt with envy at the *I like you* look they shared. (What's with the intimacy when *they don't even know each other?*)

'I'll leave you to it,' said Nurse Wilton, going across the room to open the door for Sergeant Trenchard and Dr McCabe.

(Not Dr McCabe! He was always first on the scene to patch up the boys I'd had a hope of kissing – Gianni

85

Caruso's fingers being the latest and most memorable incident – and I just couldn't take that look on his face whenever he saw me now.)

Sergeant T came clopping crisply across the floor. There was something different about her, but I felt too nervous to look at her directly. She dropped a kiss on Arnold's forehead. 'Are you all right?'

'Fine, Mum. Thanks for coming.'

'Hi, Sergeant Trenchard,' I ventured.

'Call me Hilda,' said his mum, with a pat on my arm. I felt like crying, suddenly.

'Okay,' I said, and bent to tie the lace of my trainer.

'I'm Mona de Souza,' I heard above me.

'Pleased to meet you,' said Arns's mum with no hint of surprise or recognition. 'I'm Hilda Trenchard. Hilda.'

I surfaced with a sniff to see Mona nod, smiling.

'You look pretty today, Hilda,' said Dr McCabe, tightening the armband of the blood-pressure kit round Arnold's bicep. 'And you're looking great too, young man.' His eyes flicked over to where I stood. 'Despite the head injury. Despite the wounds.'

I flushed.

There was a little uncomfortable silence.

'Elsa got hold of me this morning, Edward,' replied Sergeant T. She smiled and winked at me from contact-lensed eyes. Her wild afro was pulled back neatly into a chignon and she was wearing mascara and pale-pink lipstick. Ha! She'd had a makeover too! Good on Elsa. Arnold's mum really did look pretty.

'Blood pressure's fine,' said Dr McCabe, taking the stethoscope from his ears. He leaned forward and shone a light into each of Arns's pupils. 'No concussion, although Nurse Wilton said you were unconscious?'

'Erm,' said Arns, looking at me frantically.

'Mona,' I said, drawing her aside, while Arns muttered something about a sensitivity to the sight of blood, 'where can I get a bowl or something for Boodle the Poodle to drink water out of?'

With a reluctant glance back at the bed and a little wave, Mona took me out of the sick bay to the supply room behind the front desk. She found a large disposable plastic bowl, filled it with water from the basin tap next door and took it outside, patting Boodle cautiously on the head.

'Why do you call her Boodle the Poodle?' she asked.

'Just because she's *so* not a curly-haired pooch. Have you ever seen a bigger dog?'

Mona laughed. 'No, actually. Especially not standing on someone's wounded chest.' She went a little pink.

'I think Arnold likes you,' I ventured.

A little pink turned to bright pink.

'And I'm sure he'd love to discuss all things science with you.'

Mona raised her eyebrows in a *Really?* question and dried her hands on her skirt. Boodle's hairs were visible straight away on the navy fabric. She brushed at them absentmindedly.

'Really,' I said. 'He'll probably have to stay at home this afternoon, though. You two seem to have clicked. He'd love it if you popped round to see him.'

Mona was bright red now. 'What? Today? To his *house?*'

I nodded encouragingly. 'I'll come back in with you and we can ask him if he'd be up for a visit. His mum will be fine with it.'

'Y-you sure?' stammered Mona.

'Do you like Wham and Duran Duran? Maybe even Elvis?'

'Uh, I don't usually te– okay, yes. Yes, I do. You're going to use that against me?' Mona was now grinning.

'Nope, that's perfect. Just don't let Hilda know.'

Chapter Nine

Wednesday morning, back at the hovel

Boodle and I made our way home back down Mason, into Stanton, into North, into Beaufort and up Hill Street, all to avoid the remotest chance of encounters with St Alban's boys. It was only eight thirty, so technically I still had a whole three days before my birthday, and everything was going miraculously to plan.

No need to stress.

In a few hours I'd have just two and a half days left, but, again, *no need to stress*.

A headache was pressing against my skull, and a mindless mantra ticked through my head like the bicycle wheels spinning beneath me: *two and a half days, two and a half days . . .*

It only stopped when I squeezed my eyes shut so tightly I saw spots. Not because the spots were distracting. No, rather the near-death experience: Mrs Sidment was backing out of her drive and would have run me over for sure if Mr K hadn't yelled out from the other side of the road. I swerved away from the slow-moving vehicle and waved thanks across at Mr K. He just lifted his fedora in acknowledgement, and called, 'Keep your eyes open, Tallulah! That hound is not a guide dog!' with a disbelieving shake of his head.

So I was exhausted when I got home, but I suddenly had perspective again, thanks to Mrs Sidment's silent Lexus. And the part of me that had panicked for so long re eligible boy for kissing was quieted. Definitely. I did a few complex calculations in my head, e.g.:

$$\text{Arns} + \text{Mona} \times 1 \text{ afternoon encounter} = \text{Thurs evening date and possible snog}$$

Just to, you know, check that I wasn't GOING TO RUN OUT OF TIME. Seeing as my birthday was on SATURDAY.

Okay, breathe in, breathe out. Keep perspective! It's all going to be okay, I thought.

Boodle pushed the back gate open for me and I put the bike away in the shed, then poured water into one of Boodle's bowls from the tap outside the back door. I sat down on the step and stroked her back with one hand while she drank. Long tufts of hair came off with each stroke and I leaned against the door in the sunshine and carried on with the grooming motion.

Sigh.

I felt a Piz Buin tan coming on.

All was right with the world.

Inside, I heard the kitchen door thump open, the noise

echoing clearly through the window over the sink to my right. *Dad must be taking another sick day*, I thought idly, my hand still littering the courtyard with clumps of dog hair.

An angry voice at the sink inside made me jump nearly clean out of my skin.

'*I'm not coming back!*'

Silence.

It was Dad, sounding like I've never heard him before. Angry and upset and almost on the brink of tears. Shocked, I kept completely still, my hand motionless on Boodle. I couldn't let Dad know I was here, could I? No. Just those four words told me this was not something my father ever wanted me to hear.

'Freya,' he said then. 'It's too hard. My family will find out, and I – I just couldn't stand it.'

Find out what? What the hell was all this about? Who on this earth was Freya? Boodle lay down quietly and stared up at my stricken face.

'What do you mean *it helps that my wife knows*? She doesn't *really* know, Freya! That's just not possible!' He yelled so loudly I'm sure the window above me shook.

There was a crash then and a sob. I heard my father's slippers *shuck shuck* away, followed by the slam of the kitchen door and silence.

I still couldn't move. The sun suddenly felt harsh and bright, my skin itchy under the salt of sweat. I pressed the heels of my hands to my eyes for blissful darkness. There had to be a reasonable explanation. Anything but that my father was involved with someone else. I just had to think. *Think*.

Was Freya his new editor? And he was refusing to meet with the publisher again over some issue or another and Mum knew he wasn't going to get a book out this year and there'd be no money coming in . . .

That must be it.

I bit my lip.

But it could be anything. I'd be silly to jump to conclusions, crazy to add this to my list of worries.

I'd ask Dad later. Quietly, when he was on his own.

I took a deep breath. And another.

Dropping my hands to my knees, I noticed my fingers were trembling. In fact, my whole body was shaking. I needed a drink of cool sweet juice. A shower. A refuge. I looked across the courtyard at the annexe as I pushed myself slowly to my feet. Boodle jumped up with me and loped over to its door.

She's a mind reader, I thought.

I tried the handle. Locked of course. Then peered through the window of the living area. There were heaps of boxes and piles of old clothes. To the left of the front door was another window, but tall and narrow. It looked on to a small square area with a door to the bedroom and bathroom. To the right was the kitchen breakfast bar and living area.

It was bigger than I remembered. Right now it was dingy and horrible but with hard work it *could* be a lovely refuge.

Hard work. That's what I needed right now.

I should go and get paint, cleaning materials. But I was still frozen by the distress of my father's shouted words, still shaking.

Pull yourself together, Tallulah! Stop overreacting!

I scratched at my arm, trying to concentrate on the annexe instead of my freak father, and noticed a smear of rusty red on my wrist. Was that . . . Arnold Trenchard's blood? Ew!

I needed a shower. And before that a drink. Something strong, like Lucozade. Maybe even Lucozade Tropical.

Moving quickly and quietly round to the front of the house, I then came in noisily through the front door. 'Anyone home?' I called. There was no reply.

I sighed and dropped Boodle's lead on the hall table with the rest of the household clutter and noticed the phone wasn't there. I remembered the crash in the kitchen. Okaaay.

Shouldering my door open, I found a note from Pen taped to it.

Fatass
I'll be home for lunch. Salad?
P

Little chancer. Mum would have told her I wasn't well.

I showered first. It was beautiful. Hot water thundered over my face, hair, body till I thought of the planet and turned it off regretfully. I got into ancient tracksuit bottoms, pink, and a mustard yellow T-shirt that Pen had got me last Christmas. I'd never had such an awful gift in all my born days and our sibling relationship had taken a turn for the worse from the moment I unwrapped it.

I caught a glimpse of myself in the mirror, and grinned despite myself. I looked a lot like a pustule.

Bong went my computer, as if in agreement. Message. Carrie, Alex and Tam were on MSN.

CARRIE: Yoohooo! We're back from busking and we want the lowdown. T? You there?

TATTY BIRD: I'm here. How'd the busking go?

CARRIE: Awful. Wet. Tam got a pity tip from Alex's dad for two quid and the rest was small change. Alex is in a state about Coven's Quarter. What's going on?

TATTY BIRD: Huh?

CARRIE: It's Alex. Don't *huh* me. Coven's Quarter on the *Guardian* page 7. WHAT THE HELL? Come on, T! What's going on? Why is someone else getting the scoop on the Coven's Quarter story? Please sort it out otherwise our English grade is going to be poo and my portfolio pooier. I need this work experience to go well. Laters, okay? You'll message me?

And then they were gone. I felt a little miffed that they'd not asked about Mission Arns + Mona, but clearly I needed to see the paper. It was probably strewn across the kitchen table.

It wasn't, but the innards of the phone were – wires trailing across it like gutted intestines.

The front door slammed, shaking the entire house.

'Hello, slaves,' trilled Pen from the hall. 'Put the kettle on!'

She appeared in the kitchen doorway and took in the destruction of the telephonic device at a glance.

'Lula's gonna get into trou-uble,' she lilted, tossing her bag on the table, narrowly avoiding a glob of strawberry jam that would have stayed stuck to the faux leather forever.

I ignored her. 'Seen the paper?' I queried.

'Nope,' she said.

I checked everywhere downstairs. No way was I going up there to ask Dad. I needed to mull over what I'd overheard before I could face him.

Freya wasn't a homewrecking kind of name.

Definitely a publishing kind of name. Yes, definitely.

I gave up on finding the paper and slammed out the back door, feeling breezier already, keen for renovation.

Yanking the shed door open, I discovered cans of paint – and it was white, frabjous day! Now for brushes. I began lifting out bits and pieces I'd need. Elsa's work on Arns's room last night had left me feeling inspired.

'What are you doing?' came Pen's voice behind me.

'Preparing for the renovation of 155A Hill Street.'

'We're just 155, not A – oh, aha, I see what's up. The annexe.' Pen put her hands on her hips and stared at me belligerently. 'You've already taken over the cellar, Tallulah. Don't you think you should finish fixing that car in there before you start something else?'

'I can't do anything for Oscar till I've found a gasket for him.' I hefted up a bottle of white spirit and added it to the pile, then began wrestling with the wheelbarrow.

Pen scrunched her face into a *you're sooooo pathetic* expression. 'How could you call him Oscar? It's totally lame.'

'You'd rather I called him Angus?' I stopped tugging on the barrow handle to drag irritating tendrils back into my pony bunch.

'No!'

'Pen lurves Angus! Pen luuurves Angus!' I chanted.

'You're such a child.' Pen hoisted the front of the barrow over a bunch of DIY essentials, and set it down neatly next to my modest pile.

'Hmm,' I said. 'Thanks. What do you want, Penelope?'

She suddenly looked overly innocent. 'Shall I put this stuff in the wheelbarrow?'

'Yes, please,' I answered promptly. I knew my sister and I knew myself. Whether she told me now or later, I was going to have to give in to whatever she wanted anyway – might as well get my pound of flesh while it was on offer. 'So, Pen. Fancy giving me a hand with the renovations?'

It took us an hour to clear out all the empty boxes and paraphernalia from the annexe. During which time I'd sent Arns several messages like: Is Mona a go? Do you owe me yet? A date tonight would be perfect, thank you very much.

Pen trotted about in a disturbingly helpful way and we scrubbed and scoured the place from top to bottom, till we got to the bathroom. My sister drew the line at toilets, but she came in after a while to see how I was getting on with the cistern. (You don't wanna know.)

'I wonder what's behind that bath panel,' said Pen, tapping it firmly with her toe.

The old MDF caved instantly into a soggy hole.

'Yeek!' squealed Pen. She dropped to her knees to inspect the damage. 'Maybe some Polyfilla,' she suggested optimistically.

'Yeah, right.' I crouched down and peered in. 'Pen!' I said excitedly. 'It's an old claw-foot bath!'

We looked at each other and hefted a kick at the panel. It fell apart to reveal a puce-pink bath beneath, but, yep, it was claw-footed nonetheless. Pen began knocking the rot away enthusiastically, rattling on about what colour the bath should be repainted.

I watched her for a minute. 'You're working awfully hard for that salad, Pen.'

'I'm bored,' she admitted. Then, 'And I might live here *one day*,' the last words said with threatening emphasis.

I looked at her long and hard. 'I can't believe you're only here to make sure I don't paint anything avocado green.'

'Well . . .' Pen glanced down. 'Maybe I want to move into your old room today.'

I blinked and shook my head. 'Firstly – *why*? Secondly – it's going to take *forever* to get this place sorted out. Today is not an option.'

Pen held my gaze, unwavering: I groaned in despair, and ordered her to help pull off the rest of the bath panel.

In minutes the clean bathroom was clean no more, yet that tub was truly splendiferous.

'Cool,' said Pen. 'But you'd better get this place cleared up before Mum gets back. She'll freak if she sees you've been tearing down structures without her say so.'

'*Tearing down structures?*' I mimicked. Pen dodged the rotten clump of wood I threw at her. 'It's a good thing you want to be a solicitor, little sis, because you couldn't sound like anything else if you tried.'

'Whatever,' retorted Pen, being all fourteen again.

She clomped down the steps and out the door.

'Hey, where're you going?' I called, suddenly aware that there was still a lot of work to be done.

'To get bin bags,' Pen called back, halfway across the courtyard. 'Got to conceal the evidence.'

Ha! It was good having the law on my side.

Reaching for the broom, I began pushing the debris into a pile near the door. Pen came rustling back with a load of bin liners.

'Whoa! Stop! Stop!' cried Pen.

She was frozen in fright, her mouth open and her index finger pointing at my face. Her lips moved but nothing came out. I felt something move across my forehead and into my hair.

'Nyaaarr!' I yelled, shaking my head wildly. 'Wha-where-wha–?'

From the sheer horror on Pen's face I knew it could only be one thing.

'Spider!' she gasped at the exact moment it fell inside my shirt from its tenuous grip on my left earlobe.

I snatched at the shirt and pulled it away from my spine, arching my back and jumping even harder. I prayed urgently that I was wearing my Per Una knickers with the reputable elastic, and not one of the old twenty-in-a-pack-for-5p numbers that had lost their hold on my waist after the first wash.

'Where is it? Where is it? Pen? Pen? You've got to help me!' I pulled the shirt off over my head and whirled around. 'Is it still on me? Pen? *Pen?*'

'Uhh – uhh – uhh –'

It was no good. My sister was in full meltdown. I was still dancing around when I saw her index finger move, shaking, to the shirt that I still held in my hand.

On it was the hugest spider I'd ever, *ever* seen. People, I tell you now, that thing was not of this world. After *immense*, the next thought that sprang to mind was *hairy*, and that was followed shortly by *one nip from this thing and I'll be in A&E, spasming in death throes of an awful and painful kind.*

Frik! Frik! Frikking frik! We ran screaming into the safety of the sunshine outside.

'Aaaaaaaaah!'

'Aaaaaaaaaaaaaah!'

It's a good thing our courtyard is invisible from the Setting Sun's eagle-eye view over the town. If Mr Kadinski could have seen me leaping about topless, albeit with sensible undies still firmly strapped in place, he might have suffered a fatal coronary. It was bad enough Dad emerging at that instant.

'T, Pen, what?' he croaked from the back doorway.

'Dad, Dad, Dad,' gibbered Pen, grabbing him by the hairs on his forearm. He tried to swat her off, but she got behind him and began pushing him towards the annexe.

'What's *wrong* with you two?' Dad tried vainly to stagger back to the kitchen, but Pen elbowed him in the midriff and he kind of fell into the annexe doorway. It seems the spider had big ideas about leaving through the front door because Dad had only just stepped in there when he jumped straight back out with a sound like, 'Yoowaargh!' and did a little moonwalk in front of us. He slammed the door to the annexe shut. His face was white. 'Don't let it out!' he wheezed. And threw up over Mum's cacti collection near the back step.

At last his retching gave way to coughing and, shaking, he made his way back inside the house.

Looking over at Pen I put my hands on my hips and said, 'Okay, mainbrain, now what?'

Chapter Ten

Wednesday, needing lunch

Pen and I stared at each other in silence till Boodle the Poodle wandered out to see what was going on. She slobbered hello on Pen's leg and then Mum came home, looking hungry.

Followed shortly by Blue and Great-aunt Phoebe wielding the *Guardian*.

'Let's think about Supersize Spidey later,' I suggested, and we all trooped inside.

As I got the food on the go, Aunt Phoebe spread out the newspaper on the kitchen table.

'There,' she said grimly, stabbing at a headline on page seven with her perfectly manicured forefinger.

SITE OF ANCIENT WORSHIP DESTROYED?

Historical librarian Dr Anne Bird of Hambledon University denies the significance of missing documents necessary to stop bulldozers moving in on one of Britain's most ancient sites of mystic ritual. Coven's Quarter is set for demolition if evidence cannot be provided in time for the planning appeal meeting scheduled for Monday 19 April. Dr Bird declined to comment further, but colleagues confirm speculation that she is

distracted by the recent troubles of her husband,
renowned songwriter and poet Spenser Bird.
Is Dr Bird the best person to be heading up the
Coven's Quarter cause right now?

'Right,' said Mum, her face stricken. 'This is why the vice chancellor wants to meet with me asap.'

'What happened with Sophie this morning, Mum?' I asked, feeling desperate. 'What recent troubles? Is Dad okay? This is crazy.' The thought of this mystery woman Freya whipped into my mind. Maybe not so crazy. Who was Freya? Did this journalist know something about her?

Pen put another cup of tea down in front of Mum. 'How would this Felix Kennedy know the material is missing?'

'Your father might have been talking to strangers,' replied Mum tightly, 'down at the Rat and Parrot.'

'I can ask him,' I said, though I didn't want to. 'He's upstairs I think. Should we leave him some salad?'

Mum reached over and put the last of it on her plate. 'I'll talk to him later,' she replied, and I was deeply relieved I didn't have to face him just yet. We all crunched in silence. Even Blue, though it looked like she wanted to ask a thousand things, her eyes flitting from one face to another, searching for answers she didn't know the questions to.

Once Mum was done inhaling cucumber rounds at warp speed she said gloomily: 'Sophie has an alibi.'

'Tell all,' commanded Great-aunt Phoebe.

'Her parents say she was in her room, moving around getting ready, until her mother took her off to the dentist for her appointment at nine fifteen.'

'Her *parents*?' I yelped. 'That's not an alibi! Besides, she swiped in at eight.'

Mum looked at me squarely. 'The dentist appointment checks out, and there's no way she could have got to the library and back in under an hour.'

'Course she could! Even weighed down with all the metal piercings!'

'She lives on Stones Hill,' said Mum with finality.

'Hn,' I said.

'Big miles,' said Pen dismissively. 'So, Mum. Can you help us get rid of the spider?' My mind sifted through all the library info while Pen hatched a brave plan to catch the monster. She got the video camera (don't ask me why), I got a large bowl and some card paper, and in minutes we were good to go, with Blue as dubious wing man.

'Has it got very hairy legs?' asked Blue, biting her lip.

'Don't worry, Blue Bird,' I said in her ear. 'Pen's the only one with hairy legs.'

'*Operation Arachnid Assault showing no signs of proving successful,*' came Pen's documentary voice from behind the camera. '*Has the battalion's leader bitten off more than she can chew?*'

'You stay here, Blue,' I said, 'and hold the paper for me, okay?' She nodded, still chewing anxiously on her lip.

Taking a deep breath, I pushed the door open, and jumped back with a scream blood-curdling enough to bring Mum running over. She stood aghast in the doorway. 'That thing,' she muttered, shaking her head, 'needs to go to the zoology department. It's got to be from some tropical jungle. So . . .' she swallowed, '*huge*. So . . . so *fast*.'

She slammed the door quickly.

'Genetically modified?' came Pen's voice hopefully, like a hack on the brink of a big news story.

'No comment,' said Mum. 'It's on the loose in there. And I've got to go to work now.'

Pen and I burst into pleading wails for help, Blue jumping up and down babbling, '*Don't go! It will eat us! It will eat us!*' but Mum was having none of it. 'I can't be late, girls. I've got to inform the police now, and I should let Egginbottom know too.'

'Who's Egginbottom?' I asked.

'You are *so* blonde!' sniped Pen. 'Only, like, the town mayor.'

I slitted my eyes at her, but she just smirked fearlessly back.

'And he's also Mabel's brother. Can't believe that woman can be related to someone in office,' muttered Mum. 'Right. I'm off,' she announced.

As she turned to go, Boodle the Poodle suddenly sat bolt upright and then knocked Pen right over to streak up the path at the side of the house. *CRASHSMASH!* went the video camera.

'*NOOO!*' shrieked Pen.

There was a horrible silence.

'It wasn't me,' whispered Blue, and she scarpered to find Great-aunt Phoebe.

Mum, Pen and I stared at each other in shock.

'Dad's going to kill me,' whispered Pen.

'Yes,' I said, 'and –'

Suddenly there was a thud, barking and a loud yell from the front garden.

'Oh, for the love of God, *not* the postman again! I've told him to call from the front gate if he needs a signature,' huffed Mum, beetling up the path. I overtook her and turned the corner of the house to find Boodle rolling in the front garden, Arns rubbing her tummy with his foot.

'The dog went down.' Arnold grinned. 'Brought my killer tae kwon do sidestep and handoff into play.'

'What are you doing here?' I asked, eyeing the lump on his head from the PSG wall and jerking my head at Mum with my finger on my lips.

Arns nodded slightly.

'Everyone okay?' asked Mum, rushing up. 'Who yelled?'

'I did,' said Arnold. 'Martial-arts moves come with calls.'

I rolled my eyes.

'Is that you, Arnold?' asked Mum, blinking rapidly. 'What happened to your head? Was that Boodle?'

Arnold smiled. Boodle leapt to her feet and nudged him in the bottom with her wet nose back towards the annexe.

'Oof!' said Arns, staggering past us.

'Hey!' came Pen's voice from the courtyard. 'Watch for broken glass, Arnold Trenchard.'

'I'm going to be late,' despaired Mum.

'Take the car,' I suggested.

She nodded, sighing, and we followed Arns round to the back of the house where he was politely listening to Pen talking animatedly about him getting the spider out.

I clapped my hands to my face. 'You have no shame, Pen! You can't just hijack a visitor, and turn him into some kind of exterminator!'

'This I've got to see,' said Mum, and she sat down on the back step.

'Fine,' I said belligerently. 'But I am *not* involved.' I stabbed my finger aggressively at my sister, my eyes narrowed.

'Yeah, yeah,' she said.

Within minutes, Arns was poised with a takeaway container that I hoped would be big enough, and he'd even punched air holes in the lid. Pen pushed the door open, which I thought was admirable under the circumstances till I saw her brush past Arns a little closer than necessary, casting him a distinctly flirtatious look.

'Shameless!' I mouthed at her. 'You're *fourteen*!' and she stuck out her tongue at me.

'Where did I go wrong,' mumbled Mum, her glance flicking from her daughters back to Arns.

We waited quietly.

It didn't take long for the beast to emerge. Arns moved fast to get the container over it. The box made a cracking sound on the paving and we all gasped but it held, and the spider began scrabbling on the inside of the plastic.

'Ffff–' said Arns, then with a glance at my mum, '–fffvery, very big.'

He slid Pen's proffered piece of card under the container, then deftly flipped and whisked this way and that till at last the lid was on and the spider safely trapped.

'I don't feel very well,' he said suddenly.

'Why are you here?' I asked again. 'Why didn't you reply to my texts?'

'My mobile's dead. Got no mobie number for you and your home phone's not working,' he said. 'I had to let you know that Mona arranged to go out with me tonight. And she's bringing Ben Latter with her – he wants to meet you. Can you come? Dinner and a movie?'

'What?' I was astounded. 'B-Ben Latter? *The* Ben Latter that I have secretly fancied since I was *six years old*? Are you *serious*?'

'Oh yes!' Arns beamed. 'Your flirting efforts are going to make me look really, really good. Consider it the last step in Operation Makeover.'

'Spshslgpfff!' I hissed. 'You have no idea what this means, Arnold!'

Mum raised her eyebrows and disappeared into the house to find car keys.

My voice went tight and squeaky. 'You're nuts! Ben Latter is The One! I need a few *weeks* to get ready for a *hello* with him, let alone a *date*! Frik! Are You Out Of Your Mind? Don't do this to me, *please*!'

Mum appeared at the back door. 'I'll drive you home, Arnold,' she said. 'On my way back to work. Come on. And I'm sure Tallulah can't wait for tonight.' She gave me a knowing look and I felt my face turn puce.

'Thanks, Dr Bird,' said Arnold. 'Here's the spider.' He handed the container over to Mum and she popped it into one of her bags without a second's hesitation. Pen and I shuddered. I made a grab for Arnold, but he was quick in following Mum to the car.

'I'll come round at seven?' he called over to me. 'Then we can meet Mona and Ben at Steak City at seven thirty?' He turned to Mum. 'If you're sure that's okay with you, Dr Bird.'

'I'm delighted you'll be chaperoning Tallulah, my dear,' said Mum with a happy beam.

'*Wait!*' I called, jumping frantically on the spot. 'WAIT!'

The car doors slammed shut and Mum backed the car slowly down the drive.

'Don't I have any say in the matter?' I yelled.

Arnold rolled his window down and waved cheerily as they sped off. 'See you later!' he called, and a feeling of dread settled in the marrow of my bones.

Chapter Eleven

Wednesday afternoon, five hours till hot date

'What the hell are you going to wear?' asked Pen in despairing tones behind me. 'Ben Latter . . . You're going to have to pull out the stops.'

I made a small high-pitched sound. 'Why couldn't Arns have arranged some unscary person? I just need a kiss. And Ben Latter is never going to kiss me. Never.' I wrung my hands, forehead tightly wrinkled. 'He's going to remember me from Monday morning outside St Alban's. I was in the baggy track bottoms! All wrinkled! No mascara! Frik! *Frik!*' I sank to a heap on the ground and noticed my hands were shaking. 'I feel nauseous, Pen.'

'Well, no mascara *is* a criminal offence, Lu, but forget about Ben Latter for now.' Pen waved her arms dramatically, totally in charge. 'We need to get this room move sorted out. Time to start painting. It will distract you.'

'Painting?'

'The annexe walls and that tub. But first you're going to have to clear out the bathroom. Good thing Mum's left. She won't know you've been hacking stuff about.'

I didn't bother with backchat. Just got to my feet with a sigh and trudged through smashed camera to the annexe.

Before I stepped inside I got walloped with the washing-up gloves we'd been using. They hit the back of my head with a wet *schluk* and stuck to my neck.

'Wear those in case our eight-legged friend has a missus,' called Pen, disappearing into the kitchen.

'Frik,' I breathed, and smoothed down my goosebumps.

At four thirty Pen bellowed something at me from out in the courtyard. My arms and back ached and I was quite sure I had paint up my left nostril. I felt ragged and worn out.

And tonight I needed to be on top form.

After tonight, just two days left till my birthday.

Two days!

I had to impress Ben Latter.

I concentrated on finishing the paint job on the bath.

Another shout from Pen. I sighed and took a deep breath. 'WHAAAT?' I howled back. Then felt bad. I staggered out into the sunlight to find Pen standing in the courtyard, holding up a pretty pink camisole.

'Don't yell at me,' she said in a small voice. 'I was too scared to go in there. Any more creatures?'

'No. Sorry. Just tired.'

'How about this?' Pen danced the little lacy number in the air.

'It's see-through. Where did you find it? I haven't laid eyes on that for, like, ever.'

'Bottom of your laundry basket,' said Pen quickly.

'Ha. Not frikking likely, Pen. I'm the only washerwoman in this place and that basket was emptied yesterday.'

'OK, bottom of mine.'

'Doesn't that camisole belong to me?'

'Oh, here we go. You should be grateful I once had the intention of washing it for you.'

'*You* wore it! Clearly. And I don't remember you ever asking if you could.'

Pen sighed and went back into the house.

I followed. 'Sorry, Pen. Look, do you want to see the annexe?'

Pen laid the camisole over a chair. 'Is it all clear in there?'

'Not a single creature, not a speck of dust, not a smidgeon of dirt.'

We went out to investigate.

'Wow, Lu.' Pen put her hand on my shoulder. 'It's wonderful. And the bathroom?'

I led her into the tiny space between bedroom and living room. The little window let in lots of light and even I took a breath at the sight of the bath resplendent in grey against the white walls. There was a good-sized basin near the window and a toilet with an old-fashioned cistern mounted high on the wall. They both gleamed beautifully. Even the old pine floorboards had scrubbed up well.

'Wow,' said Pen again.

'And wait till you see what I found in the kitchen.'

Pen shot me a look and walked round the breakfast bar to investigate. 'Nooo!' she squealed. 'A teeny little fridge!'

I clapped my hands excitedly. 'And I think it works!'

'Nooo!'

'Yessss!'

Pen shut the door of it with a thud and looked at me seriously. 'Mum's never going to let a boy within a mile of this place. This is Seduction City.' She stepped back up to the bedroom, looking up at the huge skylight windows flooding the room with warmth and light.

'Forget the first kiss,' said Pen baldly. 'This could be where you get laid.'

'*PEN!*'

'Let's get your furniture in,' she said.

It soon became clear that Penelope Bird was desperate to get me out of my room. *Desperate!* She made us shuffle in and out of house and annexe like jerky silent-movie Charlie Chaplins on Red Bull.

As I headed back into the house to find some clean bed linen I heard her turning taps on and off as I went. Seemed the hot water was a living relative of the main house's – same kind of loud, thumping dialogue, but it had settled into its usual death rattle by the time I got back with the linen.

Pen emerged triumphant.

'Leave the sheets, Lula. Come with me.'

I tossed everything on to the now clear bed and followed her back to the house. She made straight for the back veranda.

This space belongs to Dad. Dad is the messiest of us all. It pains him to throw anything away. He walks along the streets of Hambledon and if he chances to spot an old spark plug, a screw, a bit of wire, it all goes into his pockets and then on to the sills of the massive windows that run the length of the veranda along the back of the house. It's a long, thin space with a spectacular view and this is why Dad likes to write out here.

And drink.

He thinks we don't know about The Green Box.

The Green Box looks like any old storage, but it can hold three quarts of lager, two vodka jacks and an expandable plastic cup. Pathetic. But I'm not going to get started on that.

To get to the desk area you've got to squeeze past an enormous trunk (Mum calls it the trousseau) and an armchair so huge it's like a mini sofa. The chair is a nice shape, but the fabric is so stained and ripped that it makes me wince every time I have to touch it, which is quite often, unfortunately, because this is where Mum has strung a kind of interior clothes line for days too wet and cold to dry the laundry outside.

'You've hung my washing. Thanks, Pen.'

'Sure. No problem. Now give me a hand.'

'Pardon?'

'With the chair. C'mon. We're going to have to hoist it to the left – okay? – like so, then angle it to the right and squeeze ever so carefully through the French doors. Do you think we'll get it through the annexe front door?'

'No frikking way.'

'What?'

'That rotting pile of sponge is going nowhere near my pristine interior.'

'Listen to you! I thought you had an eye for potential.'

I paused. It did have an elegant curve to it. I wavered. 'Okay, let's do it.'

'You can't take Dad's beer chair,' came a small, clear voice behind us. We turned to find Blue in her fabulous cloak, pulling anxiously at the hem. 'He'll be cross again.'

'Oh, Blue,' said Pen. 'It's all good! No drinking chair, no smelly beer breath, right?'

'He'll still be thirsty with no chair,' declared Blue, shrugging Pen off and heading for the stairs. 'You are going to be in big trouble.'

'Think she's going to tell Dad?' I panicked.

Pen shook her head. 'She's on our side.' She glanced at me quickly. 'But let's get a wiggle on.'

More shuffling and the chair was heaved into the back

corner of the annexe's living area. Pen collapsed on it with a groan. 'Your skin is touching it,' I noted.

'Pfff,' said Pen, her head back, her eyes closed.

'What am I going to cover it with?'

Pen smiled. The last time I'd seen that grin was seconds before she emptied all of Dad's booze from The Green Box down the toilet, and carefully replaced the empty bottles. What happened later was not pretty. Clearly Blue still remembered the incident.

'Oh no,' I said firmly. 'Whatever it is, no way.'

My evil sister opened her eyes and said, 'Great-gran's feather quilt.'

My jaw dropped. 'The *heirloom*?'

Pen nodded, still smiling.

'Geez, Pen. You're out of your mind. There's a reason Mum keeps it bundled away in the trousseau, you know.'

'Time it got appreciated.'

'You'll explain to Mum?'

'I will.' She nodded once, like some judge in a high court approving a not-guilty sentence, then heaved herself up. 'I've arranged a little surprise in the bathroom. Go on in and relax while I bring in the heirloom and some outfits.'

I turned to go, then stopped. 'Pen,' I said quietly. 'Thanks for today.'

She glanced at me quickly, then stared down at the paint splatter on her fingernails. 'It's been fun,' she said, then looked up at me with a quick grin.

I smiled back. 'Yes, but I know you've got an ulterior motive, haven't you?'

Pen's grin got bigger. 'I have. But you'd better start getting ready. It's six p.m.'

That bath was truly sublime, even though my stomach was in knots, twisting in terrible anxiety about dinner and a movie with Ben Latter. Sure, I felt comforted that I wouldn't be alone. I knew I liked Mona. And Arnold would help, wouldn't he? Though he had said he wanted to look good with me as a foil. My thoughts wandered. Who had suggested Steak City? Ew. Did Arnold know I was vegetarian?

'Time's up!' called Pen. She nudged the door open a few centimetres and put a glass of something thick and cold on the floor. 'That's to give you energy.'

I pulled the plug out with a regretful sigh and got towelling. The smoothie was . . . interesting. I emerged, gurgling up the last few drops. Pen held out her hand for the glass.

'Your outfits are in your boudoir,' she said.

'Whoa! Outfits? Pen, *what do you want*?'

Pen sighed. 'Look, it's got nothing to do with you. I just needed to get a little further away from Blue's yodelling and Dad's snoring, okay?'

'Don't lie to me,' I said, narrowing my eyes.

'Okay, *fine*!' said Pen. 'You need to kiss someone, Lula, *anyone*. Please! I'm your *sister*, and your stupid jinx problem is already becoming my problem! Jason Ferman stared at me really weirdly the other day, and I just know he thinks I'm also –'

'Hey! Jason Ferman is a freak. He was prob–'

'I don't want to talk about this!' yelled Pen.

I stared at her aghast. She looked really upset.

'Pen, I –'

'Don't,' she said. 'Just get dressed. You don't have much time.'

I went into my room and stared at the outfits laid out on the bed.

'Oh, Pen. Thanks. They're perfect.'

She came up behind me and spoke in a small voice. 'I'm sorry I yelled.'

I sighed. 'I totally understand. I wouldn't want to be infected with my reputation either. Thanks for these.' I gestured at all the clothing, wondering what Ben would find irresistible, and hating myself for caring.

'No problem. Mum's just helping me move my bed. I'll be back at quarter to, to show you and your penthouse off.'

I nodded and headed for my hairdryer. Once I'd got the style sorted I lashed on as much mascara as possible, and carefully stroked some dark shadow on to my lids, a little colour on my cheeks and shimmery gloss on my lips.

Then I picked up the flimsy camisole doubtfully. Pen had miraculously found matching undies, though not much of a priority there – what hope had I of clothing removal when kissing was still an issue? She'd put out my favourite jeans and a pretty beaded lilac cardigan of hers that I'd always coveted.

I was just putting my shoes on when a knock came at the door. I opened it with a flourish.

'You look amazing, Lu,' said Pen. 'I knew that cami would work.'

Boodle the Poodle suddenly barked from the garden. It sounded like she was at the front gate.

'Arnold's here,' I said, smoothing down the cardigan nervously.

'Okay, Lula,' said Pen solemnly. 'Remember that if Ben Latter doesn't kiss you, you'll just have to kiss him. Even if it's against his will.'

I looked at Arns over the table of flickering candles. He looked good. It didn't make me feel any better.

'When did they say they'd get here?'

'Calm down. They're just a few minutes late.'

'I'm not sure I can do this. The smell of sizzling flesh is making me feel ill.'

'Protein is an essential part of the human diet.'

'Not animal protein.'

'I can't believe you're vegetarian. Is this a soapbox of yours?' Arnold raised his eyebrows.

I looked at them closely.

'Has Elsa been plucking?'

Arns blushed furiously.

'Sorry,' I said, 'didn't mean to embarrass you. You look great.'

'Er . . .' said Arnold, then, 'Hi, Mona!' and, 'You must be Ben!' he added, springing up in relief.

Mona didn't say anything, just slid into the booth next to Arnold. I think she was smiling so hard her lips couldn't move to form words.

Whoa!

She really, *really* liked him! I could tell by the way her eyes were kind of lit up, the way she sat close, but not too close, definitely not touching, and the fact that she didn't seem able to speak. I could tell because, staring up at the perfection of Ben Latter, I felt the same way.

He was wearing a pale blue shirt with a collar that buttoned down and very dark blue jeans that hung beneath the heels of expensive brown shoes. Not trainers, not boots, *shoes*. The trendy kind that cost a lot from exclusive shops. The sleeves of his shirt were rolled about twice up from the cuffs and the tanned smoothness of his forearms made me flush. Could he see that I wanted to touch him?

Frik!

I bit my bottom lip, willing myself to stop grinning like a loon. Though his blond fringe flipped low over his forehead I could still see his eyes. They were a darker blue than I remembered, and they were looking at me.

Ben sat down next to Mona. I felt my cheeks burn. *He didn't even want to sit next to me.* Cringe! This was going to be too terribly dreadful for words. He wasn't smiling – just gazing at me intently. 'So . . . you're Spenser Bird's daughter?' he mused.

'Uh . . . yes.' I gestured at the three of them sitting in a row opposite me and laughed nervously. 'Is this an inquisition?'

Awkward silence.

'Oh, sorry,' he said unapologetically. 'It's just . . . you look familiar. You look like the library lady's kid.' He stood slowly and came to sit on my side.

It was official. I was a beet on a body. Purple complexion, features morphed into one big purple round purple purple thing that was very purple. The boy I had lusted after for ten years – The One, The Love Of My Life – barely knew who I was. *Worse!* I'd been reduced to The Library Lady's Kid, like some brat with a snotty nose.

I looked at Arns.

He looked at Mona.

Mona looked at him.

I coughed.

'I *am* the library lady's kid,' I said.

'Of course!' Ben slapped his perfect forehead. I jumped. 'Dr Bird, Spenser Bird – your mum and dad? This town is sooo incestuous.'

Incestuous? My brow furrowed. I could feel it wrinkling away and quickly assumed a *you're so unbelievably clever and interesting* expression.

'Ye es,' I said, though my parents were married, *not* related. 'How'd you know about my dad? Have you read his poetry?'

'Oh, uh.' Ben picked up a fork and put it down again. 'Doesn't everyone know of Spenser Bird? Songwriter to the stars?'

'Oh,' I said. I leaned back in the booth, wishing it would swallow me up. In London, in New York, maybe even LA, sure, Dad was wined and dined. But people in our town knew Dad for his academic status – I liked it that way. 'What's your favourite Spenser Bird song, then?' I asked hesitantly.

Ben looked at me for a long moment. Arnold and Mona were laughing together at something on the menu and I hated them for being so happy with each other when I felt so vulnerable. Suddenly I didn't care about the jinx any more. I just wanted to get away.

'I want to talk about *you*, Tallulah,' said Ben, 'not your father.'

Our eyes met.

And suddenly I got it. I got what a world of poets and musicians and artists and, mainly, Alex had been banging on about forever. It was a slam to the chest, a prickling of the skin all over, a blush from split ends to toenails, a high of unbelievable proportions. What a rush to have all that gorgeousness focused entirely on me. Me, people! Me! Meee! *Me!* I saw him all over again: the blond hair that curved perfectly over his forehead, bluest of blue eyes under chiselled brow over chiselled cheekbones over chiselled jaw. The straightest nose. And lips – I admit to you now I couldn't tear my eyes from his lips. But I must have because when I saw his smile it was in the tiny crinkles at the corners of his eyes before it hit the world's best toothpaste ad unfolding beneath.

In the instant of his grin I knew I had to have him. Nooo – not in the rampant *I've got to lose my virginity* game, rather in the *hi this is my boyfriend Ben whom I kiss all the time constantly mine mine mine* kind of game.

I blinked.

Ben was saying something. He stopped, waiting for a reply.

'Pardon?' I said.

He looked at me closely. 'You didn't hear me?'

'Sorry. A million miles away.' I tore my gaze from his face and reached for the jug of water in the middle of the table. It was too heavy to show the trembling of my hands. I hefted it towards Ben's glass. 'Water?'

Arnold's voice spluttered into my consciousness. 'Sorry, Tallulah. I should have got that.' He lifted the jug out of my grasp and filled all our glasses, then lifted his in a toast.

'To Boodle the Poodle.'

Mona and I laughed. We knew what he meant, and it was sweet. Mona kissed him on the cheek and they sat staring at each other. Wow! Had she just, like, *made the first move*? I mean, sure, it's only a kiss on the cheek, but *still*! I didn't know where to look until Ben cleared his throat and said, 'Boodle?'

I glanced up into his face and I suddenly felt with a thudding heart that this – Ben Latter with Tallulah Bird, a childish dream – was *real*. This incredible boy and me, sitting side by side, candlelight dancing over our faces . . . And not only was it real, but I felt like I *belonged* in it. He really and truly seemed interested in *me*.

'Boodle,' I said slowly, 'is my very big and hairy bodyguard.'

Ben's eyes widened. 'Wow, your dad must be bigger news tha– Oh –' He stopped. 'Ha ha, very funny. You don't have a bodyguard.'

'I like the fact you thought I did. Even if it was just for a millisecond.' I smiled sweetly.

He smiled back. 'Couldn't help it. You look like a famous person.'

'As in, here she is checking into the Priory?'

'As in, here she is checking out of the Priory.'

'Oh, ha ha to you too, mister.' I laughed.

'You talking rehab already, Ben?' asked Mona with a teasing grin. She looked at me and rolled her eyes. 'Ben is a chemical freak,' she continued. I glanced at Ben. His eyebrows had drawn together and he shifted uneasily. 'Always talking about what this or that compound can do for a person. He's been banging on about how he's going to wow everyone with his big paper at the opener to the Science Fair on Monday.'

My eyes were fixed on Ben. His beautiful mouth had pulled into a strange line that I didn't like, even though I wanted to. Mona's voice droned on – '. . . latest thing is . . . addiction . . . always out . . . Fort Norland like the back of his hand . . .' I wished I could look back at her, but I was transfixed by the marring of the lips, how very red Ben's face had become. He was furious.

'But I think that's great,' I said desperately. 'Scientific research – must be so exciting. Helping addicts.'

'It *is* great,' said Mona. 'Don't be cross with me, Ben. Someone's got to tell Tallulah how fantastic you are.'

Ben smiled uncomfortably.

'So . . .' said Arns. 'Everything ready for your big exposé next Monday, then?'

'Just about,' said Ben shortly.

We sat in silence. Arns coughed.

'Just going to the bathroom,' said Mona, and she slid out of the booth and disappeared.

'Well, you obviously don't want to talk about it,' I said brightly, turning to Ben, 'but I think it is amazing that you're doing something so relevant.' Ben looked at me blankly. 'Did Mona say you do work at Fort Norland? Community projects with drug addiction.' I waved my arms enthusiastically. 'That's what you're involved in, right? Drugs?'

Ben pursed his lips. The scary line was gone. 'Absolutely,' he said, his skin colour returning to normal. 'It *is* important. Narcotics ruin too many people's lives.' He lifted his glass for a few gulps. 'I don't like talking about it – all very confidential. Sorry if I sound like some kind of boring do-gooder. Most people would rather I was an interesting bad guy, but that's just not who I am.' He fiddled with his fork self-consciously. I had a strong urge to kiss him sweetly on the cheek and pat his shoulder. Okay, that's a lie. I wanted to jump his bones.

Then Arns said, 'Don't worry, Lula's one of the good guys.' He winked at me as he took a drink from his glass and I thought, *Noo, Arns! Me being one of the guys is not helpful right now.*

'Good, maybe,' said Ben. His smile made my heart jump out of my chest. (Seriously. My entire left breast moved.)

'But absolutely not one of the guys.' His eyes ran the length of my body and my whole self blushed.

Ben put his hand on my forearm as he lifted the water jug and my heart did its little samba dance again.

'Another drink?' he asked, leaning closer.

Chapter Twelve

Wednesday night, Steak City

'Absolutely delicious,' said Ben, between mouthfuls.

I wondered if he'd say that after his lips had met mine. *Stop it!* I told myself. *Focus!*

Smiling at him, I pushed a crouton to the side. (No way I was going to risk trying to spear one of those little bullets. There'd be an incident and Dr McCabe would be involved for sure.)

'Tell me what it's like having a famous father. I bet you have to study his poems in English class.'

'It's not like that. He's not a big celebrity. But I'm really proud of him,' I said defensively.

Putting his hands up, palms facing out, Ben leaned back and said, 'Absolutely! Absolutely! But, you know, creative temperaments . . .' He took another drink. 'Is your mum the calming influence?'

'Mum's very organised,' I said. 'But she's creative too.'

His eyes crinkled in a smile again and I wondered suddenly if he could see how much I liked him just from looking at me. I shot a look over at Arns and Mona, who were talking quietly together.

'So you're the eye of the storm?' asked Ben. He looked at

me intently and I began to talk, not about anything really serious – I couldn't even tell my closest friends about Dad's drinking – but even just nattering on about how my family all rubbed along together felt like deep revelations. I'd just got to Blue and her eccentricities when:

'Absolutely,' murmured Ben. He checked his watch, fiddled around inside his jacket pocket and said, 'Listen, I've got to run – I'll get this – unless you guys want coffee or dessert or anything?'

Huh? He was leaving?

Arnold and Mona tore their eyes from each other and blinked at us.

'I thought we were going to see a movie,' said Arns, looking over at me.

'I'd love that. Soon?' said Ben, looking at me. I nodded dumbly. 'Can I call you?'

And suddenly, instead of feeling outraged that he was leaving me to gooseberry the lovebirds *on our first date*, I felt flattered that he wanted to see me again. *Omigoodness, second date! On our own!*

'Sure,' I said, forgetting to blink seductively.

'Thank you,' he said softly, close to my ear, and then he kissed me on the cheek and left, stopping at the door to settle the bill.

The restaurant rattled on even though its most beautiful, *most* incredible customer had just left.

'Well,' said Arnold. 'Anything you said, Lula?'

'What?' I asked, a big smile on my face.

Mona punched lover boy in the arm. 'I thought that went really well!' she enthused. 'Ben's never interested in any of the PSG girls, but he was really wrapped up in you, Tallulah!' I glowed. 'Hm?' she said, turning to Arns, with a question on her face.

'Yep,' said Arns. 'Ben is *wonderful*. Let's get dessert.'

'No time before the film,' said Mona crisply. 'I bet Ben had –'

'Yes,' said Arns abruptly. He seemed cross. 'Selfless community project work to do, right?'

Mona checked her watch. 'I think his little group meet around about now.'

'Very diligent,' I said, still grinning like a crazy person.

The grin lasted all the way to His Majesty's Theatre, Hambledon's prehistoric cinema, until Mona, facing the billboards, said, 'Ooh. Keira Knightly. Orlando Bloom. I feel like a romcom.'

'What about Matt Damon?' I asked desperately.

Mona and Arnold turned to look at me at exactly the same moment with exactly the same expression on their faces: *hey, little sister, are you nuts?* kind of thing.

'How many times,' said Arnold patiently, 'can Mr Bourne find a new identity?'

'Same old,' agreed Mona, at one with her man.

'You go,' I said. 'I'll head home.'

'Nooo!' said Mona. 'Come on. This'll be fun. You can do Matt Damon with Ben on your next date. He'll be so incredibly impressed you're not into chickflicks, unlike us PSGers.'

I hesitated.

Arnold threw me a pleading glance. Why, I didn't know. I mean, he had this infatuation all wrapped up – he really didn't need me.

'Okay,' I said reluctantly, then kicked myself as Arns's face fell. Ohhhh. He'd been pleading for me to go. Duh! 'But I'm not sitting with you lovebirds,' I added hastily.

Arnold looked instantly cheerier and splashed out on treating 'his two ladies' (puke) to tickets, and Mona got the chocolates, so the film experience would be a pamper-me session. I should be grateful.

We had plenty of time before the movie started. Mona's schedules were clearly a good thing. I had a feeling she was super-efficient. Arns would like that.

The theatre was just that, a theatre. Of the oldest-fashioned sort. The seats were red leather-effect vinyl, and stretched away down and up again to a wide stage and red crushed-velvet curtains that soared to an incredibly high ornate ceiling. Wall lights shaded in dusty velvet lined the red and gold papered walls, and dimmed promptly at the start of the film. They were at full wattage now, and Mona startled Arns and I with a little shout: 'JACK!'

She giggled at the fright we'd got. 'My brother,' she explained. 'Over there.'

'Your cousin Alex is always going on about Jack,' said Arnold quickly, shooting me a look. 'She's one of Tallulah's best friends.'

'Freaky! We're all connected, and we didn't even know each other earlier today!' said Mona. 'I'll have to waylay Jack after the movie and introduce you. JACK!'

The faraway figure turned and waved before settling into a seat in the midst of a group of what looked like university students – all of them girls. I got a glimpse of dark floppy hair falling over an eye, a tall rangy frame, a flash of white teeth. Even from here I could see that Jack was tall, dark and fffff! handsome. No wonder Alex wanted him for her glam-mag empire; he'd add serious gloss to any enterprise.

'Right,' I said. 'I'm going to bag a seat over there.' I pointed to the distance. 'Thanks for the chocolates,' I said, and headed down the aisle.

'Sure you don't want to sit with us?' called Mona.

I shook my head and waved a farewell, choosing a row halfway between Mona and her brother, an acre of space in either direction. I ripped open my bag of Maltesers with relish and got crunching. Sooo good. All was right with the world.

The movie was sweet, though Keira's long black hair and porcelain complexion had me hating myself. Perhaps if I grew mine . . . I gave myself a mental headshake. Like, hello? I had the patience of a flea. All that upkeep would have me on Prozac in no time. And me with dark hair? Nope. As the credits rolled up I sighed and stretched. A teary episode had made my eyes bloodshot and I could feel my nose had geared up to twice its normal size, with nostrils swelling closed so I couldn't breathe.

'Tallulah? You okay?' Mona had appeared at the end of my row looking concerned.

'Hab I got bascara od by face?' I mumbled, shuffling, embarrassed, to my feet. 'So glad I didn't see this with Bed.'

Mona handed me an aloe-vera facial wipe without comment, and began wittering. 'It was quite sad when Keira . . .'

Facial wipes. Geez. She *was* organised. I swiped the panda-look away from around my eyes, checked I had everything on me and started moving towards the aisle.

'Jack!' Arns and I both jumped out of our skins and Mona laughed. Again. 'You guys are quite wound up,' she noted, as the group of students neared.

I saw that most of them were very Keira-looking. Loads of hair. Miles of perfect skin. Gorgeous bodies, gorgeous clothes. I gritted my teeth. 'I'b goi'g to head hobe,' I said, with a blocked nose. 'Thanks for the boovie.'

'Oh, er, I'll, um, if it's okay with you, Mona . . .' started Arns.

'Absolutely bot,' I said firmly. 'I'b fibe to walk hobe ob by own.'

'Sure, but your mum is scary, Lula.' He paused as a chivalrous thought occurred to him. 'And I'd never take the chance anyway. You know, of something happening to you.'

The student group had arrived. Jack was taller, darker and handsomer than I'd thought. He reminded me a little of the guy Carrie had taken to that year-eight dance with me and Stan Pavorovich. While I'd wound up at the hospital with Stan, Carrie had ended up crying in the girls' bathroom because her partner had danced with every girl except her. What spiked that memory? The self-confident air he had? The way the girls' voices went up a notch around him? Ugh.

'See you girls tomorrow,' said Jack, turning to his posse.

One of them hung back. 'You're not walking me home, babes?' she asked.

'Oh,' he said. 'Aren't you going back with Sarah and Ems? I just want a word with my sister.'

'I can wait,' the girl said.

'I don't want to hold you up, Jazz. You go on. I'll see you tomorrow?'

We watched the dialogue, heads bouncing back and forth like tennis spectators.

The muscles in Jazz's jaw clenched for just an instant, then, 'Sure,' she muttered, and headed up the aisle after her friends.

'Another stalker, Jack?' whispered Mona, trying not to laugh.

Huh, I thought. *Probably he's just tired of her. Ready for the next one. Sarah, Ems, whoever.*

Jack bit his lip. 'She's sweet,' he said, then, 'You okay, sis? Less stressed?'

'Yes,' she replied. 'This is Arnold Trenchard. He's a science whizz and has explained the whole thing to me.'

'I owe you big,' said Jack, shaking Arnold's hand. 'I thought she was going to go nutso.' He dipped his head in Mona's direction and then looked at me. He didn't say anything.

Yep, I thought bitterly. *Lookee here – I'm an invisible girl, a haze in the air, not beautiful enough for your radar.* I blew my nose loudly into an old tissue I'd found in my coat pocket.

Preerrrp.

'Tatty,' said Mona, 'this is my brother Jack. He goes to uni here.'

I held out my hand for a handshake. Jack looked startled.

'Oh, Jack' – Mona punched him on the arm –

'enlightened girls shake hands too, you know.'

'Sorry,' said Jack. 'That's not why – I mean, I didn't – uh . . .' He shook my hand. Firm, decisive. 'Tatty.'

Then he looked me up and down, and laughed.

How frikking rude was this guy! I looked at him in shock. Usually, I didn't give my nickname a second thought, but . . . Was he actually implying that I *was* tatty? And not in a dishevelled, incredibly cool kind of way?

Whoa.

I blinked, took a calming breath and tuned in to what he was saying: 'What are you guys doing now?'

'We were just debating,' replied Mona.

'I'b headi'g hobe,' I said quickly, just wanting to get away. 'Thanks for the boovie, Arns, and the sustenance, Boda. Dice to beet you, Jack.' That last bit took a lot of willpower, let me tell you. Clearly I'd been schooled in manners somewhere along the line. Unlike the person I'd just met.

'Not so fast, Lula,' said Arns. 'We need to walk you home.'

'Boda will be late back to school then,' I said. I blew my nose again. They all stepped back, but I grinned happily. I could breathe at last. 'I'm fine on my own. Really. I'll have nine-nine-nine on redial and I'll text you when I'm back safely.'

'No,' said Arnold. He looked reluctantly at Mona.

'Maybe your brother could walk y–'

'Perfect!' said Mona. 'Jack, you wouldn't mind walking Tatty, would you?'

My jaw dropped.

Jack looked amused. 'No problem.'

Mona grinned. I felt my face warm and cast about in my mind for anything, *anything* to not let this happen. No way was I spending a moment with a guy who thought I looked like a tramp. I wanted to pretend I'd never met him, and think about Ben instead.

Omigoodness! Ben Latter. His blond hair, his perfect face, the way his eyes had looked past mine, into my thoughts. The energy rolling off him that made me kind of crinkle inside. The lurch of my stomach when I saw him, when he spoke.

'I really,' I said firmly, '*really* would rather walk home on my own.'

Then I caught the look on Arnold's face. The boy was desperate for time alone *in the dark* with Mona. He held her hand in a vice grip. I could see white knuckles and everything. He coughed.

'I'm not that bad,' said Jack. 'My cousin Alex can vouch for my character.' A slow, lazy smile stretched over his face and my stomach lurched. He's making the bile rise, I decided.

'Fine,' I said. 'Can I come out now?'

Jack was standing in the space between rows so I couldn't get into the aisle. He stood aside and swept low into a bow as I walked towards him.

Mona and Arns were ecstatic, I noted bitterly. They hugged each other close and hurried to the exit, desperate for a bit of full moon and the cover of darkness. I forced a smile while we said our goodbyes.

Jack and I watched them swing down the road together, Arnold talking quickly, waving his free hand in the air, explaining something.

The air shifted and felt colder. I pulled the softness of the cardigan round me and regretted the lacy number beneath.

'Let's hit the road, Jack,' I said wryly, but he didn't laugh.

He slung an arm over my shoulders and countered with, 'Sure, T-Bird.'

The skin prickled on my neck against the warmth of his arm. I stepped away and threw him my best bad-ass look. 'Only my dad calls me that.'

'Why does no one call you Tallulah?' he asked. 'Alex never said why you're Tatty.'

I crossed my arms and looked him in the eye. 'You seem to have your own ideas about why I'm called Tatty.'

'What?' He had the grace to look confused.

'In the cinema,' I said hotly. I swallowed. 'You gave me the old sneery looking up and down in there.' I nodded at the theatre behind him.

Jack stepped towards me. He suddenly looked younger. 'Geez!' he exclaimed. 'Cut me some slack! It was just a shock meeting you, that's all. After all this time hearing about you from Alex. I wasn't being sneery. I was just surprised to see you there. Alex said . . .'

He paused and I felt my outrage sieve slowly out of me. Oh, *cringe*. Had I misread the look and the laugh?

I turned and began walking up the hill. Jack strode alongside. 'Hey,' he said, and bumped me gently with his arm. 'I'm sorry I gave you the wrong impression. Sometimes I – well, you know, um – I may seem rude, but it's a shyness thing. Really. Or um maybe I'm just not good with girls.'

'I'm not good with boys,' I said before I could think, then bit my lip. *How could I have said that out loud?*

We checked for traffic on Beaufort Street and crossed over.

'So, why are you called Tatty?' asked Jack.

'A long time ago,' I said uncomfortably. 'An unfortunate outfit in pre-school. You don't want to know.'

Jack grinned. 'I know more about you than you think,' he drawled.

'Don't go there,' I snapped. 'I'm still cross with you.'

Jack wisely bit his tongue and I snuck a look over at him. You couldn't get two boys more different than Jack de Souza and Ben Latter: Jack all dark angles and weird energy; Ben so lit-up and fluid and magnetic. I could see why Alex liked Jack, though. He really was amazingly gorgeous. If you liked that whole rugged and scary thing.

'– like you,' Jack was saying.

'Sorry?'

'Alex,' repeated Jack. 'She's a lot like you.'

'You've got the wrong girl,' I replied. 'I'm nothing like Alex.'

'That's not what I meant.'

'That's what you said.'

What was wrong with me? I couldn't stop sniping at this guy. *I just want to be at home, thinking about Ben*, I whined to myself.

We were walking fast, my arms swinging like a chimpanzee on a cross-country event, but Jack kept his hands in his back pockets, his long legs carrying him along next to me easily. And I could walk really quickly. I picked up the pace.

Jack laughed. 'Would you rather run?'

'I like to walk fast.'

'I see why you weren't bothered about heading home alone – you could outstride any attacker.'

I stopped abruptly. 'Look, thanks for walking me home. The thing is that I've had a pretty crazy day' – something made my voice catch; I coughed – 'and was hoping for some space. I'm just desperate to be in bed right now.' Oh, frik. Did I just say I wanted to be *in bed*? Did I say *desperate*?

Really, there was no hope for me. At. All.

'Um, in bed, you know, *sleeping*,' I added hastily, my face on fire. 'Let's cross the road.'

I checked for cars and I swear I heard him laugh, but when I whirled to face him with narrowed eyes his face was perfectly composed.

'Why?' asked Jack.

'Because we need to get to the other side,' I muttered.

Jack grinned and we walked over the still, wide street, the moon casting shadows on our faces. 'Why'd the sheep cross the road?' he asked.

'Surely,' I said, 'a university student can do better than crossing-the-road jokes? I'm losing faith in our academic system.'

'A sheep is many steps above the common chicken,' said Jack, his voice deepening with the seriousness of his tone. 'Our system of learning has taught me this and much more. Do you know why snot is green?'

'I beg you. Spare me. Please.' I could see the chimneys of the Setting Sun now.

We crunched through the gravel on Mrs Sidment's front pavement in silence and still neither of us had spoken as we rounded the corner up to Dr Thurwell's, but when we hit Mr and Mrs Jones's garden-gnome collection Jack came up with, 'Yow!'

'What?' I asked.

'Nothing,' he said quickly, then, 'That gnome with the mallet. Kind of takes you by surprise, you know. The life-size bulgy eyes.'

'Does anyone else know about your fear of garden gnomes?'

'Come on.'

'Nothing to be ashamed of, you know. It's a proper condition. With a name and everything.'

We were on the home straight now.

Jack cleared his throat. 'So you know about phobias?'

'All about phobias. My sister has arachnophobia. Ask me anything.'

'Well, I'm not interested in phobias as such. More interested in, like, unreasonable fears. Maybe even worries about strange superstitions, curses, jinxes, you know the kind of thing.'

I thought uneasily about how much time Alex spent messaging Jack. What did she fill her conversations with? Hilarious anecdotes at my expense? She wouldn't have told him I was an unkissed social oddity? FFFF! No . . . No, she wouldn't. But, still, there was clearly other stuff out in the open. Oh, frik.

'Alex says you've had a run of bad luck that's got the boys of Hambledon High spooked and –'

'*Alex*,' I interrupted quickly, 'has plenty of her own fears to deal with.' Like how she was going to endure all the barbaric torture I was going to inflict.

'Don't take it personally,' said Jack hurriedly. 'She's not, like, betraying your confidences or anything. This is all just from conversational chitchat.'

'That chitchat,' I said, 'will have to stop.'

'No can do.'

'Yes can do.'

'Nope. I need the fluff.'

'Pardon?' (Such excellent manners. Even at this stressful time.)

Jack smirked. 'For my column.'

'Dear God.' I was horrified.

'*Mizz* magazine.' Another smirk.

'You wouldn't.'

'I surely do.'

'What did Alex say? Oh, wait. Don't tell me. You never reveal an exclusive before it hits the shelves.'

'Exactly.'

We were at my front gate. I thought about how Alex knew me better than my own mother. She knew my fears and phobias. She knew my bra size and my body fat percentage. She knew who I loved, who I hated. She knew A Whole Frikking Lot.

'And you should know,' Jack said quietly.

'Pardon?'

'About confidential sources. You should know, seeing

as I'm *your* source.'

I still looked confused.

'The information I gave Alex for you. About Mona needing help for the Science Fair. Info does not come cheap. You owe me, Tallulah.'

And with that he brushed my cheek with his lips and loped off down the road, leaving me speechless.

Chapter Thirteen

Thursday morning, hard at work

I was in my usual spot in the 600s the next morning considering, as usual, my navel. And The List. And the fact that there were just TWO DAYS LEFT TILL SATURDAY! Could I risk pinning all snogging hopes on Ben Latter? Would it be morally reprehensible to start working on a standby in case he didn't call me again before my birthday? I stared at the names with a rising sense of panic. I couldn't concentrate. Frik! It was too damn noisy in this library – noisy with the sound of Arns, whom I now hated with a terrible passion, laughing intimately into his mobile in the 700s. Why couldn't he take his irritating self somewhere far away from me? Like the 000s of reference? Why hadn't Ben called me yet? Didn't he like me? Did he think that camisole too tarty? Not tarty enough?

Okay, hang on. I know how that just sounded. It sounds like I'm ranting and all grumpy with Arns and everything because Ben hasn't called. No, no. I'm not *that* pathetic.

I was just grumpy because I was tired.

I was tired because of . . .

Let me explain.

*

Back to Wednesday night

So, Jack leaves me at the front gate and I stand there feeling all disorientated and confused and wanting to speak to Alex *immediately*. Jack disappeared down the road and I fumbled in my bag for my phone. I was thumbing my way through my contacts when I heard soft footsteps coming towards me.

My head jerked up from the bright light of the phone. I froze and my eyes squinted to search through the overhanging branches.

The sound of footsteps stopped.

I got the feeling someone over the road was watching me.

I tried to swallow, but I couldn't. I wanted desperately to look down at the phone and hit CALL, but I was too afraid to look away from where I'd last heard those steps. Why had they stopped? Had they followed me home?

Come on! Just a neighbour having a wee, I told myself. Stop scaring yourself. Put the phone away. Get on the other side of the gate.

Inch by inch I backed into the gate, until it screeched open. I slammed it behind me and stumbled down the steps, fumbling for my house keys. Then I remembered I just had the single key for the annexe. Oh no. Have to go round the dark corner, down to the dark back of the house, into a dark separate dark accommodation all my own. Ffff! My fingers scrabbled for the key and I gripped it like it could inflict mortal damage. I flung myself round the side of the house and stopped again, feeling that I needed to wait and listen.

The sound of steps came quietly up to the garden gate. I tried not to whimper, but I think I may have. The footfall was different now, so much surer than before.

He knows his prey is defenceless, I thought wildly. *Trapped in the shadows. No one to come to her aid.*

The gate opened, ever so slowly.

The streetlamp would be shining right on whoever was there.

I gritted my teeth and put my head back round the corner to take a look.

His back was to me, carefully pushing the gate back into its latch, but I'd know that fake Chanel handbag anywhere.

Dad.

Dad?

(How is it that my father, a man in his forties, could fall in love with a Coco Chanel handbag? My mother thinks it's funny. While I don't want to dwell on this matter, I reckon she should insist that he throws it in the bin. (Or into my welcoming arms. (It's a great bag. (But not for a man.))))

I ducked back round the wall, my heart still pounding.

Yowzer!

What was my father doing scaring the beheeners out of me in the pitch black of night? What was he doing coming home at this hour anyway? For once there was no whiff of alcohol following him along, so he hadn't been out for his evening binge.

I heard the bleep bleep bleep of mobile phone keys being pressed. Then Dad's voice saying, 'I'm home now, Freya. Thanks for tonight.' A low laugh. The phone clicking closed.

My body went cold, my mind a total blank, thoughts whizzing so fast I couldn't work out what I was thinking at all.

The front door opened and then it shut.

I was shaking now. I couldn't move. I wanted to go inside to my old room. Somewhere safe and warm and familiar. I didn't want to be alone out in the annexe.

And then I heard a voice hissing in the darkness of the front garden, and hesitant steps.

Oh. Dear. God.

Another late-night lurker? What are the chances?

'*Sffggssinashflgl!*' came the voice again, nearer by.

Silently, stealthily, I felt for my key, and wondered if I could make it over the courtyard, unlock the annexe door, get inside and lock the door behind me before I got pillaged. I could taste blood from the inside of my cheeks where I was biting down.

The quiet went on and on. There were no more footsteps. My hammering, yammering heart started to slow to a sustainable rhythm. I'd imagined it. Clearly. I held my breath and strained my ears.

Then that hissing voice was suddenly against my ear – '*Sffggssinashflgl!*' – and I nearly dropped dead right there. An icy hand clenched my bicep and pulled me round to face a dark figure, cloaked from head to toe in a black rippling fabric. I could see no face.

From the shadows where the mouth would be came a question:

'*Where did he go?*'

'Oh, for frik's sake!' I said, my fear flooding away. 'Who's *he*? What the hell are you *doing*, Pen? What's with the sinister garb?'

'Sinister?' she squeaked. 'Hardly! This is Agent Provocateur.'

I grabbed her black satin sleeve and frogmarched her back to the front door. 'You'd better tell me what all this is about, Penelope, or I'm going to go straight upstairs to check if Dad is still awake.'

'Damn!' Pen slapped her forehead. 'Dad! It must have been him I heard, not Ang–' she stopped short. 'Not *angry* housebreakers, ready to burgle us.'

'Ang–? Nice try. Expecting company, you little tramp? Ang– . . . Hmm. I'm guessing Angus? Please tell me not Fat Angus from the St Alban's rugby team? The guy with the cauliflower ears? *This* is why you wanted my room tonight? Easy access to the front door away from Mum and Dad's room? So you could seduce *Angus*? Are you *nuts*?'

I was just warming up to big-sister mode when Pen flicked me on the nose and hissed, 'Tallulah, don't you go getting your big sensible pants in a twist. I'm just a lot more organised about my first kiss than you are. That's all it's gonna be, *a kiss* – a kiss before I get branded with the Jinxed Witch Girl label too. Okay?'

Back to Thursday a.m., clearly still hard at work

And so that's how I had a sleepless night.

Okay, so maybe that's not all . . .

More on last night – sorry, but you need to know

My nostrils were partly to blame for the insomnia. Sometime after two I woke up to craft a plug from a small wodge of Andrex Aloe Vera for my left nostril that was streaming stuff down my face. The plug worked well until about five a.m. when I woke, coughing, to find it stuck to my cheek. I *knew* that bliddy camisole was a mistake! This head cold had better be vaporised by the time Operation Ben Second Date rolled around. I paused to consider before flopping back on my pillows.

It would mean Vicks VapoRub on the chest.

It would mean Lemsip.

It would mean, perhaps, a woolly scarf for a time.

Frik.

I shuddered.

My mobile rang. It was five in the morning! I pushed myself up off the pillows, coughing, and picked up the phone.

'Hello?' I croaked.

'Oh. Nasty,' came the reply.

I stiffened. 'Who is this?' I croaked again, then coughed at full volume, making no effort to turn from the receiver.

'Youch. I deserved that. It's Jack. Just calling to make sure you got in okay.'

I lurched to the side of the bed to see my clock. Yep. 5.06 a.m.

'It's *dawn*! Are you out of your mind?'

'No, no, not I. It's just that . . .'

Cough, cough. (Me.)

'I – uh – I –' Cough cough. (Him.)

'You've got a cold?'

'Me? No, I just, I –'

'Oh, *man*. Will you – *please!* – just get on with it!'

'Okay, maybe I am going a little mad. It's just that I left you at the front gate, which Alex would flay me alive for, but I had to, you know, because I didn't, you know, want to kind of muscle my way to your front door and then there'd be that whole do I come in for a coffee thing –'

152

'Don't even –'

'Anyway,' said Jack hastily, 'against my better judgement, I leave you at the front gate and then I'm walking home and I see this guy loping along, must've been a transvestite, and I –'

'Don't worry,' I said through gritted teeth. 'A glitzy bag? I know him.'

'Yeah, well, I was going to say I wasn't worried about him, just the other bloke.'

'What other bloke?'

'There was another guy heading up the road after Handbag Man –'

'Please don't call him that.'

'Sorry. Why? Is he a neighbour? Anyway, I wanted to turn round and check you were safely inside and not erm outside, you know, potential victim and everything.'

'Jack.'

'Yes. Tallulah.'

I tried to think of something to say.

'Did guy number two have very misshapen ears?'

'I don't know. To be honest, at that point I'd got to your neighbour's – you know, with all the gnomes – and I was a little distracted. Everyone around me had odd ears.'

'Jack, you're supposed to be a supersleuth kind of journalist!'

He coughed. 'I am usually. I'm really quite brilliant.'

I shook my head disbelievingly, and reached for the toilet roll. I worked up another plug and said, 'I dow who the odder guy is. I can look after byself, but thanks. And thanks for walki'g me hobe. Tell Alex to call be, okay?'

'Yeah, about that.'

'Hnh?' (Frik! Now the right nostril was going full faucet on me!)

'Could you not say anything to Alex about me walking you home?'

'*This* is why you call be at five a.eb.!' I squeaked. 'You wanted to get to be before I spoke to by friends!'

'Nonononooooo,' said Jack quickly. 'That's not what this is. I was truly worried about you.'

'So why are you ondly calli'g dow?'

'It's taken this long for Alex to wake up and give me your number.'

I smiled, picturing Alex's sleep constantly interrupted by a persistent voicemail alert.

Justice!

'Okaaay,' I said, pulling the duvet up around my neck and settling my aching head back against the pillows. 'Here's how it is, bister. I tell by friends everythi'g. It seebs one of theb,' I added darkly, 'passes on that inforbation, but I ab dot one to judge. I will be speaki'g to Alex, sternly, of all that has passed in the last twelve hours and I will be expecti'g a full explanation.'

154

'Fine,' said Jack sadly. 'Bring on the humiliation.'

'Pardon?'

He sighed. 'She said I should work out a way to kiss you. At some point. Before Saturday.' He sighed again. 'But I –'

'But you couldn't bring yourself to stoop so low,' I snapped. '*I, Mister Don Juan*,' I was shouting now, nostrils miraculously clear, '*am PERFECTLY* UNAVAILABLE FOR A PITY KISS, A PITY DATE OR A PITY *ANYTHING!*' I reached a full-blown shriek and slammed the phone down really hard, hammering my thumb in the process. 'And I'm hardly likely to feel humiliated by confiding in my friends,' I said petulantly, sucking my pained thumb.

I picked up the receiver and dialled Alex's mobile. 5.14 a.m. Lovely.

'Unhughlkle?'

'Alex, it's me.'

'HJKehe.'

'Wake up. Jack's just called. What have you said to him? Does he know I've never kissed anyone? I do not like this boy. Were you thinking I should put *him* on The List?'

'Wait.'

'You sound like a toad.'

'Tatty, I feel' – cough, cough – 'like a toad. An aged toad. A toad facing oncoming headlights on a distant Arizona highway.'

'So you should, you cow. Jack walked me home last night and, for your information, *there was no kissing*.'

'Oh, glory, I knew it.'

'Alex!' I shrieked. 'I'm your friend! You should not sound unsurprised! I *am* worthy of a kiss!'

Alex sighed. 'Calm down, crazy person. I said *I knew it* because Jack would struggle to kiss someone he likes. And, no, I did not tell him you'd never been kissed.'

'You didn't? Whew! I couldn't take any more humiliation. You came close to an early death. Hang on, what do you mean he'd struggle to kiss someone he likes?'

'It's just . . . he gets the jitters. He can kiss loads of randoms, but –'

'Nice,' I said.

Alex sighed again, and then said, '*Yes, it could only be Tatty Lula at this hour*,' to someone on the other side. Clearly my conversation with Alex had woken Carrie and Tam up too.

'Hey!' I said. 'Focus, Alex!'

'Sorry, Lu. The reason he didn't kiss you is obviously because he likes you.'

'Oh, that I doubt. Plus he's only just met me!'

'Bet you ten bags.'

'Peanut or chocolate?'

'Half and half.'

'Fine. No. Not fine. Cancel that. It's not worthy of a

bet. I'm focusing on Ben Latter. Alex, last night' – my voice ascended into a squeal – 'I went on a date with Ben Latter – and Arns and Mona but forget that – and I think Ben really likes me! Ben Latter! *Ben Latter!*'

There was a whole lot of shouting and shrieking and amazement between Hambledon and the city. Then I forgot all the night's strangeness and how tired I was and got totally caught up in the *he said she said* rundown of the evening and Jack didn't even come into the picture. My story ended with me in the cinema and Mona and Arns snogging some rows back and then we got into a whole discussion about the cinema and what was showing and how hot Matt Damon was. And then those three went back to sleep and I started a production line of nose plugs to see me through a long day of library.

Thursday a.m. I promise not to hark back to Weds p.m. – okay?

So here I am now, hating the world cos I'm bored of nose plugs and I'm tired and cross. I wait until the second hand limps round to finish off the minute that clicks the big hand on to the hour of twelve and push myself to my feet.

Officially one and a half days until I am sweet sixteen and never been kissed.

Frik!

Even though Ben *felt* like a sure thing, was he . . .?
I mean, he hadn't even called me yet . . . Was there still a chance of us kissing before Saturday?

Ffff!

We had to!

Time for another layer of VapoRub!

I pasted it on and breathed happily through clear nostrils.

I was staggering along towards the staffroom – readjusting my scarf to keep my throat covered even though it resembled a kind of neck-brace thingy – when Ben hove into sight at the 300s.

There was nowhere to run.

'Tallulah!' he said, walking smartly up to me with a smile. There was no hesitation in his lean in to kiss me gently on the cheek. It was suave. It was smooth. It totally made my knees buckle.

'Hey,' he said, looking at me closely. 'Are you all right?'

'I've got the sniffles,' I said with a watery smile.

Arns said afterwards that Ben took a step back then, but that's just mean. I maintain he took a step back at the *next* second when Arnold said, 'Hi, Ben!' really loudly as he walked on by.

'Sooo,' said Ben as Arns disappeared round the book stacks.

I drank him in. Sun streaming through the high arched

windows turned his hair ski-slope white. He was in his school uniform, immaculate navy blazer, tie perfectly knotted, crisp shirt collar. And, again, very good shoes. Extremely shiny. He shifted, coughed and smiled again. I dragged my eyes from his mouth to meet his gaze, and only just stopped myself from giving a lustful sigh. Gulp.

He looked away. 'I forgot you said you worked here.'

Then I noticed he had an armload of books – *Addicts Unravelled* and *Families Anonymous* blah blah. I blushed. I mean, I hadn't said anything, but I'd just assumed he'd come here to say hi to me and how presumptuous was that? The call of the library was stronger than last night's date. I hated myself ten thousand times more. Was that possible? Yes, infinitely so.

'I had a nice time last night,' said Ben, flipping back his blond fringe.

I looked him in the eye and tried to smile.

'It's great seeing you here, saves me a phone call.' He laughed.

I still had my fake smile stuck on.

'Would you be keen for supper tomorrow night?' he continued. 'Just us . . .'

'Uh,' I blurted. 'Th-that w-would be great. Sure. Fine.'

'Great.' He laughed again. 'I'll see you at the steakhouse again. The Booth. Seven thirty?'

I nodded and he ducked his head to kiss me on the cheek

before hurrying away to the front desk.

I was still standing there, wearing a psycho smile, when my mother came to find me five minutes later.

'Fancy a sandwich?'

We trundled into the staffroom and found Arns at the tea urn.

'Dr Bird! A cup of Earl Grey?'

'You are so lovely,' she said to him sweetly, and he blushed.

'Mum,' I said fiercely. 'Sandwich.'

She rolled her eyes and handed me a fiver. 'Shall we all sit over there?' she asked mildly, pointing to the only free table.

Arns flung himself into a purple chair, Mum found comfort in an orange, so I'd have the remaining poo green. No biggie, I know, but that shade is so – *infectious*. My head cold would be rampant after half an hour. I could still have a blocked nose come tomorrow night. Frik! How does a girl kiss without a secondary air supply?

'Egg mayo?' asked the lady at the bar and I nodded yes.

'And an Earl Grey, and freshly squeezed orange juice, please,' I asked.

She smiled. 'You'll be wanting to kick that cold before the weekend.'

I looked at her blankly. *How could she know about my hot date?*

'Yes, dear. All the schools coming back, the rest of the

students. Frey's Dam party. New term, Monday.'

'Oh!' I nodded vigorously. I had to get a grip. Not everything was about me.

I managed to carry everything back to our seats, and carefully handed Mum her tea. She sighed her thanks, looking worn out. 'You okay, Mum?' I asked.

Mum nodded. 'Just stressed, Lula. Two meetings this afternoon, thanks to that newspaper article. Esme Trooter and her lot are coming in at two. Then Vice Chancellor Gordon. I don't have any answers for them.'

Arns's eyebrows went up. 'Esme Trooter?'

'She is the town campaigner,' I explained, rubbing a little VapoRub under my scarf. 'You haven't heard of her?'

'I don't do much campaigning,' replied Arns.

'Neither does she,' I said darkly, taking a big bite of my sandwich and chewing furiously.

'Lu . . .' said Mum in a warning tone.

'She makes a lot of noise,' I clarified. 'About everything from Mr Ranfulshuffer's new conservatory to what they're feeding the cats up at the RSPCA.'

Arns looked appalled. 'What are they feeding the cats at the RSPCA?'

'The point is, dear,' said Mum, 'the pensionable population of this town are going to have my guts for garters. They're the only ones putting up a decent argument against Harry Harrow's development, but they'll get nowhere without the historical documents. They need them to prove their case.' She hefted herself out of the chair and collected her bags together. 'I need to talk to Mike,' she muttered, and left without saying goodbye.

'What does your mother have in the bags?' asked Arns. 'Is she one of those ladies who just, you know, has *bags*?'

Nodding my head, I rolled my eyes, my mouth too full to speak.

Mum's office is not altogether private. It's in the middle of the historical library section, and while it's got lots of lovely dark wood panelling, complemented by an enormous antique desk, the rest of it is miles of clear glass, barely single glazed. There are about eight permanent librarians, and often part-timers like me too. We could all hear Mum perfectly as her voice rose ever so slightly.

'Detective Sergeant Trenchard has confirmed that your fingerprints numbered among those on Sophie Wenger's access card. And you were here Saturday morning. Do you have any idea how that looks, Mike?'

I tried to look busy with some filing near Tweedy Mabel's desk. She was as mesmerised as I was, and the twitches had escalated. Her arms creaked up and down restlessly, fingers tapping against the spectacles, adjusting the gold chain behind them, fluffing her minimal hair. The rest of the staff had the decency to move to a ten-metre perimeter.

Stinky Mike laughed. 'God, Anne! I just came to get my jacket! You saw me leave – I didn't take anything else with me!'

Mum stared at him, her expression inscrutable. 'Mike, Security find it suspicious that Sophie's card was swiped in, not yours, and that yours was swiped out, not hers.'

Sweat was glistening on Mike's sloping forehead. He wiped the back of his hand against it and trailed it dry on his trousers, shifting his weight from one foot to the other while he shook his head vehemently.

'I came in with that gaggle of guests through the front door. This is outrageous. Anne, I –'

Mum held up a hand. 'I know, I know. I hadn't realised you came in with the historians. I thought you were already here.'

'You're mistaken!' Mike's face was getting flushed.

I glanced at Mabel to find her looking at me. She glanced away quickly.

'Would you tell Security to cross me off their list of suspects?' Mike continued. 'We've all picked up that girl's card at some stage. She's always leaving it lying around.'

Mum sagged into her chair. 'You were never really a suspect, Mike. I told them it was ridiculous.'

They spoke more quietly, then Mum got up and saw Mike to the door.

'We're still at square one,' she said clearly, her voice

carrying right across the office. 'I'm going to call Security and CCTV footage will need to be checked to see if we can find out who took Sophie's card,' she added.

Arns came to stand nearby. 'Wow. Didn't know there were cameras in here, Dr Bird.'

'Oh yes,' said Mum, pointing to a small lens mounted in the far corner of her office.

Mabel and I gaped openly at the office now.

'Good idea,' said Mike. 'We need to get to the bottom of this.'

'I'll call you back in when I've had some answers from Security,' said Mum.

Mike turned to go, his mouth set in a narrow line.

Then Mum's phone bleeped and she picked it up. 'Hello? Yes, I'm expecting her. *Ten* colleagues? No, there's simply not enough' – she held the receiver away from her ear then listened again – 'Oh, all right. Bring them up to my office, please.'

Five minutes later Security trooped our town campaigner extraordinaire into Mum's office. Esme Trooter had brought along ten OAPs, our over-the-road neighbour Mr Kadinski, predictably, being one of them. He gave me a small finger wave, and I gave him one back. It looked like the pensioners at the Setting Sun had one last mission left in them. If Mum weren't so stressed about it all, and if I weren't so worried about what was going to happen to my favourite place in all of Hambledon, I would have found it quite funny.

But, even without Esme Trooter shrieking at Mum in front of everyone, it was very, very unfunny indeed.

And that was *before* Vice Chancellor Gordon arrived.

Chapter Fourteen

Thursday afternoon, the dwang hits the fan

Vice Chancellor Gordon is a huge and hairy man. Very dark, brooding eyebrows, upright posture, sharp eyes – all befitting of The Boss Of All Hambledon University. He is frightening, unapproachable, unforgiving, but highly regarded by everyone. Whatever he does, he does well. And what he did this Thursday afternoon, once he'd got rid of the pensioners from Mum's office, was Tell Her Off. From what I could see, she didn't say much. Just nodded a lot. But then, at one point, Mum shrugged her shoulders and he went slightly mad at that. He started pointing and wagging his finger and I didn't like it. Not one little bit.

Before I could think about what I was doing I was marching over, thudding on the glass of the office door and barging in.

'Excuse me, Dr Bird,' I said with dignity as Dr Gordon stopped in mid roar, 'I've got the Prince of Wales on the phone and he can't hold on much longer.'

Mum nodded calmly at me, her hand going to the phone on her desk. 'Is it about the Highgrove papers? Or Camilla's family tree?'

'The press is pressuring the palace for feedback on

the Highgrove issue,' I said importantly.

The multiple-coronary purple was receding from Dr Gordon's face. I could see him collect himself: *I'm yelling at a valued member of staff in front of everyone*, was the thought I saw flit through his mind.

I shut the office door behind me and went to the nearest desk to ring Mum's extension. From the corner of my eye, I saw Dr Gordon put a hand to his forehead and mumble something.

Mum nodded and then I saw her gesture at the camera mounted high on the office wall. Dr Gordon looked relieved. He said some more stuff, shook her hand and left, giving me a nod on the way out.

I reached for my pot of VapoRub and took a hit. This much stress required clear sinuses.

Mum picked up the phone. 'Thanks, Lula. I couldn't have lasted another second.'

'Are you okay?' I said into my receiver.

'No,' she replied. She sat down and stared blankly at her in trays.

'What's with the camera?' I asked.

'Dad's old Polaroid,' she said quietly. 'I put it up this morning, hoping it would scare someone in this office. The Security guys are convinced the theft is an inside job.' Our eyes met across the office.

'Cunning,' I said.

'Desperate,' she countered. 'Mike is my friend. There's no chance he's got any connection with the developers. And he didn't turn a hair at my camera ruse. Dr Gordon's right. I'm clutching at straws. There's no way Mike took those papers. Maybe I should rethink Sophie Wenger. Maybe her dentist-appointment alibi is a sham.'

'What's the deadline for supplying the council with the documents? When will it be too late?'

'Monday morning, ten a.m.'

I kept quiet, then, 'Check Sophie's personnel records,' I whispered. 'And cross-reference them with the planning application. Maybe . . . maybe there'll be some connection to Harrow Construction? Maybe her dad is Harrow's plumber or accountant . . . or . . . I don't know . . .'

Mum blew out a frustrated sigh. 'Hardly, Lu, but I suppose we've nothing to lose. Actually, I've got one more trick up my sleeve. Are you ready to see me in action?'

I raised my eyebrows as Mum hung up with a quiet click and got her bags together. She locked her office door behind her, and cleared her throat loudly.

Everyone in the office stopped what they were doing and looked up.

She bent her head to acknowledge their attention. 'Thank you, everyone, for your help in trying to find the Coven's Quarter documents. I'd like you all to continue with your usual projects from this point because Security has confirmed that the surveillance disks I have locked in my desk drawers are sure to have information with regard to the missing papers.'

A small cheer went up.

Mum smiled, and before anyone could ask further questions, she said, 'I'll be examining the disks with the vice chancellor and the head of Security tomorrow. Could I ask you all to ensure my office door stays locked as an extra measure?'

'All our access cards open your door, Mum,' I said, not following her logic.

'Yes, but only ours. And the perpetrator is hardly one of us! The locked door is a good extra measure,' she concluded blithely.

'And no better safeguard than that camera you've got there, Anne.' Mabel's high-pitched voice was as clear as a bell.

Mum grimaced. 'I'm afraid it's not working right now, Mabel,' she answered. 'But it's a good thing it was recording when we really needed it. I'll see you all tomorrow.' And she was off.

I heaved a sigh, staring into Mum's office. This was not a very sophisticated trap. And, without any method of surveillance, all totally pointless. I looked around. Everyone knew Mum kept her drawer keys in her pen pot, but nobody seemed interested in the security of the disks.

They were already focused on catching up with their usual projects.

I stared blankly at my computer, wondering about Mum's plans. On the screen in front of me was the uni home page, with the different faculties all listed down the left-hand side. *Hmm*, I thought. *Sophie does drama club here, doesn't she?*

Even though they're at school, not university, the Hambledon pupils using the uni drama department have, like, *headshots*, and *portfolios*, and *CVs* and things. And because their classes are held here on campus, maybe . . . Clicking on Drama, I moved quickly through the different menus.

And there she was, along with a load of people from all the schools in Hambledon, including Barbie from PSG, and – wait for it! – Vincent Harrow, son of Harry Harrow, the developer who wanted to ride roughshod over Coven's Quarter. I looked at the photo of Vincent. It didn't take a genius to suss that Sophie would fall for this guy:

1. He was strangely attractive.
2. He was as goth as you could get without facial piercings.

And if he needed to get something sorted for his dad, then there was a motive, and opportunity, for document snatching. Who could tell me if Vince and Soph were an item?

I logged out and grabbed my bag to hare off to the 300s on the second floor in search of Arns.

'Er, Tallulah?' came a voice from behind me.

Stinky Mike.

I forced a smile.

'Yes, Mike?'

'Could I have a quick word? I see you're on your way –'

'Sure,' I said quickly.

'I was just wondering. I feel so' – he shifted from foot to foot – '*helpless* about the missing documents. I thought maybe we could help your mother find them?'

I blinked in disbelief. 'Uh, *how*?' I asked, on the brink of downright rudeness.

His eyes narrowed, and I smiled hurriedly. 'I was just wondering about Sophie,' he murmured. 'Could she have mistakenly filed something from your mother's office maybe? You know her better than most. She's in some of your classes at school, isn't she?'

I was thrown. Was Mike really trying to be helpful, or just pointing a finger? 'I don't know her that well,' I replied grudgingly. 'It *would* be good to know who she's very friendly with.'

'It would,' Mike agreed.

We looked each other in the eye.

'Look,' Mike sighed. (Yowzer. That blast of breath was not pleasant. We're talking a garlic salami with fishpaste combo.) 'If those documents don't come to light soon, I'm going to be in just as much of a tight spot as your mother – you know, as I'm second in command.' He looked out at me from under his wiry eyebrows with a yellow-toothed grimace. 'Can you find out anything about Sophie?'

'The security footage will confirm everything, though, won't it?' I suggested mildly.

Mike didn't bat an eyelid. 'Sure it will,' he said. 'But further proof would be good.'

'I'll make a few calls,' I replied.

(I've ALWAYS wanted to say that for real!)

It was all quiet in the 300s when I finally got up there. I checked every stack, but Arns was nowhere to be found. I texted Alex instead. My watch said three p.m. Two hours till home time. Trapped here until then. I ground my teeth in frustration, and unscrewed my pot of VapoRub. Right. I'd have to go and slump in the 600s. Stare at my lardy navel for a while. Put some VapoRub on it. Maybe go and see if Jessica Hartley and Jason Ferman were still snogging down in the 000s. Or, seeing as they were staying clear, photocopy my nostrils. Hey, that could be fun. Maybe I'd do that first.

In the end I checked on the snoggers before I went

anywhere else. I wanted to research head angles. My hopes for the date with Ben were high.

Jason and Jessica were thankfully still at it when I got there, but all I could see was the back of Jessica's head. I was about to creep down the next stack to get a profile look at them between shelves when I saw where Jason's hand was.

Yikes!

I bolted.

Wasn't that, like, tenth base?

In my headlong flight from perversion in the book stacks I ran smack bang into a hard and bony ribcage.

'Wheck!' I yelped.

'Erghupf!' said Arns, winded.

'What the frik are you doing?' I hissed. 'We've got to get out of here!'

'Jessica Hartley and Jason Ferman?' he croaked.

'You don't want to know!'

I hustled down to the photocopy room and Arns limped behind, wheezing and cursing all the way.

'Oh, stop it!' I commanded as we burst into the copy room. 'Pull yourself together.'

He fell gratefully into one of those plastic bucket-shaped seats on spindly metal legs and it collapsed predictably to one side, leaving him sprawled on the ground.

I laughed.

Correction.

I *howled*. Until tears ran.

'You are not normal,' muttered Arns.

I staggered over to help him up and he ankle-tapped me just as I bent over to grab his outstretched hand. I went down hard, but skilfully got his shoulder blade with my killer right elbow.

'AAAAAAAAA!' he yelled.

That just finished me. I was laughing so much I couldn't breathe and he was swearing, trying to get up from under me. I bet we would have come to blows if Tweedy Mabel hadn't tottered in.

'Well!' she huffed. 'Goodness me!'

I couldn't speak.

'Mabel!' shouted Arns. 'Thank God! Please get her off me!'

So not fair!

Mabel turned tweeded tail and ran.

'Arns,' I said, getting to my feet hurriedly, and straightening my clothes. 'Have you ever seen Sophie Wenger hanging out with Vincent Harrow?'

'Not since Debra Hansen's birthday party.'

'Oh yes?' I sat down carefully in the bucket chair. It held.

'A scary selection of those drama-club girls were trying to get Vinnie to do a strip tease –'

'No way!'

'Indeed way. You need to get out more, Lula. Even I know about this. Your friend Alex was very disapproving.'

'I had the pox. Didn't go anywhere that weekend.'

'You didn't miss much. Debra's parents came home just as those girls threw Vinnie in the pool. He was really peed off. Mascara and eyeliner everywhere.'

'Very goth.'

'Wet goth. Bad hair.'

'I can imagine.'

'I believe Sophie grabbed Harrow Jr's nipples through the wet T-shirt at one point.'

'Ew.'

'What's relevant?'

'Hm?'

'Why are you asking about the drama clubbers?'

'Vinnie *Harrow*?'

'Duh.' Arnold slapped his forehead. 'Harrow Construction. Who would know for sure whether Sophie and Vincent are on speaking terms?'

'Alex,' I said. 'I've already texted her.'

Arnold nodded and pulled out his phone. He probably had a hundred unread texts from Mona. I checked my watch: 3.25 p.m. So much time to kill. And I couldn't very well copy nostrils with Arnold around. I went back to worrying about my chances with Ben Latter and whether I'd better reconsider The List.

'How old do you think Billy Diggle is?' I asked him suddenly.

Arns looked taken aback. He shoved his phone in his jeans pocket and stared at me blankly.

'Is he too young to have kissed anyone yet?' I persisted.

A familiar noise filled the room.

'I think that's your Mona Phona ringing,' I said.

Arnold took the call while I tried to remember which year Billy had started at secondary school. Oh, frik. *Had* he started at secondary school?

Arns hung up with a smile. 'She loves me,' he sighed blissfully.

'Please, please, boil your head,' I begged.

I checked my watch again, sighed, got up from the chair and photocopied my nostrils. I had no dignity left, after all.

When Arns's phone buzzed with, like, the billionth text of the day, I headed down to the staffroom. In the back of my mind was a persistent niggle about whether Mum had got anything out of Personnel, but somehow I just wanted the whole issue to go away. I suddenly had an urge for some quiet time and packed up to leave.

Back at the homestead I pulled myself over the back gate and went straight to the cellar doors. The key turned noiselessly. I pushed in through the right-side door and stretched in a tentative hand to find the light switch.

A blaze of light and there he was. Oscar. 1971 Morris Minor Traveller. Beeyoodiful. My pride and joy. I felt a rush of gladness and pulled the door closed behind me. There was something calming about being down here just beneath the house. The creaking planks overhead were the floorboards of the rooms above, the walls around me part of the solid foundations of our home. Dust and grit were thick on the ground, but that didn't matter too much in the world of motor mechanics, unless you were in the habit of dropping spark plugs. Most of Oscar's engine block was on a small workbench to the right of him, waiting for the gasket I couldn't find or afford, but I stepped round that and slid into the front seat. I breathed in happily, a smell of wood polish and old leather still lingering inside, and promptly sneezed so hard I was glad my nostrils had been photocopied in case reconstructive surgery was necessary. 'Bless me,' I moaned quietly, wiping my eyes.

'What was that?' I heard just above me.

I jumped so high my right knee whacked the bottom of the steering wheel. Ffff!

'Cellar door is probably open downstairs,' said Mum. 'Tallulah has been a bit scatty lately.'

I was about to yell up to them in outraged denial when Dad said, 'Not scatty enough not to notice how terrible I'm feeling. Or what's really going on.'

I kept quiet. Really going on? Okay, what *was* really going on?

'You're doing fine, Spenser. Just keep it together. Please. I don't want the girls getting hurt by any of this.'

The hairs on my forearms prickled up and slowly my whole body went cold. My nose itched again, but the next sneeze vanished when I blinked hard and angrily.

'I don't think I can do it, Anne.'

There was a scuffle sound, like Mum suddenly moving a little away, and that must have been right because her next words were muffled and quavery. 'Don't you dare, Spenser. After everything we've been through . . . You just fix this, you hear? Fix it! Our girls . . . They're so impressionable now. Teenagers – and little Blue! Who knows –'

More scuffling.

Dad saying, 'Now, Anne, come on. I don't –'

I didn't hear the next bit, until Mum started raising her voice. '. . . all under pressure. Don't even think . . . what's with . . . Freya?'

Dad muttered something back. I couldn't hear Mum's reply, but my heart flashed hard and cold as stone at my father's next words:

'I can't be there for you, Anne.' Steps away. '. . . so sorry.'

Mum: 'I understand, Spenser.'

What?

WHAT?

She shouldn't be *understanding* him. She should be beating him into a pulp, pips and all.

How could he betray her?

How could he blithely shrug off any responsibility to support us?

How could this man, so unfeeling, so offhand, be my *dad*?

Suddenly the cellar didn't feel cosy and secret and refuge-like at all. I felt as if I were trapped in an igloo miles beneath the surface of the earth, desperate to get out. But there was no way I could leave now. Not until Mum and Dad had moved away, further into the house, and I could exit through the back and come in through the front, like I wish I had in the first place.

I hugged my arms to my body and curled low over Oscar's wide wooden steering wheel, tears splashing on to the polished walnut and spattering the embroidered hearts on my jeans till they turned so dark and soggy you couldn't see them at all.

Chapter Fifteen

Thursday p.m. Just over one day left

My self-piteous, shambling arrival at the front door an hour later coincided with Pen's high-on-life version.

She batted my tremulous key away with her own steadily aimed one, and slammed into the house in record time.

'Hello, losers!' she yelled as she shrugged off her jacket and dropped her bag to the floor.

'Find anything to wear this morning?' I asked when she sashayed to the kitchen in my low-rise jeans and skinny-me shirt, adorned with tiny pearl beads and flowers that *I* had personally sewn on.

She turned in the doorway and lowered her left lid in a sultry wink. 'Thanks, darlin',' she drawled, rolling a shoulder and glancing down at her ensemble. 'Angus came back from the city this morning. He said I'm the best thing he's seen all week. I might get you to do me some more of these funky vintage pieces.'

I dropped my bag with a deadpan expression and stomped menacingly towards her.

'Take my clothes off now,' I growled.

'Ooooh, I'm soooo scared,' wailed Pen, and she

disappeared into the kitchen.

Now, do not underestimate me, dear reader. Most would have sprinted after her and ripped the clothing from her thankless form, but not I. Oh no ho ho. I slipped into Pen's bedroom and quietly removed her mobile from her bag. If my failing parents would not take a firm hand, then it was up to me to Instil Discipline. No sister of mine would run rampant about the place, not on my watch. Nuh-uh. *Bring it on, Pen, for I am ready.*

I shut Pen's door quietly behind me and headed for the kitchen.

Dear God.

Mum had done chicken-liver stew. My stomach turned and I nearly ran from the room, but I knew what Must Be Done.

'Mum,' I gushed, 'this smells wonderful.'

Pen shot me a baleful look and lifted her fork in a rude gesture.

'Careful with the cutlery, Pen,' I suggested mildly. 'Don't want to take your own eye out.'

Her nostrils flared and Dad coughed as if he were about to say something. But it seemed the cough turned into some sort of heave, because he bolted from the table and headed for the bathroom across the hall.

Pen rolled her eyes. 'Dad's illness is, like, so old,' she complained, fiddling with the trim at the sleeves. I watche her work a bead loose and tried to calm my breathing.

It was no good.

'Leave the frikking beads,' I snapped. 'They take at least a minute apiece to sew on.'

Pen ignored me. 'Has Dad got Aids?' she asked Mum curiously.

My jaw dropped. If it wasn't for my excellent hinge joints, the bottom of my face would have landed on the floor.

'I think the correct term is HIV, Pen,' said Mum. 'And, no, it's just a fluey thing.'

'Oh,' said Pen, clearly disappointed.

'Your daughter?' I said to Mum, waving the salt cellar at Pen with meaning. 'She needs help. Clinical help.'

Pen yawned ostentatiously. 'Fu-unny,' she drawled.

'Conniving to get Fat Angus in the sack is the first symptom of which we should all take note.'

'*Tallulah!*' cried Mum. 'That's enough! Just ignore her, Pen,' she continued, finally sitting down.

'Okay, Mum,' said Pen meekly, pretending to eat the stew while slipping forkloads to Boodle under the table.

'Where is Great-aunt Phoebe? Is Blue in bed?' I asked.

'Blue's asleep,' confirmed Mum. 'Phoebe rushed off when she remembered a dinner drink she'd scheduled ages ago.'

Pen caught my eye. Yeah, *right*. Mum's stew had sent Great-aunt Phoebe running for sure.

We sat in silence for a while, listening to Dad vomit.

'He puts a lot of volume into each retch,' I noted at last. I gripped my fork so hard the handle hurt my palm.

'Tallulah!' exclaimed Mum again. 'What is with you tonight? I'm glad I'm not on the receiving end of your bad mood.' She stood up from the table and turned to the sink to start rinsing and putting stuff in the dishwasher. Pen sprang into action, and Boodle obliged as her plate appeared under the table. Scoff, scoff, scoff.

My foul food was congealing. I stared at it numbly.

'Personnel had nothing much to say about Sophie,' said Mum, clattering dishes into the washer. 'We're going to get answers soon, though.'

'Riiight,' I said doubtfully.

Mum bent her head over the stew pot, blackened at the edges, and began to scrub like a woman possessed.

I looked at her closely. Uh-oh.

'Mum, what have you done?' Pen asked sternly.

My mother looked distinctly shifty and ripped off the rubber gloves before shoving the crusty pot on the bottom rack of the groaning dishwasher. She swiped a wisp of hair from her forehead leaving Fairy foam upon her brow. 'I told everyone that the disks from the CCTV footage were in my office for safekeeping.'

Pen's eyes widened. 'Yes?' she urged.

I pushed my food into a grave-like mound, and nudged

a potato into headstone position. The sound of retching was still coming from the bathroom.

Mum pulled a container of ice cream from the freezer and thumped it on to the table. 'I asked that my office door remain locked till I got a chance to look them over.'

'Oh,' Pen said, disappointed. 'But, Mum, you told me earlier there are no tapes. And you won't know if anyone does rummage in your office, because you don't really have a working camera in there.'

'Two words,' said Mum, holding up three fingers.

Pen raised her eyebrows.

'Maybe three,' she added. 'Mr Kadinski's clock!'

'Clock?' I muttered.

'Yes, alarm clock with hidden spy camera and twenty gig digital video recorder combi package!' she trilled.

'I'm not hearing this.' Pen shook her head in disbelief.

'But wait!' said Mum. 'That's not all! This is the ultimate video surveillance system at an affordable price, providing up to sixty hours of constant video recording by a high resolution camera integrated in the alarm clock.'

'Noooo,' moaned Pen.

'You've planted a hidden camera. In your office.' I was incredulous.

Mum beamed triumphantly. 'Someone will try to get those disks. And I'll see exactly who it is.'

'Four bags of Maltesers says it's Sophie Wenger,' I said.

'It will be so good when you have evidence to prove it – I just want this planning dispute over with.'

'Please.' Pen shot me a scornful look and said in her most pompous voice, 'Secret tapes are inadmissible. You know nothing of the law. Don't go there.'

'Stop with the pseudo-solicitor speak, Pen. I've seen enough telly to know what's admissible,' I said darkly. 'I can see I'm going to have to take this matter into my own hands.'

Dad staggered out of the bathroom.

'Other matters too,' I added, through a lump in my throat.

'Whatever,' said Pen disrespectfully.

I bit my tongue and clutched her mobile for comfort. It helped. Revenge would be sweet. I was going to think up something terrible. Like ringing Angus and saying –

But Pen was not done being forty: 'It looks like you should be doing extra school work to get your marks up!' she said, waving her index finger in my face. 'Or getting that heap of junk in the cellar to start! Or actually not damaging the next guy who comes along so that you at least get a kiss before you turn sixteen!' Pen was now the most worked up I'd seen her in a long time. I blinked. 'Any minute now your weird-ass jinxy reputation is going to start affecting *me*! If it gets any worse, guys will wonder if *I'm* in the same boat as *you*!'

'Mind your own business,' I said, my voice tight and strained.

'I *am*!' yelled Pen. 'Don't you get it?'

'Take it easy, Pen,' said Dad from the doorway. We all turned to look at him.

'Yes,' said Mum. 'Lula's got a date tomorrow, anyway. Nothing wrong with being a late starter.' She beamed at me kindly and I felt like screaming. 'With Bill? Ben?' she asked.

'Ben,' I said, nodding wearily.

Mum took the rubbish to the dustbin outside, and Pen escaped with Boodle for a walk.

'A date?' said my father mildly.

'Hn,' I replied.

'Me too.' Dad laughed. 'Though I shouldn't.' He sloshed himself a glass of water at the sink and staggered across the hall again, leaving me gaping after him in disbelief.

What? Was he *drunk*?

The frikker had just told his own daughter he was going on an illicit date. *How? The? Hell?*

Clearly, only one path was open to me. Vengeance. Bodily harm. More vengeance, more harm.

Okay. Make that several paths.

I shoved my plate into the dishwasher so hard it smashed.

All at once everything seemed just too, too much. I wanted to scream and shout and cry all at the same time, to forget everything – have everything back the way it was before Grandma died.

'Lula?' came Mum's querulous voice from outside. 'You all right? What broke?'

'Your heart, in case you hadn't noticed,' I muttered, too low for her to hear. And left the smashed plate in the washer, eyes too full of tears to manage a clear up.

'I'm going to catch up with Pen and Boodle for a stroll. Back in a bit,' called Mum, but I barely heard her. Dad's voice was on repeat in my head: *A date? Me too.*

And I hadn't said *anything* to him. All this . . . *hatred* at Dad and *NOTHING* – *not . . . one . . . word* – would come out of my gaping, useless, gobby mouth.

So, then, with my head in no place at all, my senseless body took over. I pushed away from the dishwasher and went after my father. He was just closing the bathroom door behind himself as I got into the hall, and suddenly it felt like I'd been hit with a jab of adrenalin because the next second I was pounding on the door, just as the latch clicked to lock on the other side.

'You fff–! You rr–! You shh–!' I shouted stupidly. And I pounded, and hit, and thrashed, and punched till my fist felt soft and pulpy.

'T?' came Dad's voice, and then, 'Wait, I –' and more retching.

'You PIG!' I screeched. I took a step back and kicked the

door as hard as I could. All I could think was that I wanted to get in there, shout at him and see what he had to say for himself. I wanted to see him squirm. I wanted to see him understand that messing up our weirdy family was not going to happen. He needed to sort everything out – there'd be no understanding *I knows* from this quarter. No sirree.

The door bounced in its frame and I stood back and levelled another kick. The panel I connected with cracked through, taking my foot with it. I hopped uselessly, my leg stuck and my heaving sobs sounding loud, with Dad's retching coming clearly through the shattered panel. Falling on my right hip, I kicked with my left foot, splinters both giving and pulling at my ankle, tearing my sock. As the wood panel fell out and away I could see my dad squashed in against the wall next to the toilet. He was hanging over the toilet bowl and his whole body shook and convulsed with the retching from his chest. His head was down, his hands holding the seat tightly.

My foot came free then, and I pulled it out of the door, but I didn't move. The adrenalin shot had gone and I was frozen by that small square picture of my father reduced to something I couldn't hate. At all.

And then he looked up. His eyes met mine through the shattered square and he wasn't shocked at the smashed door. Not angry. Not outraged.

Broken.

Broken so completely it caught at my throat.

There was nothing I could do. As my father turned away to heave again, I rolled to my knees and pushed myself up from the ground, wincing at the pain in my fist and ankle. My entire body was shaking like a leaf, and I somehow made it to the back door. I didn't know what I was doing till I found myself outside the cellar again in a daze. I went in slowly, quietly shutting the door behind me, leaving the light off while I felt my way round the workbench to Oscar's side. Opening the driver's door, I slumped on to the seat behind the wheel, but this time I couldn't cry.

In the last hour everything had got so unbelievably jumbled that the tears were squashed down low. Deep down it hurt. And my chest hurt too. And my head.

And my fist.

And especially my foot.

Heaving a shaky breath, I moved my ankle carefully and sagged into the seat, listening numbly to the muffled sounds around me.

After a while, Mum was back. Then, minutes later, Boodle's panting breath came snuffling round the cellar door and Pen said, 'C'mon, Boodlington-love-bunny-snuggly-hugs.'

Boodle followed her up the back steps to the kitchen door.

It wasn't long before I heard a call from inside th

house: 'Je-hee-pers! Mum! What happened here?'

I winced. Pen had found the bathroom door.

It sounded like Mum followed her straight to the scene of my crime. She rattled the doorknob. 'Spenser?'

Shuffle, shuffle.

Pen's voice, lower down: 'Dad, it's not like we can't see you in there.'

I hunkered down in the car seat and pushed the heels of my hands against my eyelids. Could I live down here? Like Anne Frank? For, like, ever?

In the house above me, Dad came out of the bathroom. 'Dad?'

'Spenser?'

'Don't ask me,' he rasped. 'I'm going to bed.' I listened as his footsteps receded above, Mum and Pen obviously standing very, very still.

Then they spoke together, the sound loud in the quiet: 'Tallulah.'

'I told you she had problems,' said Pen.

'That child . . .' said Mum, in her special *I'm going to eat my offspring* voice.

Hoo boy.

This was not going to be a happy time.

It must have been at least an hour of solitary I confined myself to. Sitting in the dark, listening to the plumbing roaring and banging, the bathwater gurgling from the downstairs bathroom, Pen dirging tunelessly (she knows better than to sing in public), Boodle whining at the back door for a last wee in the Great Outdoors. I wondered whether Mum was worried about where I was. Maybe I should face the music now. Get the pain over with. Confront both parents about what was going on.

I shifted in the deep leather seat to get out, but my ankle protested with a jolt of agony so extreme I went eeeemph, and fell back. It was a sign, I thought. I should stay where I was. But I was interested to see if there was blood from the door incident. I wiggled my toes and slid out of the car. While I fumbled for the light switch I heard the back gate squeal and I stopped in my tracks. Who was coming in? Or going out?

My family were all inside, I was pretty sure of it.

Unbidden, Pen's words before supper flitted at me: *Angus came back from the city this morning.* So it hadn't been him that Jack had seen hanging around our house last night, after all. *Who, then?*

Footsteps sounded ever so quietly outside, moving slowly to the back steps, then stopped about a metre from the workshop door. The crisp night air carried a faint whisper: 'Subject is not in her room, not in the cellar workshop.'

I was too frightened to think how totally nutso this was. *Subject?* I mean, wha–?

Who was this?

I inched back into Oscar and hunched down behind the steering wheel.

Then I *really* thought I was going to lose bowel control because whoever was outside moved carefully over to the cellar door . . .

Frikfrikfrik!

. . . and opened it.

Fffffff!

I was frozen inside the car, shaking like a leaf and staring at a dark silhouette in the doorway. Tall. Male. No handbag. No satin robes. A stranger.

A stranger looking right at me.

I couldn't breathe.

He reached into his inside jacket pocket and images of gun shoulder holsters flashed through my mind. There was a faint rustle of clothing and then a barely discernible click before he said softly: 'Subject has not progressed on mechanical project. Confirm halt in all this activity since programme commenced on March eleventh.'

Another click.

I hadn't blinked and my eyeballs were starting to hurt, but the next second I squeezed my eyelids shut because the figure moved suddenly and then, thrusting at his jacket pocket, he flicked on one of those mini Maglite thingies that has, like, a floodlight glare from a torch the size of a lentil.

The bright light focused on the workbench and started moving over the body of the car. Any minute now he would see me sitting here like a corpse, and, who knows, maybe that's how I was going to end up.

And then, *then*, someone chose that moment to ring my darling sister on her mobile, which was still in my pocket. The sound of 'Kumbaya' echoed loudly across the cellar and in a flash Mr Sinister was gone.

The back gate was vaulted with a clatter, then silence.

I rummaged for the phone in a state of shock.

'Hello?' I rasped.

'Pen babe?' said Fat Angus. 'You okay?'

Now here's why I should be a secret agent: even with adrenalin pumping, with white knuckles clenching, I had the presence of mind to take revenge on Pen.

'Angus,' I whispered, letting the shakes reach my voice, 'I think I'm pregnant.'

No reply.

Then Fat Angus said, 'Tatty Lula? Is that you?'

(Okay, so that didn't work. Maybe not a secret agent. Maybe a secret agent's shoe polisher.) Clearly Angus's mangled ears are damaged only on the outside. And who said a rugby prop had to be a meathead? I was seriously impressed.

'Yes,' I said.

'I might tell Pen about this,' mused Fat Angus.

'I was just messing around,' I muttered. 'Listen, I need your help.'

'Yeah? This plus my silence on the aforementioned pregnancy thing is going to, like, cost you big.'

I winced. 'Fat Angus, does your brother still do the odd bit of detecting?'

'Bludgeon?'

'Yes. You've only got one brother.'

'You saying I don't know my relatives?'

'Sheesh, Angus! Calm down.'

'What you want?'

I paused. 'I think someone's following me around.'

'Yeah right. Like you're that hot.'

'Pardon?'

'I mean, no offence, you're fit, but, you know, you're not your sister. Proper brunette, like. Some guys I know like that beach-babe look, but I'm into au naturel, you know?'

Please. God. Stop me from speaking.

I climbed out of the car, noting that my hand and left foot felt sore but not totally damaged, and shuffled out of the cellar.

'Angus,' I said firmly, 'someone has just opened up my –'

I was going to say *workshop door*, but news that I liked motor mechanics would not help my snog-a-boy plots. I'd be classed as WEIRD faster than Fat Angus could say 'I like a good scrum'.

I chose my words carefully as I walked up the back stairs, and explained about last night and the night before. Angus didn't sound convinced, but said he'd ask Bludgeon if he had any 'thoughts on the matter'.

Crossing the courtyard, I found Pen waiting impatiently for me outside the annexe.

'I knew you had it!' she hissed, snatching the phone from me before I had time to say cheerio to her boyo.

'Angus? Angus?' she said, after a quick look at the screen. 'Did you call me? You do know you've been talking to my psycho sister, not me, yes?'

I unlocked the annexe and stepped inside, shoving the door closed behind me, but before I could get the latch on, Pen's fierce little shoulder had butted against the panelling and sent me staggering into the kitchen counter.

'Bye-bye, Angus,' she crooned, and hung up the phone. She backed the door closed behind her with a thud. 'Right, Lula.' Pen's eyes were narrow and slitty. Yeesh. I was ever so slightly fearful. 'What's with the strange behaviour?'

Chapter Sixteen

Still Thursday night. Will it *ever* end?

'Well?' said my evil sibling, hip shunted out, foot tapping, like some Victorian chaperone on the rampage. 'What explanations for your recent madness? Is it drugs?'

'I don't have to answer to you!' I spat back, outraged. Pen took a breath. 'And don't even *think*,' I hissed, 'of saying you speak on behalf of your client, Dr Anne Bird, because I have currently lost my sense of humour. And *she* has lost her mind.'

Pen came towards me, wagging her index finger. 'Tallulah, Mum is seriously worried. She thinks you may need a spell at Fort Norland for drug addiction. She sent me to check on you.'

'*What* drug addiction?'

Pen paused. 'Okay, that's pushing it, but you're *not far from it*, Lu!'

'Would you please leave?'

'Not until you tell me what you were bothering F– I mean Angus about.'

'He didn't tell you?'

Pen examined the perfect cuticles on her right hand. 'We didn't really have time to converse. He had to go.'

'Hm,' I said. I was, again, a little impressed by Fat Angus and his discretion. Maybe the guy had hidden depths.

I walked behind the little kitchen counter and yanked open the door of the minuscule empty fridge.

'You got chocolate?' Pen leaned over the counter from the other side and tried to look down into my fridge.

'Why are you still here?' I asked, pushing the fridge closed with a thud.

Pen paced restlessly. 'I know you've got Maltesers somewhere. What happened to *sharing is caring*?'

'Hgrph,' I snorted. 'You threw that lesson on its ass the day you poured out all Dad's booze from The Green Box. Couldn't you have left him a tipple to keep him happy?'

Pen whirled round, her face outraged. '*I was trying to help him!*'

We stared at each other hotly. This was an issue we'd never truly thrashed out.

I turned the kettle on with a snap of the switch. 'Dad has to help himself,' I said to Pen. 'You meddling just makes it worse!'

'You doing *nothing* makes it worse,' retaliated Pen. 'You know, I was here to help you too, Tallulah. WELL. You can FORGET IT.'

I felt bad instantly. But what's a girl to do when an apology can't come out in the nanosecond it takes for a younger sister to slam out the room? Heaving a heavy, shaky sigh, I headed for the armchair and reached under the heirloom quilt. The bag was fantastically heavy. I sighed again. I'd been doing so well. I pulled the heirloom back in place and collapsed on the chair, taking a hit of five Malteser balls in one go. Soooo good. Munch, crunch, munch, crunch. Mmm. I had another two mouthfuls and stopped only when all the surfaces of my teeth were levelled by impacted honeycomb.

Just as the sugar high was about to kick in, Pen turned the hot tap in the kitchen on full throttle and the pipes went berrrsERK.

WUGGABANGWUGGABANGBANGBANG!

I bit my cheek with the shock of the first WUGGA and the rusty taste of blood killed all the comfort of the chocolate binge.

My hand strayed back for another hit, but I restrained myself and moved to lock the door, then checked all the windows and made sure every curtain and blind was completely closed.

The pipes were quiet now. As my heart slowed I got behind my computer and logged on, simultaneously thumbing out a text:

Goils, I'm online.

EGMONT PRESS: ETHICAL PUBLISHING

Egmont Press is about turning writers into successful authors and children into passionate readers – producing books that enrich and entertain. As a responsible children's publisher, we go even further, considering the world in which our consumers are growing up.

Safety First
Naturally, all of our books meet legal safety requirements. But we go further than this; every book with play value is tested to the highest standards – if it fails, it's back to the drawing-board.

Made Fairly
We are working to ensure that the workers involved in our supply chain – the people that make our books – are treated with fairness and respect.

Responsible Forestry
We are committed to ensuring all our papers come from environmentally and socially responsible forest sources.

**For more information, please visit our website at
www.egmont.co.uk/ethical**

Mixed Sources
Product group from well-managed forests and other controlled sources
www.fsc.org Cert no. TT-COC-002332
© 1996 Forest Stewardship Council

Egmont is passionate about helping to preserve the world's remaining ancient forests. We only use paper from legal and sustainable forest sources, so we know where every single tree comes from that goes into every paper that makes up every book.

This book is made from paper certified by the Forestry Stewardship Council (FSC), an organisation dedicated to promoting responsible management of forest resources. For more information on the FSC, please visit **www.fsc.org**. To learn more about Egmont's sustainable paper policy, please visit **www.egmont.co.uk/ethical**.

'Th-thanks,' I stuttered, yanking my bag away so my dress could drop back to the knee.

'I could see ya knickers,' she said again, with a great deal of satisfaction.

How long had I been striding along with my GREY GRANNY KNICKERS ON SHOW? HOW LONG? I ask. HOW LONG?

Ali: Yikes. Yep – that's pretty high up there on the embarrassment scale. Maybe it'd been like that since you left the house. Imagine how many people –

[Samantha shoots dagger eyes at Ali]

Ali: Err. Right, sorry. Okay. Just one more question before we wrap things up. Who would you fall for? Jack or Arns? Or Fat Angus perhaps?

Samantha: Ha! If I went anywhere near Fat Angus, Pen would do something terrible to me!

Ali: Samantha! Pen is in your head!

Samantha: Exactly. Brain damage!

Ali: Arns or Jack?

Samantha: Can I tell you after *Lula Does the Hula*? I think there might be more we need to know about those two . . .

I put the phone down within fingers' reach and ran through my messages. Nothing exciting, sob sob. I keyed in a quick one-liner:

TATTY BIRD: I'm being stalked.

And within seconds I had a reply. But not the one I wanted.

CARRIE: Fantastic!

TATTY BIRD: Er, nooo. I thought I was going to *die* earlier.

CARRIE: Who is it?

TATTY BIRD: Dunno. Bludgeon's going to find out.

CARRIE: You called Bludgeon? You didn't! Fat Angus's brother? That guy with no neck?

TATTY BIRD: You should know. He's no. 3 on The List!

CARRIE: We thought you'd get lucky with that maimed guy long before no. 3!

TATTY BIRD: Well, no, actually. There's no way I'd kiss Bludgeon. NO WAY. But him helping me now is a good thing.

CARRIE: BLUDGEON? A good thing?! How?!

TATTY BIRD: Hey! He has his finger on the pulse of crime in our town.

CARRIE: Oh ha ha. Finding out that Jessica is snogging Jason Ferman and ratting her out to Dennis Wiseman is not a finger on the pulse. Everyone knows about recent activity in the 000s.

TATTY BIRD: Fine, fine, but he's my only hope.

I filled them in on what had been happening and demanded their immediate return. I n*eeeee*ded them.

CARRIE: Look, Lula, we'd be back asap, but – hang on. This is going to take too long. Tam says she's got free minutes on her phone.

A second later my mobile rang.

'You think you've got problems,' said Tam in answer to my 'Hello?'.

'I *know* I've got problems, babe!' I exclaimed.

Tam's hand went over the receiver. '*She just called me babe*,' she said to everyone with her, clearly concerned.

'I can hear you, Tam!' I yelled.

She came back. 'Sorry.'

'Forget it. What's going on there?'

'I'm going to give you a five-second version of Alex's latest, okay? Ready?'

'Yeah.'

'Alex's dad took us all out to dinner and Alex snuck out and snogged the dishwasher guy.'

'Everyone is kissing except me!' I wailed. 'Is he hot?'

'Who?'

'The dishwasher, Tam, the dishwasher! Geez!'

'Who cares. Mr Thompson saw them and he's seriously peed off. We're grounded.'

'Ouch,' I said.

'Don't even. Ever try earning a pfennig busking from a second-floor apartment?'

'Oh. Geez. That bad?'

'You have no idea! This holiday is a total washout!'

'It's not my fault!' came Alex's voice over the line.

'It's never your fault!' Tam yelled back. Then nothing.

'Tam?' I ventured. There were snuffles on the end of the line. Could have been sobs of frustration. Could have been hysterical laughter. 'I'm going to go now,' I continued in a lonely tone. 'I might call a few people here to see what they think. I'm probably overreacting.'

Tam squeaked goodbye and I quickly keyed through my phone contacts, hitting call when I found the name I was looking for. There'd been something niggling at my subconscious and it was time it got out in the open.

'Tallulah Bird?'

'Hi, Jack. Are you really an investigative journalist?'

'Yep. Need anything exposéed?' I could hear the smile in his voice.

'*Why are you creeping around me and my house?*' I demanded.

I was convinced I was right in my suspicions, but the shock on the other end sounded real enough. 'Wha–? Wha–? Lula – Wha–?'

Either he'd thought he was deep undercover, or he really didn't know what I was going on about.

I didn't give him a chance to explain. Bludgeon would find out the truth, I was sure of it. Hanging up with a hard pelt of thumb to red-receiver button, I deleted his number, thumped my mobile down on the desk and logged off from the computer.

I needed a bath.

Time for Pen to hear dem pipes.

All the lights were out and I was keeping my eyes closed to persuade myself that I was drifting off after a relaxing bath when my mobile rang. I snatched it up.

''Lo?'

'Hi, Tatty, it's Bludgeon.'

'Wow. Didn't expect to hear from you so soon. Or' – I checked my watch – 'so late.'

'A sniper never sleeps.'

'Okaaaay.'

''Eard you got lurker problems.'

'Stalker, he's a *stalker*. Why won't anyone believe me?'

'Oh, I believe you, darlin'. We been followin' up on somethin' that's been goin' down in your neck o' the woods. Not high on the pile at the mo cos of other stuff, you know, goin' down.'

Purlease spare me the Hollywood speak, I thought.

'That Mr Kaplinsky from the wrinklies over your road –'

'Mr Kadinski?'

'That's 'im. 'E's been on the blower every five minutes about some bloke 'angin' about. I 'ad to put my best boy onnit. Yeah?'

'Ye-es,' I said slowly. 'What did your best boy come up with?'

'Your dad with a 'andbag, for one. I'm gonna keep that one on file, like,' said Bludgeon with a girly giggle.

Oh, geez. 'What about Jack de Souza?' I asked tightly.

Bludgeon laughed. 'Nah. Not 'im. Mr K saw 'im round yours last night so I checked him out first. Not much gets by you, eh? That Jack's been in the IT building all night.'

'All night?' I asked. 'You sure?'

'Got a guy working campus security what told me.'

Great. So there really was a stalker, and it wasn't Jack. 'Anyone else?' I asked, rubbing at an ache behind my eyes.

'Coupla leads, but I reckon it's a random crazy from Fort Norland. One of 'em's escaped, like. You shouldn't worry.'

'No, Bludgeon. The guy in my cellar sounded like he *knew* me. He . . . mentioned my . . . uh . . . hobbies that not many people know about. He was *taking notes* of what I've been doing since the eleventh of March.'

'You sound freaked out.'

'I *am* freaked out, Bludgeon!'

'That's why you called me. I can 'elp, love. Leave it in my in tray. Now, let's talk payment . . .'

I nipped that in the bud with a quick reference to how we were virtually brother and sister, what with Pen and Fat Angus moving in on each other. It worked.

I was asleep in minutes, with strange dreams of Mr Kadinski sprinting down the road, his clothes on fire, at twice his usual height and yelling obscenities at creeping shadows in the dark.

Chapter Seventeen

Friday five a.m. Last day of being fifteen

Waking up was unexpectedly effortless and by the time the room was filled with a faint pink light I was raring to go. I wiggled my fingers. Hand okay! I tested my ankle. Perfect! I inhaled nervously through my nose. Clear!

Whoohoo!

Pulling on my running gear I felt my quads bulge as I flexed out in the bare minimum of a warm up. I stretched again to tie the annexe key to my shoelace, sighing happily at how limber I felt, then moved quietly out of the door, pulling it closed noiselessly behind me.

The main Bird residence was still, silent, and there wasn't a sound in the air except for peepings from birds and the scurrying of a blue tit on a housing mission. Taking a deep breath of cold air, I padded round the house to the front gate and jumped it to prevent its telltale squeak. *Superfit action woman!* I thought, and headed up the hill at a slow walk. Lifting my eyes to the dawn sky as I crested the rise, I caught sight of a twitching curtain from a Setting Sun window. *Could only be Mr Kadinski*, I thought with a grin. Did the man never sleep? I twisted my body round to the left and right, arms outstretched, and thought about which way to go. Past St Alban's was my favourite route, but with boys there it was a no go. Exhibiting flabby bits at full wobble capacity to potential snoggers was not an option. At this time of day, though . . . I'd just turned in that direction when I heard a door slam hard, cracking through the silence like a pistol shot.

'Wherrff!' I squeaked, jumping a mile high before squinting back at home.

Hang on. It must be Mr Ka– I tensed to start running straight away but too late.

'Tallulah? Please come here,' he called.

Damn the aged!

Groaning under my breath, I stomped through the retirement home's front gate and up the garden steps, towards the house.

'Hi, Mr Kadinski,' I muttered.

'Tallulah, I've been trying to talk to you all week. Can you give me a hand down?'

'Sure,' I muttered again, and shoved my forearm under his.

'That's what I love about the youth,' he said, smiling. 'Such gracious respect for the elderly.'

I sighed. 'Sorry, sir,' I said. 'Just a bit tired,' though that was a lie.

'Yes, I remember the teen years being particularly wearying.' He smiled again and I saw how bright his grey eyes were. They twinkled out from beneath his thick white hair, topped with a charcoal fedora, no specs required. We started down the stairs and I said, 'Hey,' before I could stop myself.

'Yes, young lady?'

'You don't need my help on the stairs.'

Mr Kadinski laughed. 'I'm an ex-marine, you know. Special Forces. We have bodies of fine tempered steel.'

'Wow,' I said, thinking, *Special Forces, suuuure.*

We'd already got to the bottom of the steps, the grass of the lawn wetting my trainers and darkening the suede of his old-man shoes.

'My fine physique is not my only asset,' he said. His face was serious. I looked closely for some sign of humour. There was none. 'My mind is one of the finest in Britain.'

I bit my cheeks to stop myself from unseemly guffaws. *Finest mind in Britain, wha ha ha!*

'Go on, laugh,' he said bitterly. 'Then talk to me when Bludgeon McGraw comes up with a vast array of dead ends.'

'Wha—?'

'The old-man shoes are just a cover, you know. Your grandmother trusted me to take care of things for you, Tallulah.' He tipped his hat at me and began walking slowly in the direction of town. 'I'm off to the police station now to check on something I left with them on Tuesday.

Come by this afternoon for some answers to your problems.'

He'd gone several metres before my whirling brain could take in what he'd said. How on earth had he known I had problems?

Yes, Bludgeon had said Mr Kadinski'd reported a lurker.

Okay, but how had he known I'd even spoken to Bludgeon?

Probably Bludgeon.

I sighed. I'd never make the Special Forces. I was a little slow. Though maybe I just had post-traumatic stress from last night.

I couldn't face running past Special Agent Kadinski, so I headed up the hill, the way Boodle and I had gone on the bike. I'd take the same route as then, and sprint past PSG, St Alban's and home, thinking about Ben Latter the whole way round.

A grin pulled at my mouth as I thought of how close we'd come to kissing on Wednesday night, and before I knew it I was flying up towards the woods.

Something odd happens to your persona when you're pushing yourself to the max through a sleeping town. A strange sort of ownership creeps over you. King of the Road! A Chariot of Fire! By the time I'd vaulted our creaky squeaky gate again, I was seriously pumped.

I Would Talk To Dad.

I Would Get Results From Bludgeon.

The Coven's Quarter Paperwork Would Appear.

And tonight there would be the World's Most Awesome Kiss With Beautiful Ben.

Eeeeeeeeeeeeeeeeeeeeee!

The library was busy that morning. Or maybe it just seemed that way because for once Mum and I got in before nine. Everyone was milling about in the staffroom getting coffee and stuff. We were among the first to punch in for hot chocolate, keen to get to the office to check for webcam files and open desk drawers.

'Bring it on!' hissed Mum, skedaddling up the back stairs in front of me in a particularly voluminous deep red caftan.

'What's with your Christmas dress, Mum?' I puffed.

'Decided it needed more wear. Plus, I'm power dressing today,' she puffed back.

The fire door banged against the wall as we flung ourselves into the historical-library offices. We were the first in.

'Yesss!' I said. Evidence would be undisturbed.

Mum hit the light switches and fluorescent tubing hummed and flickered into life.

We gasped.

The glass in her office door was shattered from top to bottom and a trail of chaos led from her desk to the fire door where we stood now. A high-tech digital alarm clock matching Mum's description of a complete video surveillance package was lying smashed on the floor.

Mum moved slowly to the nearest phone.

'Security?' she said. 'We have a situation. Can you come up immediately?'

Even I was dispatched to stay in the staffroom while Mum went through everything with the Security guys. Mike looked disgruntled to be bundled away with all of us. He harrumphed and muttered to himself, refusing to congregate round the coffee machine – lounging on the sofa instead with the *Financial Times*. Mabel approached him at one point, and he said something so sharp and abrupt that she scuttled away faster than a beetle from a steel-toed boot.

I was soooo desperate to know what was going on I thought my head would explode. Then Sophie Wenger walked in and it nearly did.

The girl was limping, and when she finally took off her gloves, after Claudia Hautsenfurg asked her if she should turn the heating up, we could all see a myriad tiny red cuts covering her left hand.

I remembered that Alex hadn't replied to my text about Sophie and Vincent Harrow, and pulled out my phone. My thumb danced hard and fast over the keypad with renewed demands before I shoved my mobile back into my pocket.

Arns caught my evil eye at Sophie and ambled over.

'Don't,' he said, pouring himself his, like, fiftieth espresso.
'Arns, you are going to be so wired.'

'Like you're not.'

'I have a lot of natural energy today, I'll admit.'

'Today's a big day for you,' conceded Arnold with a nod.

'I'm pretty focused on a number of issues,' I said, meeting his eye. 'One, *my* main suspect is about to be fingerprinted and called to account for her whereabouts last night, and made to explain where certain key historical documents have gone to.'

'I *knew* you'd jumped to that conclusion. The chickens have not hatched.'

'Arns, they have hatched and are already at full egg-laying capacity. Secondly, my d–' I stopped myself. What was I thinking? The Dad issue was a personal one, and though Arns and I had shared *a lot* in the past few days, parental politics would be kept strictly confidential. 'Secondly,' I began again, 'what to order at Hambledon's finest slaughterhouse tonight?'

'Does Ben know you're vegetarian?'

'Don't think so.'

'Right. I guess you don't *look* vegetarian.'

Arns sipped his espresso thoughtfully and headed for a small sagging sofa vacated by Mrs Simmons who was going home in a huff.

'You can call me when all this silliness is over with,' she said to Mum's PA, Sally Penridge, and left in a flurry of scarves, chiffon and far too much Chanel No. 5.

Arns coughed. 'That fragrance,' he said hoarsely, falling into the sofa.

'Alex would confirm it as Chanel,' I said decisively.

'It needs discontinuing.'

'Forget that,' I said rudely. 'What do you mean I don't *look* vegetarian?' I put my hands on my hips and stared down at him aggressively.

Arnold glanced at me: a quick, nervous flick of his eyes. He coughed again, and took another sip of coffee. I swear his pupils were a pinprick in diameter.

'Just . . . that,' he began, then stopped. 'Vegetarians . . . they're generally quite . . .' he winced, 'spindly.'

I plumped down on the couch so hard Arns's coffee slopped from its tiny cup into the cushions. He winced again.

'I knew it! You're saying I'm not thin? Are you calling me fat? What are you implying, Arnold? You do realise this is a critical time for my self-esteem, right? *Critical!* I'm about to be Sweet Sixteen! *Never Been Kissed!* Not Good! *Not. Good. AT. ALL!*' I was whispering fiercely and my frantic hand gestures had caught the attention of Sophie Wenger. She ambled over and sat in a straight-backed wooden chair opposite us.

'Settle down,' said Arnold to me out of the corner of his mouth.

'How're you guys?' asked Sophie, dropping her bag to the floor and lifting her tea for a quiet drink.

'Fine, thanks,' I replied. 'What happened to your hand?'

Arns's foot crept across mine and pressed down hard.

'Uhh, I cut it,' she replied.

'Exactly,' said Arns. 'Doing any good drama productions at the moment?'

'Duh,' said Sophie after a slow blink at Arns. 'Term starts on Monday?'

'Right, right,' said Arns, flushing. 'Well, I'm just going to –' but before he could leave me with the criminal goth, one of the Security guys came into the staffroom and said:

'Can I have everyone's attention, please?'

The room's murmuring chat immediately quietened.

'As most of you know, it seems there was some kind of disturbance in Dr Bird's office last night and we need to get to the bottom of it. Fingerprints have been lifted and we have three good ones and a partial that are not Dr Bird's. We will be fingerprinting you all in turn, and asking a few questions, just as a first port of call.'

An angry buzz erupted immediately.

The Security guy grabbed a dirty cup and teaspoon

and whacked at the china with the spoon.

Chink, chink, chink.

The talk in the room wound down. 'Could Sophie Wenger step this way first, please?' he continued.

Sophie stood up so fast her chair fell back. Her face was whiter than usual and her hands shook as she reached for her bag. Arns picked up the chair as she walked across the room in complete silence. You could have heard a teabag drop.

But when the door closed behind her Arns could barely make himself heard in the pandemonium that broke out.

'IT'S NOT HER THAT MADE OFF WITH THE DOCUMENTS,' he yelled in my ear.

I rolled my eyes. 'How do you know? Anyway, I think you're losing the plot, Arns,' I said loudly back, noise levels returning to normal. 'Arriving late for work, for one.' I looked down my nose at him, my eyes wide and knowing.

'Ha! I'd forgotten about my tardiness in all the disruption here,' he replied.

'Yeah,' I said, bracing myself for a boring tale of how he'd got a puncture on Albert Street or something.

Arns put his cup down with a bang and turned to me, leaning in with scant regard for personal space. 'I was right on schedule, Lula, locking up my bike in the basement, when a car pulled in right next to me. Eight forty-five.'

I closed my eyes to indicate extreme state of boredom and general uncaringness.

'I was about to stand up,' he continued, 'when I heard the guy open the door straight into the car next to him.'

'Ouch!' I said. 'That is such a wronger. Did he leave a note?'

'Well, I stayed down low to check, and then someone got out of the bumped car and started really going at this other guy.'

'What? Like fighting?'

'No, Tallulah, no.' Arns's turn for the slow blink. 'He was just hissing at him in this stressed-out, familiar-sounding voice, but trying to keep quiet at the same time.'

'Like, *whispering*? That's odd. I'd've been *yelling* about my car.'

'That's what I thought. Then the first guy told him to suck it up and asked if he had The Stuff.'

'The Stuff?'

'Yes, that's how he said it.'

'Okay.'

Arns paused. 'Then the second guy said of course and he wasn't going to hand it over till the transfer had gone through.'

'No! This is so Hollywood!'

'I know! And even though my legs were cramping, I just kept as still as a stone.'

'What a man,' I smirked.

Arnold closed his eyes. 'You wouldn't understand, being such a stranger to exercise yourself.'

'I'm going to let that go,' I said hotly. 'You have no idea about my training programme.'

'Programme?' he snorted. Rude boy.

'What happened then? Were there threats? Safety catches taken off powerful weapons?'

Arnold shook his head wearily. 'The first guy said, "Fine, then you're going to have to hand it over to him yourself tomorrow morning."'

'Where? When?'

'They walked away. I couldn't hear, but I've been thinking . . .' said Arns.

Then Tweedy Mabel wandered closer, almost as if she were trying to hear what we were saying, her face more like a praying mantis than ever. I couldn't believe she was related to anyone on earth, let alone the town mayor.

'Hello, Tallulah. Hello, Arnold.'

'Hello, Mabel,' we chorused respectfully.

Oh no, please don't make us converse, I thought. 'Hey, Ams, I thought your bike was out of action,' I said, hoping she'd move on.

'I can fix a puncture, Talluluh,' replied Arnold, killing the conversation.

Then the Security guy was back.

'Tallulah Bird?' he called.

My turn now? Great. Just great. Now we wouldn't get a chance to talk to Sophie at her most vulnerable.

'Sophie,' I mouthed urgently to Arnold, but he shook his head in that *I'm not going to waste my time* way he does more often than I'd realised before. I stamped on his flip-flopped foot hard as I got up to go.

'Oops,' I said lightly, 'sorry,' and headed for the door.

Chapter Eighteen

And so. Still Friday morning

A small area had been set aside for interviews near Mum's office. Up close the damage looked even worse than my first impression. The thing I hadn't noticed earlier is that Mum's desk was actually broken, not just in a crazy mess. The front right leg had snapped and if it hadn't been for the drawer unit beneath it, itself badly damaged, the whole thing would be on the ground, empty in trays and all.

'Frik,' I said, with meaning.

'Step this way please, Miss Bird,' said the Security guy, and he led me over to Mum.

I sat down in the chair he gestured to. 'You okay, Mum?' I asked.

'I'm fine, Lu,' said Mum. She did not look fine. 'Just thought I'd ask for an independent opinion from you because Dr Gordon can't be here for several hours, and I'd like to get the office put to rights as soon as possible, quite frankly.'

'You want my opinion? Not my fingerprints?'

'Those first,' said the Security guy, and he began rolling the top of my fingers over a purple pad of ink, then rolling them one by one on a white page with TALLULAH BIRD:

PART-TIME LIBRARY WORKER typed at the top.

'How did your desk break, Mum?' I blurted out. A thought occurred to me and I looked at the Security guy. 'I don't remember seeing it broken when we first came up this morning. Were you guys a little clumsy with your investigation in there? That desk is two hundred years old, you know.'

'It wasn't them,' said Mum, and she dropped her head in her hands.

'Mum?' I asked, suddenly uncertain.

'Could we have a few minutes, please?' asked Mum. The Security guy nodded and hovered uncertainly outside Mum's office doorway.

'What's going on?'

'Sophie Wenger –'

'I knew it!' I raised my arms in triumph. 'Call me Jack Bauer! Call me Bond – James Bond! Call me Supersleuth!'

Mum was not smiling. 'This is not easy for me to explain, so I'm just going to spit it out.' I dropped my arms. 'It turns out that Sophie Wenger is, um, prematurely – and I must stress that I think this is most unnatural, Tallulah – she is . . . um . . . sexually active.'

'Exactly! Mum, I sent Alex a text because I think Sophie Wenger is going out with Vincent Harrow – Harry Harrow's son! Alex will know for certain. As soon as she gets back to me, we –'

Mum held up her hand for silence. 'Will you just let me finish?'

'Sorry.'

'Sophie came into the building after hours, with a friend, and had intercourse on my desk.' My eyes bugged out so far I thought if I blinked I might lose them. 'And during the, um, *rigours* of their action, the desk leg broke. The desk obviously crashed down, damaging my drawer unit.'

'Yowzer . . .' I breathed.

'Precisely. When the couple eventually got off the desk, that spider you lot trapped at the annexe had already begun to crawl out of the drawer.'

'You hadn't taken it to the zoology department?' I whispered. 'It could have died! How did it get out the box?'

'The first drawer literally smashed open, and obviously the box along with it.' Mum shook her head. 'I can't believe I'd forgotten all about that spider.'

'Then what?' I asked, impatient.

'Well, panicked by the commotion they'd made, and with the spider on the loose, Sophie threw herself out of the office, but she tripped because her, um, *clothing* was around her ankles and she fell into my office door.'

'Oh, geez.'

'Sophie's partner abandoned her, concerned that Security would be on their way with all the noise, and he crashed into several desks on the way before he found the fire doors.'

'Oh, man.'

'Sophie was quite thoroughly, um, tangled, and cut up, but she saw the spider crawl under the drawers –'

'Sweet . . .'

'– across the office –'

'Frikking . . .'

'Up the walls, and round the top of the doorframe.'

'Mercy.'

'She left promptly – hasn't seen or spoken to her partner since.'

I had too many questions to be able to speak. My skin was so raised with goosebumps I was afraid it would hurt if I moved.

The Security guy appeared out of nowhere. 'Some story, huh?' he leered. 'She won't say who loverrr boy is, but we'll get to the truth.'

Ugh.

Mum's eyes narrowed. She was about to say something but then he waved my sheet of fingerprints. 'You're clear,' he said.

I ignored him, my eyes still uncomfortably far from their sockets. 'This is such a mess, Mum. Was Sophie in there for action or info?'

Mum rubbed her forehead. 'I thought you'd be able

to tell me that, Lu. I don't know. I just don't know.' Our eyes met. 'Mr Michael Burdon next, please, Frank,' said Mum, turning to the Security guy. Then, 'Go home, Lula. Have some lunch and relax for a bit.' Her head tilted ever so slightly in a meaningful nod. 'Maybe chat with Alex. The office may be back to normal on Monday, but there's going to be no work for you to do here until everyone's been questioned and the office properly examined and cleaned.'

'Sure,' I said uncertainly. Was she telling me to check out Alex's info? She nodded at me again. She was.

I gave Frank the meathead a cheery wave and winked at Mum, pulling my bag to my shoulder before taking a last look at the office on the way out.

I got a text from Alex on the way home.

Sophie and Vincent in love. Matching tongue studs.

So was Vincent Harrow shagging Sophie Wenger in Mum's office? Pretty damn likely. My pulse quickened. *Video surveillance*, I thought to myself, and began to thumb my phone to thank Alex.

Before I could press send I got another message.

Psycho girl. I'm not stalking you. Don't flatter yourself.

I flushed crimson as I hit delete. Right! Out-and-out hatred for Jack de Souza was the only way forward. He *was* the lurking type – I was sure of it! It must have been him! I texted Bludgeon and nearly fell into an open water-mains manhole on Hill Street so my message only got as far as:

Any news on the stalk

before being sent. Knowing Bludgeon, he'd think it some kind of secret code and would puzzle over it for hours. I shook my head and tried to think positive. Maybe Mr Kadinski could shed some light . . .

So for the first time in nearly sixteen long and terrible years, I headed voluntarily up the steps to the Setting Sun.

Mr Kadinski was in a rocking chair on the veranda in a shady corner. You couldn't even see him from the road.

He had a newspaper over his head and torso and wasn't moving. I only recognised him by the shoes. There was a truckload of pine needles stuck to the mud on the bottom of them.

Hmm. Pine needles. 'Have you been to Coven's Quarter, Mr Kadinski?' I asked.

The newspaper rustled slightly. Other than that – no motion.

'Mr Kadinski?'

'Huh.'

'Hambledon doesn't have many pine trees.'

Mr Kadinski snatched the paper from his face. 'So. Now you want to talk.'

'And you don't.'

'I've decided to keep my nose out of it.'

'Out of what?'

Mr Kadinski coughed and folded up the newspaper carefully. 'I knew your grandmother, you know. When she was still a Hewson.'

'Wow,' I said. 'Did she ever put a jinx on you?'

He laughed. 'Not exactly.'

I looked at him carefully. 'You sure about that?'

This time he really hooted, and I found myself smiling in response. 'Sit down,' he said, nodding to another rocker beside him. I obeyed, and he went on, 'Coven's Quarter has some sentimental value to me. Quite a lot, actually. That's where Sally Hewson and I first kissed. And we'd still be together if it weren't for your father's father.' His expression darkened, but I could see he was only half serious. 'He had a way with words, just like your award-winning parent, and I guess I really had no chance.'

I felt suddenly sad.

'But no regrets,' he said, catching my eye. 'I can't imagine my life now without the ecstasy of Lorraine Greenwood, who followed soon after.' He whistled.

'Ew,' I said.

He held up a placatory hand. 'I do apologise; I digress. The point is that I don't want Coven's Quarter disappearing in a molten pile of concrete. I've been trying to corner you all week to say I overheard something in the woods on Monday morning.'

'Really!' I leaned forward in excitement and the rocking chair almost catapulted me out into the Sun's begonia bed.

'Two men arguing about not being able to get documents out of the library. I'm convinced one was Dirty Harry himself, the developer. A short stocky man with pale hair and a square head. Light-coloured eyes, big lips, drinker's nose. Sound familiar to you?'

I shook my head. 'Never seen Harry Harrow, but if that really was him he sounds nothing like his son. Who was the second guy?'

'Now that man . . . I can't quite place him. Distinctive kind of waddle to his walk. But the worst is I think they saw me. *And*, ever since, there's been someone hanging around the area.' Mr Kadinski sighed and leaned back in his chair, his face turned up to the veranda roof. 'Yep. They definitely saw me.' He turned his head to look at me seriously. 'I heard Harrow say that the council will never get to see the documents. I got it all on my cameraphone, and took it to the police first thing Tuesday morning, but they've done nothing with it. Nothing. Can't even confirm the identity of the other man.' He sighed again. 'It's maddening – we know enough to confirm Harrow is behind the missing documents, but not enough to prove a case against the development.'

'Yes! You've got video evidence! Could the other guy have been his son, Vincent?' I asked, excited. 'I'm almost certain it's him that has the documents. There's a girl that works at the library with me –'

But Mr Kadinski was already shaking his head. 'No, it couldn't have been him. The man was nearing middle age. I've seen him somewhere before, I'm sure of it. Big, balding.'

My mind buzzed with who Harry Harrow could be linked with that was old, big and balding.

Yep.

Half of Hambledon.

A figure appeared on the road below. Big, partially old, not balding. Carrying a handbag.

'I've got to go,' I said to Mr Kadinski. 'Can you chase the police again? Do they know how urgent all this is?'

'Someone there has undoubtedly put a spanner in the works,' he replied, springing out of the rocking chair. 'We're on our own, Tallulah. What's your mobile number?'

I told him and he nodded.

Yeah, right. Before a disbelieving thought about his special-agent mental abilities could cross my mind, he repeated the number off pat before disappearing into the

Setting Sun's gloomy interior with a wink and a touch of the forefinger to his fedora.

'Wha–?' But he was gone.

I hurried down the steps. There were a few things I wanted to ask Dad before he got his head down a toilet again.

I got in as Dad came out of the bathroom, his face as red and sweaty as usual, but smelling a little less.

'Hello,' he said mildly, and pushed his hair back from his face. 'How's it going, T-Bird?'

'Like you care,' I replied, anger surging as I dumped my bag in the hall and walked towards him, hands shoved deep in jeans pockets.

'Course I care. Been a bit self-involved what with being sick and everything, but, you know, I'm still same old, same old.'

'No, you're not!' I said, fury tightening my throat. I swallowed it back, remembering how he'd looked when I'd kicked through the bathroom door.

'Look,' said Dad, sitting down near my feet, his back against the wall, 'it's all a bit complicated at the moment, but soon we'll be able to talk about everything openly.'

I took a step away from him. 'I'm listening,' I snapped.

Dad ran both hands through his hair, sinking his head down to his knees. His voice sounded hollow: 'Let me chat to your mum first. She thought it best we wait a few days, just till I can get my new life on track –'

New life on track? Good God! In a few days?

My jaw dropped. I stared at him incredulously. *What the hell was going on here?* I swallowed and held my hands tightly. Losing my temper would get me nowhere. Mum loved this man and, though I hated him now, I knew I loved him too. I thought of Blue, her soft littleness and acceptance of everything; of Pen; of my big sister, Darcy; Aunt Phoebe; Grandma Bird . . . A family that I wanted my father to be a part of.

I sank down to face him. Tears of grief and frustration and anger welled up. I blinked them back with an effort and blurted, 'Dad, whatever has happened is in the past. You need to make good now. Fix it. Please.'

Dad looked at me for a long moment. He cleared his throat. 'I'm trying, T. I really am,' then he ran his hand through his hair again.

'You're not trying hard enough,' I croaked. 'This is not just about you.'

'It's not easy,' said Dad. 'The thing is, I have got to move on from where I am now. If only the nausea would stop.' He shook his head miserably and a flare of anger jerked me to my feet. I looked at him – feeling so sorry for himself when Mum must be feeling torn apart, going on bravely as if our father simply had the flu – and I wanted him to suffer far more than he was already. How dare he talk about moving on, as if we were just a boring job for him, or a bunch of tired friends he no longer had much in common with? What was this? Mum had no right to cosset him when he was about to destroy our family!

'Poor Dad, feeling so terrible. Must be the stress of it all really getting to you,' I shouted. 'Well, you miserable sod, you make *me* feel sick. You *disgust* me.'

My face was hot and red, tears prickling behind my eyes. I was horrified by what I'd said. I'd never spoken to my father this way and as soon as the words were out I wanted them back. Even though they were true, they just didn't sit right, out in the open. I needed to get away, clear my head, calm down. I turned to go, but Dad grabbed my ankle.

Swiping my tears away, I twisted back to face him, crying openly now.

'You *don't* understand,' he said, his voice quiet. 'I *know* you don't.' He didn't look angry, or dismayed, just vaguely confused. Like I was telling him I no longer liked chocolate.

Well, what was confusing about me telling him he was disgusting?

He let go of my ankle then and I escaped to the annexe, Boodle following close behind. It was comfortable being collapsed on the squashy armchair, bingeing on my secret chocolate hoard and watching tears soak into Boodle's fur.

My head hurt from all the crying I was doing, from all the crazy plans I was now hatching to stitch Dad up on his adulterous night out. Maybe I could defuse the entire situation by catching this Freya person on her own and telling her to just bog off.

Eventually I couldn't shed another tear. I couldn't come up with any more brilliant solutions. The future looked bleak.

Boodle sighed and stood up. I thought she was going to ask to be let back out again, but she put her front legs right across me and hopped her back legs up on to the other side of the armchair, so I had ten tons of hairy hound on my lap.

Oh, Boodle, I thought. *Is this a big hug?*

Her heart was pounding *doof doof doof* on my thighs and its slow thud calmed me. I stared into her enormous brown eyes and noted how concerned her ginger eyebrows looked. I hugged her close.

'Oh, Boodle. There's nothing I can do about Dad, is there? *Nothing.*'

What I *could* do was go out tonight and wow the socks off Benjamin Latter Esq. It was just hours until my sixteenth birthday.

I sighed and pushed Boodle off. She left graciously, her plumed tail waving gently back and forth. Before I closed the door, she turned to look at me and her expression said,

Call me any time. I'm here to help.

'Thanks, Boodle,' I said, and I could have sworn that dog nodded kindly in reply before flopping down in the dappled sunlight of the courtyard.

As I threw the empty Malteser bag in the bin my computer gave a deferential BONG.

Message waiting.

Click.

ALEX: What happened with Jack?

[Uh-oh.]

TATTY BIRD: What do you mean?

ALEX: His interest in you has, um, *waned*.

TATTY BIRD: He never *was* interested in me, Alex! What do you mean *waned*?

ALEX: Nothing.

TATTY BIRD: Tell me!

ALEX: Nuh-uh. You lost out, that's all. Jack de Souza is a magical boy.

TATTY BIRD: *You* snog him, then!

ALEX: Uh – we're related? Ew!

TATTY BIRD: Didn't stop you craving him before!

ALEX: Till I realised! Now that I think about it – ew ew ew!

CARRIE: Hey, Lula, I've been checking out the Science Fair site.

TATTY BIRD: You are so gloriously *saaaad*!

CARRIE: And it says Ben Latter is presenting new research on the opening day of the fair – Monday.

TATTY BIRD: I know – maybe I'll go along to the lecture! Listen, better go – it's nearly two and I've got to figure out what I'm going to wear tonight on my hot date. This is it, girls! Tallulah Bird's first kiss, with just hours to go till the birthday clock chimes. Talk about leaving it till the last minute. Bye, lovebugs!

CARRIE: Wait! Lula? Lula?

Chapter Nineteen

Friday afternoon, just HOURS before I'm sixteen

Before I could lose myself in the heady delights of preparing to escape a lifetime jinx of spinsterhood, my mobile rang. It was Mum. She said that Sophie's parents had asked the police to search their home for evidence that she had taken material from the library. Sophie had been quite distraught at the accusation and nothing had been found.

Vincent Harrow's family had not, predictably, been quite so co-operative, but Arnold's mother had got a warrant for a basic premises search, and nothing had turned up there either, bar some blank DVDs carefully labelled in Mum's writing: SURVEILLANCE DR B OFFICE 9–12/4/2009. Vincent Harrow had had to admit he'd been in Mum's office with Sophie, and claimed the disks must have fallen into his open satchel when the desk collapsed. Given there were no fingerprints on them, that was the end of that.

The video files from Mr Kadinski's phone would have to save the day. If they could be analysed in time. That was a job for tomorrow, though. When I was a Frenchly kissed woman of the world.

Eeeeeeee!

An hour later, out of the bath, back down to earth

And so. What to wear.

I surveyed potential outfits. Oh, frik. I needed Pen. I had the jitters, badly. What I really should be doing is following Dad on his hot date this evening, not setting off on one of my own. Why the stress of a family breakdown on tonight of all nights? Maybe Bludgeon could tail him . . . No. No way. I couldn't let anyone else know about Dad's affair until I knew every detail myself.

Blowing out my cheeks, I glanced anxiously through my bedroom window at the sunset. It was beautiful out there. The sky was still blue enough to be day, but the clouds had turned pink, peach, gold, silver. It was getting late. A hedgehog or something was going nuts in the long grass of the neglected garden, and Boodle was nosing around for frogs.

I turned back to my chest of drawers in growing frustration. Where was my useless sister when I needed her? Still sulking, for sure. Unkind thoughts began to surface (prompted largely by the sight of the pustule T-shirt in the last (resort) drawer) when I heard Boodle's snuffling change to a happy *woorrf, woorrf*. Yay! Wonderful Pen was back! I'd welcome her with open arms! Hug her close! Kiss her beautiful cheeks!

A knock sounded on the door.

Cool. *She* was coming to *me*. Forget those crazy

thoughts. She'd be apologising first. And so she should, dammit. Hitching my tiny towel close round my body, I jumped down the steps into the living area and flung the door open.

Arns's eyes sprang out on stalks.

'Good God!' he said.

'Pen!' I said.

'Noooo,' he said, slowly shaking his head. He thumped his chest. 'Me Arnold, you Tallulah.' Then, just as I was about to push the door closed, Boodle flung herself in, knocking me and my minuscule towel flying. I had the good sense – and special-agent lightning-fast reflexes (cough) – to twist as I got flattened, so all Arns saw was my naked butt. I turned to look back at Arns, gaping in the doorway, about to squawk, 'Close the door!', when he leaned in, grabbed the door handle and shut it with a decorous click.

Scrambling into the bedroom, I pulled on my plainest black bra and knickers, grabbed the first shirt and skirt I could find, and headed back to the door. I yanked it open to find Arns in exactly the same spot.

'Dude,' I said. 'What the hell?'

'Don't even,' he said, and staggered in. 'What was *that*?' He fell into the armchair, staring at me like I'd offended him in some unspeakable way.

'I thought you and Mona were learning about life at your place,' I said sarcastically, my cheeks on fire.

'*That* is called a butt, a bottom, bum, arse, ass.'

'Not *that* – and I saw a good deal more than *that*, so you can just call us quits on the nakedness front, Tatty Lula – I'm talking about answering the door in a towel!'

I came round the kitchen counter and yanked a drawer open, searching for teabags. Finding a knife, I snatched it up.

'You saw nothing!' I hissed.

'I saw nothing,' agreed Arnold, hands up in classic murder-victim defence pose. Another Arnold look that I liked. It made me smile.

Throwing the knife back in the drawer, I said, 'I'm out of tea. Hot water?'

'Thank you,' said Arnold graciously. 'So, I take it you were getting ready? Isn't it a bit early?'

'I've got to be there in an hour and a half!'

'What? He's not picking you up?'

I paused. 'Nooo. But he's got The Booth!' I clapped my hands together fast.

Arns nodded and picked at his resized sweatshirt. 'Huh. Will he walk you home?'

I stopped clapping abruptly. 'We're not going to kiss in the restaurant, are we? And not just on the pavement. So the only option *is* a walk home.'

'We-ell, he didn't last time. Y'know. I had to.'

'But you didn't.'

'No. That was Jack.'

'No.'

'No?'

'No, that was Spawn of Satan. We speak not of him.'

'Okay. But Ben of Satan? We can speak of him?'

'Arns?' I was startled. 'Ben's a nice guy. You're joking right?' The kettle grew loud then died back as the water boiled. I poured a careful measure into a mug emblazoned with MORRIS MINOR CONVENTION 2008 and handed it to Arnold.

'Yes, yes, just joking,' said Arns, offhand as he examined the cup. 'Why don't you like Jack? I think he's cool. He said to Mona that he doesn't know why you th—'

'If Ben doesn't walk me home,' I interrupted, feeling panicky, 'I'm taking myself off the snog-plot scene completely. It's got to happen.' I felt flooded with determination. 'Come see what the options are,' I said, heading into the bedroom.

'Uh . . . see *what* options?'

'Oh, please. Don't be afraid.'

Arns heaved himself out of the chair and followed me into my room. Instantly it didn't feel like a good idea. The room was small and he felt a little close, stooping towards me under the eaves. I stepped back hastily and banged my heel on the drawer hanging out at the bottom of the chest. I said a few things to numb the pain.

'Colourful,' said Arnold, looking around for a good place to stand. He moved down the side of the bed closest to the door, while I stayed at the foot.

'What, the clothes?' I was confused – every item on the bed was black.

Arns raised his eyebrows.

'Oh, yes, I'll wash my mouth out with boric acid, I promise,' I muttered. 'Now, in the absence of Pen, which outfit?'

'*You* are asking *me?*'

'I'm desperate.'

'Nice. Thanking you.' He sighed and shook his head ever so slightly. 'Hm. That,' and he motioned with his index finger to a bundle near the pillow where he stood.

'Poloneck and jeans? Are you out of your mind? That's what I wore to the library this morning! Just haven't chucked it in the laundry bin.'

He took a thoughtful sip of hot water. 'Slattern.'

'Hey!' I said. 'Watch it! You're supposed to be being helpful!'

'Actually,' he said, 'what I came to tell you is that I never finished explaining about those guys in the underground car park.'

My mobile rang, and I jumped, hitting my head on the eaves. 'Frreeemph!'

'You are so highly strung,' said Arnold calmly.

The phone stopped ringing.

I bent over the chest of drawers, parting my hair to see if there was blood. 'I think there's blood.'

Arns came over and peered down. 'There's no bloo–'

Rrriiiiiing riiiiiiing – riiiiiiiiiiiiing riiiiiiing! the phone began again.

At the first *rrrr* I jumped, startled. Calm Arns did not. There was impact.

Rrriiiiiing riiiiiiing – riiiiiiiiiiiiing riiiiiiing!

'WHY?' I yelled, furious. 'WHY DO YOU ALWAYS HURT ME?'

'It's not *me*!' said Arns, indignant. 'Good heavens, Tallulah!'

Rrriiiiiing riiiiiiing – riiiiiiiiiiiiing riiiiiiing!

'Don't say good heavens!'

'Pardon?'

Rrriiiiiing riiiiiiing – riiiiiiiiiiiiing riiiiiiing!

'You sound ancient! Just don't say it!'

'Your head. I think there might be blood now.'

Rrriiiiiing riiiiiiing – riiiiiiiiiiiiing riiiiiiing!

'Keep away from me!' I glared at Arns and moved to answer the phone. 'What?' I said rudely. 'Oh, hi . . .' I turned away from Arns, hunching over slightly. 'You get any more info?'

'You got someone there?' asked Bludgeon on the other end.

'Yep.'

''Kay. Just keep quiet while I talk.' I rolled my eyes for my own benefit. 'Turns out the escapee from Fort Norland 'as been picked up in Neston, in the Wirral. 'E was noticed. Not a large town.'

'Spare me the geography lesson, please,' I muttered.

''Ey! This is free info, like. You wanna gimme lip then we'll renegotiate, eh?'

I snuck a look at Arns. He'd picked up a small silky black camisole and was holding it at arm's length. I couldn't work out what was going on his head. 'So what are you saying?' I asked Bludgeon.

'I'm sayin' I'm workin' on oo you reckon's bin eyeballin' you. But yer gonna 'ave t'gimme more t'work on 'ere. Y'know?'

'I thought you said Mr Kadinski'd seen him. Can't you get more information from him?'

''E's not answ'rin' 'is phone.'

'Oh.'

Bludgeon sighed. 'Jus' take care is all. Ain't never 'ad any stiffs on my watch.'

'Lovely!'

'I tells it 'ow it is.'

Arns had moved on to a very short skirt. He was holding it against his hips with an expression of disbelief on his face. His lips were moving, but no sound was coming out.

'And?' I asked crisply as I hung up.

'What . . .' he managed, 'does this cover? Is this supposed to be a *skirt*?'

I bit my lips, but the grin crept out. 'The truth now. You were born in 1928, Arnold, weren't you? And cryogenically frozen so that you could appear in this age to remind kids of today that anything ending above the ankle is slutty and' – I paused dramatically – 'daaa*haan*gerous!'

'I just can't think how it'd be comfortable. That's all.'

'Comfort is not a priority for me tonight, Arns. It's my birthday tomorrow. I'm about to be sweet sixteen and never been kissed. I can't be branded like that for the rest of my days. Ben will be kissed whether he likes it or not,' I said bravely.

Arnold sighed. 'It doesn't feel right.'

'Pardon?' I asked. 'What doesn't feel right?'

'Something . . .' he mused.

I waved him off with a flapping hand, and snatched up a soft black bolero cardi, loosely knitted so it was almost lacy. It hugged my chest and the sleeves came down way over my hands, so it gave me a demure feel, even though the black lace effect with my skin underneath was kind of, um, decadent-ish.

'Better,' said Arns.

I looked at him from under my eyebrows. 'Go and sit down in the armchair,' I advised. 'Near the kitchen.'

'Cool.'

I put a pale grey stretchy camisole on first, with tiny silver beads all along the neckline, over the straps and round the back, then the bolero cardi, then fishnet stockings – black of course, dark blue jeans and shiny black patent-leather pumps with grey satin piping and a small bow.

Next came deodorant – lots of; perfume – little of; make-up – less of. I attacked the hair with the straightening irons and was doing so well until Arns called:

'I'm bored.'

'And my arms are tired. You could be of use. Hey! I haven't told you about Sophie Wenger!'

Arns appeared in the doorway.

'You look nice.'

'Thanks. She *is* seeing Vincent Harrow and they *were* the ones in Mum's office. Can you kind of pull the irons through my hair like I'm doing here?'

'I'm not sure. It looks really scientific.' He was already moving over. 'So what's the next step?'

'Mum's asking Security to get the police involved again, so you'll have to give us the goss from your mother. Main thing is that we get the papers back before Monday. That's the final appeal date. Nothing at Vince's house, though, and nothing at Sophie's, but they *must* have stashed them *somewhere*.'

'So we have the weekend,' said Arns absently. It was quiet

while Arns read the instruction manual for the straightening irons, refusing to 'operate a machine without suitable instruction'. When he was fully instructed, I sipped a glass of water while Arns swept pieces of hair gently through the irons. I started to relax.

'Who was on the phone earlier?' he asked after a ten-minute discussion on the merits of semi-skimmed over full-fat milk.

'Uh, a guy I know.'

'Bludgeon. What are you talking to him about?'

'Geez!'

'I wasn't eavesdropping. He's loud. And I have detective parentage. No disguising that accent out here in the provinces either.'

'He thinks he's down with the Londoners.'

'He does try hard,' conceded Arns. 'Are you worried about that time you thought someone followed you home? Or are you digging the dirt on Ben?' His face lit up in a smile.

I looked at Arnold in confusion, examining his reflection carefully in the mirror. 'Dude. Do you not like Ben?'

'What's not to like?' he said carefully. 'It's just that Carrie said –'

Rrriiiiiiing riiiiiiiing – riiiiiiiiiiiiiiing riiiiiiiiing!

'Every time!' said Arns through gritted teeth.

'I need to get that,' I said apologetically.

'*Voilà, madame,*' said Arns with a flourish, releasing me from the straighteners.

Tripping over his feet, I nearly brained myself on the wall. I whipped up my phone and said, 'Hello?' while staring at him accusingly.

'What'd I do?' mouthed Arns.

A faint voice came down the line. 'Tallulah? Tallulah?'

'Mr Kadinski?' He sounded far away and then the line went dead.

'Weird.' I dropped the phone thoughtfully on the bed.

Arns switched off the straighteners at the wall plug and then looked at me with his head on one side. 'You're looking *fabulous,*' he said in a salon-executive accent.

'Wow, you'd be a great hair stylist!' I exclaimed, checking my reflection in the mirror. I liked what I saw. Straight and shiny blonde hair tipping elegantly past the shoulders, big blue eyes perfectly shadowed and eyelashes doing the business after a *lot* of subtle layering. Lips good – they did look unkissed, but that couldn't be helped. *It would all change in a matter of hours*. Body looking slim, athletic, flab of chocolate gut strangely absent in clingy camisole, no hips – that too could not be helped – long lean legs, if the Gap label jeans were anything to go by, and pretty feet.

This was as good as it got. If it didn't work with Ben . . . My throat went dry and I reckon the pulse hit 220 and stayed there till I made myself think of Jason Ferman's skin condition to calm it back down to a resting 58.

I came down the steps and gaped in shock.

'Delicious with hot water!' said Arns smugly round a mouthful of my chocolate stash. 'Why do you hide them here?'

'They'd better not be finished!' I wailed. 'How did you find them?' I snatched at the bag and stared mournfully at the remaining three.

'Stay calm, Lula. You ready to go? Might as well walk you to the meat market. And tell you what I came to say, which is that the guy with the aggressive door in the library car park had mayoral number plates on his car. I'm not up on local politics, but it could have been the mayor himself. What do you think? Does he drive himself? What does he look like?'

'Thanks,' I said, distracted. 'I'd love company on the way over. Let me just knock on the kitchen window to let Mum and Dad know I'm off.'

Here I was . . . in The Booth. I stroked the red velvet seats, examined the silver cutlery, sniffed at the red rosebud in the vase. The Booth was enclosed by panelling, with a huge picture window on to the world outside. The glass was frosted up to halfway, so the tiny space was contained, yet flooded with lamplight from outside, intimate, but not claustrophobic.

Perfect.

My hair had behaved too. Smoothing it down, I winced as I pressed against the bump near my parting from Arns's forehead. Did I have a bruise too? I was wondering about this and whether to examine the menu before Ben arrived when Mum walked past slowly as if she were looking for someone.

'*Mum?*' I exclaimed.

'Oh, hi, Lula!' She smiled brightly. 'Where's Sven? Or is it Ben?'

I sighed. 'Not here yet. What are you doing here?'

She looked at me mournfully. 'You forgot too.'

'Forgot what?'

'Our anniversary.'

My face flooded with colour. Oh no. Mum and Dad's wedding anniversary. 'Mum!' I stood awkwardly and gave her a clumsy hug. 'Congratulations. How many years now?'

'Ha. Twenty.'

'Wow. This is like a huge anniversary! A big deal.' My voice faded. 'You're not here to celebrate on your own, though.' I went white. I could feel the blood just draining away. Dad's hot date. How could he forget his wedding anniversary for a floozy? Stupid question. I'd kill him. I really, really would. Standing up his wife on their twentieth anniversary.

'Your dad will be here. I just wanted to make sure he hadn't wandered past me. He's not been himself, y'know.'

'I know.' My voice was grim.

'He's getting better, though.'

'Mm.' Something occurred to me and my eyes widened. 'Mum! Did you check the clock? For the surveillance stuff?'

Mum sighed. 'I got no picture, a muffled pornographic soundtrack of Sophie and Vincent for five minutes and then after the desk collapsed nothing at all.'

My face fell, but Mum clucked reassuringly. 'Well, I'd better get back to the table, leave you to Ken. Sorry, keep forgetting his name – Sven.'

'*Ben*,' I ground out.

'Yes, have a lovely time, dear,' and she wandered off after one last look around.

Sitting in The Booth on my lonesome I thought of the last time I was here and suddenly missed Arns and Mona. Double dating was a whole lot less terrifying. I concentrated on the opposite bench, wishing the happy couple would miraculously appear there. They did not. I shut my eyes, took a deep breath and tried again. When I opened my eyes, Ben Latter was staring at me, only the tabletop between us.

'*Yeep!*'

'Didn't mean to give you a fright.' He picked up one of my hands, clenched on the table, and raised it gently to his lips. My entire body broke out into such mad prickles I thought my hair might actually be lifting off my scalp.

'Hellohiohthereyouarehaha!' I gabbled.

'Finethanks'n'you?' he replied automatically, his eyes flickering over the rest of the restaurant. The Booth was very secluded, though his seat had a bit of a view of the other tables. Mine had virtually none.

'I'm fine, thank you,' I said, and took my hand back.

Ben looked at me properly then, and I flushed as I smiled at him, meeting his gaze. He looked like he was about to give me a compliment when a very skinny, very gorgeous waitress headed over to our table.

Please go somewhere else, I willed, but no. Beeline for us. She handed the menus over and asked us what we'd like to drink with a very *lingering* look at Ben. I know she thought her lustful stare was returned, but Ben was just gazing blankly, trying to decide between orange or apple juice.

'Still mineral water for me, please,' I said when she deigned to look in my direction.

Once the drinks order was out of the way, Ben turned to his menu straight away, so I examined mine also. It would have to be that Caesar salad again. With croutons.

Ben coughed. 'Well, I know what I'm having!'

'Yes?' I smiled.

Through the enormous picture window at my elbow, I caught sight of a shadow slowing on the pavement outside. I glanced up above the line where the frosting stopped and met the blank eyes of Jack de Souza for an instant before he walked past.

I knew it! It *had* been him following me all over the place! Bludgeon's info had been wrong. The realisation had my heart yammering away, my palms sweaty. I was relieved it had only been him, but I felt angry and betrayed too. What was he up to? Writing me up as a case study for a teen mag? The problem page, no doubt. My blood boiled.

Ben had replied and his eyebrows were raised at me now.

'Sorry, Ben.' I felt so brave saying his name. How weird? 'What did you say?'

'Said it's got to be the rare fillet. You?'

The image of a recently blooded tongue moving into my mouth nearly made me gag. I swallowed hard, but my voice still came out like a croak: 'Uh, probably the Caesar salad.'

'C'mon. Be daring. That's such a girly thing to order and you don't strike me as that girly.'

'Oh?'

Ben leaned over the table, and I shifted forward slightly too. 'You seem to have . . .' He paused and I found it difficult to breathe. Our faces were only inches apart, and I could see a tiny nick on his cheek where he'd cut himself shaving. I wanted to touch it. With my lips. *Get a grip, Tallulah!*

I drew a shallow breath, and Ben smiled slowly, staring at my mouth now. Oh, glory be. *Was this going to be it?*

But Ben was speaking again. 'You seem to have more to you than meets the eye.'

I smiled politely. The cliché was a disappointment, even though Ben's proximity was not. I wondered what he'd do if *I* kissed *him*. My smile grew into a grin and I tried to bite it back, but Ben said, 'You don't think so?'

'Er, what do you mean?'

'You don't think there's more to yourself than meets the eye?'

I cleared my throat, confused. 'Oh, right. Of course there is – that's true of anyone I reckon.'

The moment had gone. I straightened up a little and fiddled with the beads at my neckline, then checked that my hair was still behaving. Catching myself fidgeting, I stopped. Ben was watching me. He nodded. 'I know people,' he said, and nodded again.

'So there's more to you already,' I said. 'The scientist who's also interested in people.' I beamed.

'Absolutely,' said Ben, and he leaned towards me again.

I held my breath. He pushed the small vase of flowers out of the way and reached for my hands.

COUGH! 'Decided what you want to eat, then?'

Oh, frik. That bliddy skinny waitress was back.

'Caesar salad, please,' I said abruptly.

'Fillet steak, please, Susan,' said Ben, and he explained how he'd like it grilled. She laughed sweetly and said she'd put a word in for him with the chef. His meal would be as good as if she'd cooked it herself.

'I'll have to try that sometime,' said Ben in a low voice as she bent to retrieve our menus, predictably exposing cleavage that had recently seen a tube of self-tan.

Heat flushed my face and as soon as she'd departed I said tartly, 'Do you want to try her home cooking tonight? I can tell the maître d' that I've got a headache.'

'Feisty!' said Ben, and he leaned back, his arms behind his head, showing off a very decent chest. 'Forget that, Tallulah. I just didn't want to embarrass her.'

'If you're interested in people, you'll be glad to learn that leading them on is not a good placatory gambit.'

Frik! What *was* that with the vocab? Did Pen just creep into my head? I could have bitten my tongue off. (Or maybe not. I was no stranger to tongue pain after that episode with Arns.)

'Intelligent too,' crowed Ben, and he brought his arms down suddenly, propping his elbows on the table. 'You are fabulous.'

I was not fabulous. I was gobsmacked.

And suddenly I didn't know what on earth to make of Ben Latter. He was very good-looking, very well groomed, very assured. He should be perfect, but Arns's little wayward comments about my hot date, and that quick look from Jack de Souza through the window, had unsettled me maybe.

Oh, frik. Did I have issues? I did. I had issues. Maybe I was really an ice maiden and now that I was so close to physical contact with a boy I was grasping at straws to find a way out.

No. Not true.

'Thank you,' I said sweetly, though it grated. 'So, tell me how all your research is going. Are you ready to present your findings on Monday?'

'Wha–? Oh, yes. Yes, I am.' He coughed.

'Are you nervous about it?'

'Me? Oh no. I'm used to public speaking. You know, being house captain and all that. Got to do a lot of chat to large audiences.'

I couldn't let it go. I'd have to tease him. 'Oooh, house captain,' I said, but then I stopped in my tracks.

I could NOT believe it.

Guess who was standing across the crowded restaurant!

No, numpty, not Jack de Souza.

My father, that's who! *Here* on his hot date! A petite woman with a short chic glossy bob stood alongside him, smiling up at his face as he bent to kiss her with a laugh and a grin.

How could he bring his mistress to the most popular

restaurant in town? On the night of his wedding anniversary? The man was clearly so sickened by his own disgusting extramarital behaviour that he couldn't even do the extramarital bit properly!

Half the town was here this evening, and he *knew* I was going out tonight – did he think I'd be at Pizza Hut? (Okay, well, maybe. Dad still thought I was ten.)

I watched as my father straightened and searched the restaurant. Would he see Mum and *leave?*

Omigod. What if Mum saw Dad? On his hot date with Freya!

I half stood.

'Tallulah?' Ben was looking at me in astonishment.

'Gosh, sorry. I thought I saw someone I knew.'

He laughed. 'Wouldn't surprise me.'

'Oh.' I laughed too. 'Yeah, it's a pretty small town. I meant someone I had to talk to.'

'Can it wait? I'm enjoying myself here. I still don't feel like I really know you. I don't even know about your hobbies.'

'I-I'm so sorry. It'll take me just one second.'

Ben smiled politely, but he didn't like it, I could tell. Too bad. This was critical.

I scampered after my father. He was heading straight for the men's bathroom. Ms Homewrecker was nowhere to be seen. I grabbed the back of his shirt at the door.

'Dad!'

'T-Bird!' He looked surprised. 'What are you doing here?'

'Go home!' I said fiercely. 'Right now. Mum is here and I won't have you hurting her feelings.'

'Oh, you're here on your date. How could I forget?' He grinned at me delightedly. 'Why would I hurt your mum's feelings?'

'Dad, I *know* about you and Freya.'

'I thought you did.' He sighed.

I couldn't believe he wasn't more shocked. More shamed. 'So leave! Now!'

'You don't want your hot date to see your poorly father?' He laughed bitterly. 'Where is this guy, anyway?'

'Dad . . . please. Listen, it's your anniversary . . .'

'Exactly. A big one too – twenty-one years, T. I'd hoped to get The Booth.'

I blinked at his miscalculation, but wasn't surprised. Then wondered – *was* he actually meeting Mum here? Was *she* his hot date? An image of my mother swam into view, rumpled white hair and flowing caftans, alongside the Ms Homewrecker I'd seen my father kiss a minute ago, with her glam hair and sparkling smile.

'*I'm* in The Booth,' I said firmly, and raised a trembling finger, ready for accusation.

'What? No. You're too young for canoodling!'

'Dad! I'm not canoodling!'

'You should be at Pizza Hut. With aaaaall –' he made a big whole-world gesture with his arms – 'your friends.'

'Not gonna happen,' I hissed. '*Go home.*'

'Where's this Sven, then?' growled Dad. He retraced his steps back into the restaurant and peered across the way to The Booth.

Predictably, he could see nothing.

Sirens wailed outside, cutting through the polite restaurant chatter. Something smashed in the kitchen and heads swivelled from the picture windows to the crash, then back to the windows as the flashing lights of a fire engine sped past. Voices went up a decibel, and a few people half stood in their seats for a better view, but the vehicle was gone.

I saw that Ben had stood too. He didn't sit back down, though, but started to edge out of The Booth. Dad gasped, then clutched my arm when Ben turned to look around.

'That's *Sven?*' he hissed.

Chapter Twenty

'Not Sven, *Ben*! Ow, Dad. What's *wrong* with you? He's looking for me now. I've got to go. *And you do too!* Take your baggage and *go home.*' The last sentence came out tearful and I took a few deep breaths to prevent ruining either composure or make-up.

'I'm not proud of the situation I find myself in, T,' Dad muttered back at me, 'and we'll talk about that later, but I want you to know right now that I'm not happy about you seeing Ben.'

'Oh, *now* someone remembers his name!'

Something crossed Dad's face then, and he had an old look about him that I recognised. It was like we were back where we'd been last year, before he'd started drinking like a sailor on shore leave. 'T,' he started, but I saw Ben coming towards me and broke away.

I headed Ben off halfway across the restaurant, and laid my hand on his forearm in what I hoped was a proprietary gesture that could be seen by my father in the wings.

'Now *I* need a loo break,' grinned Ben. 'I'll see you back in The Booth. Keep my seat warm.' He winked.

I felt my entire stomach flip over, and smiled back.

Thinking quickly, I decided to take Ben at his word. I'd sit in his seat, thank you, from where I had some view of everyone else in Meat City. Everyone except Dad and Mum, though. I leaned out quickly for a wider view and my head caught the corner of Skinny Sue's tray.

Ouch!

Oh geez.

The tray went flying and my special-agent sight slowed the crash to give me an eyeful of how carefully crafted Ben's orange juice was, replete with little parasol and cherry on a stick. My plain-Jane bottle of water and empty glass slid into it and I shut my eyes as the whole lot landed on the floor.

I opened them and whispered, 'Sorry!' as Skinny Sue stared down at her white shirt stained with orange. Her eyes went slitty and mean, and I tried really, really hard not to smile.

'Susan!' said a fat man, waddling to the rescue. 'Have you been on the vodka again?' he muttered in an angry voice that carried too far, providing more entertainment for everyone still watching.

I noticed that Mum's head had popped up over a partition. She was looking at me and gesticulating madly.

Oh, frik.

No time to lose.

I slipped past the debris and made for her table.

'Mum?'

'Lula – I've just had a call. Nothing to worry about, but I need to get home. Can you –'

My heart clenched. 'Is it Blue?'

'No, no, silly. I'll explain when you get back.' I started to say something again, but she stopped me, her hand on mine. 'Tallulah. I want you to have a lovely time.' She smiled conspiratorially and I rolled my eyes. 'Can you tell your dad to get home as soon as he can?'

'Doesn't look like he's coming, Mum,' I said quickly.

'He'll be here,' said Mum firmly. 'Keep an eye out for him and let him know I've gone home.'

'You sure Blue's okay?'

'Blue is very, very okay.' She smiled and I believed her. 'And Pen. Now enjoy yourself. See you later.' She bustled out and I felt a weight lift from my shoulders.

Phew. A bit of space to deal with Dad. I glanced over at The Booth. Skinny Sue was looking put out, facing up to the fat man and pointing in my direction.

Now was not a good time to return. I'd do a circuitous route – back past the kitchen; maybe I'd see Dad and pass on the message.

It was a relief to get behind the wooden partitions that screened the bathroom and kitchen entrances and exits from the rest of the restaurant. It was quieter here, and dim. I was about to round the corner to the kitchen area when I heard Dad's voice, very agitated.

'You're a loser, and I don't want you near my daughter!'

'Who're you calling a loser, mate?' came Ben's voice, suddenly sounding belligerent.

'Don't call me mate!'

'Don't call me loser!'

Dad and Ben?

'Stay away from Tallulah. She doesn't need your crap in her life.'

'I wouldn't talk if I were you! Take a look at yourself.'

'I'm not interested in your opinion of me.' My father's voice was low and very, very angry. 'It's *my* opinion of *you* that counts, because there's no way my daughter is going to go out with an a–'

'Now you just hold your horses, mate! I'm not –'

DOODLIIDIIDIPPDIPIPIPDOODLEEDOOOOO. A ridiculous ring tone interrupted Ben's angry response.

I took a chance and peeked round the corner. Dad was rummaging in his Chanel bag for his phone. He found it and flipped it open.

I couldn't help a grin at Ben's outraged face. He didn't like being ignored. Dad knew what he was doing, stirring this guy up.

'Hello, Anne darling,' said Dad, and my hatred of him flooded back at his hypocrisy. '*What*? Okay. I'll be right there. Love you, bye.' He shut his phone and dropped it back into his bag. 'I'm needed at home. I want my daughter back by eleven. AT MY FRONT DOOR. No funny business.' He was eyeball to eyeball with Ben, who suddenly looked a little cowed. 'And this is the last time you see her. Understand?'

'Whatever,' said Ben sullenly, and he swung away from Dad, back to The Booth. I saw our waitress sashay over to him immediately.

Dad now came careering round the corner, leaving in haste. He didn't even notice me skulking in the gloom. I bit my lip, thoughts whirling.

Something had happened at home, but it couldn't be bad if my sisters were okay. I was going to put that out of my mind. Dad had just shortened all available snogging time. Eleven p.m.? That was so unfair! Last week Pen got back at two a.m. and no one had said a word.

I stomped back to The Booth. Right. I had work to do. And if Dad disapproved of Ben, then so much the better.

'She returns!' laughed Ben. 'You take playing hard to get to another level! Look, our food's arrived.'

I sneezed. My salad had been so liberally peppered it looked like a load of volcanic rock. 'I see you got another glass of OJ.'

'Susan says you headbutted our drinks.'

'Now that's not very nice, is it?' I replied, raising an eyebrow. Ben sliced his meat with precision and raised one in reply. Very sexy. Very, very attractive. 'I didn't see her there, that's all. Did she remember my water?'

'Nope.' Ben laughed. 'Please have some of my orange juice. There's more than enough.'

'Certainly is. She likes you – Susan.'

Ben waved his cutlery airily. 'The one I want to charm is right here.' He quirked both brows and I melted.

'Uh . . .' I replied, and sneezed again.

I picked up my cutlery and looked hard at my salad. Under the pepper, croutons covered every square centimetre of my plate. I started to move them into a tidy heap in the top left corner, scrutinising everything as I did so.

I did not trust this food.

Aha! Just as I'd thought! *That!* That right there! *That* – was not dressing. *That* – was saliva for sure.

'We were talking about your hobbies?' said Ben intently.

'We were?'

'Yes, I know nothing of them.' He fiddled in his jacket pocket and when I met his eye, he flushed shyly and looked at his plate.

So sweet! I thought.

'Mm,' I said, 'I like singing. *Atshoo!*' Singing was socially acceptable, though Tam called my voice throaty – and not in a good way.

'Right!' he said. 'I didn't know – I mean, wow. Are you good?'

261

'Not at all,' I said, and we both laughed.

'Is there something you like doing that you're no good at?' I asked him.

'No,' he said, and we laughed again. This was so lovely! This was worth waiting for – what others didn't get a chance to see – how beautifully Ben's personality measured up to his gorgeous exterior.

I looked at his lips – yummy – and then looked away quickly, but Ben had caught my glance. He dropped his knife and grabbed my hand, running his thumb in a slow circle, ever so lightly, in my curled palm. The intimacy of it took my breath away. A pity because he leaned over the table then and if I'd had oxygen in my brain I would have moved towards him and that would have been it! The first kiss!

Did it happen?

It did not.

I blame the pepper for that sneeze and fully acknowledge that being an inch away from that kind of velocity is a big turnoff.

'I'm so sorry!' I gasped.

'Bless you,' said Ben, expressionlessly wiping his face with a serviette swiped from my place setting.

He replaced my serviette and sat back.

'I –'

'Don't worry about it. Listen' – he turned to rummage

in his bag (very respectable boysy satchel) – 'could you help me out with something?'

'Sure!' I blurted.

'A friend of mine is doing some research for the Science Fair and he's running a bit behind schedule. He was supposed to get a load of questionnaires answered, but hasn't had a good response. Could you do one for him . . .' He rummaged some more '. . . It's in here somewhere. Could you?'

'Fill out a questionnaire for you?'

'Pardon?' Ben was flushed from bending over his satchel. He pulled out a wad of stapled papers. 'Not for me. For my friend.'

'Sure,' I said again.

'Don't look at it now,' said Ben hastily. 'Let's not ruin the mood.'

What mood, I thought moodily. I pushed my pepper and crouton salad away from me.

'Should we just go?' asked Ben, reaching for my hand again, and dropping his voice to a husky whisper. Although maybe all that blood from his food was sticking in his throat.

'Let's have dessert,' I said decisively.

'That might be a problem,' said Ben.

'Why?'

'Our waitress has gone home.'

I looked at him hard. No, I couldn't do it. I couldn't kiss a bloody mouth unless it had been thoroughly cleansed by something before me. 'We need chocolate,' I said.

Ben grinned and nodded. 'The lady shall get whatever she desires,' he said, hailing the fat man across the restaurant.

Pudding had been sooo good. So, so good.

And it was such a novelty having someone interested in *me*. All we did was talk about me, my life, my friends. It was wonderful . . .

Then after very much chocolate mousse we took a slow amble home.

'You're completely different to any of the girls I've ever been out with,' said Ben, taking my hand.

'Uh-oh,' I said, thinking, *Get ready to take this on the chin*.

'I really like the way you were open about your jealousy when Susan was flirting with me,' he continued.

'Er,' I said, wondering how best to put my violent response to him.

'You were very *male* about it. Y'know, just said what you felt. Is that a trait learned from a strong paternal figure, or is that something you've inadvertently learned as a child growing up in a house where the father is perhaps not so very' – he paused – 'manly.'

I was a little astonished. Okay, a *lot* astonished.

'W-w-wha– Pardon?' I asked.

'Oops – too much psych talk,' laughed Ben.

'I can understand the psych talk,' I said sharply. 'I'm just thinking that my dad is actually a very masculine guy, more's the pity.'

'Hm,' said Ben. 'Okay. And your mum? She seems sweet.'

'She has a marshmallow outside and a titanium inside,' I said firmly. 'And my sisters are totally different to me. We bicker lots, but actually . . .' I warmed to the topic. It was fun putting my blood relatives under the microscope. Putting Ben straight. I didn't want him to misunderstand the family he was getting into. (So to speak.)

'And your friends are important to you?'

I stopped and looked at him seriously. 'I've got sisters, y'know, that I love with all my heart. But my friends . . . I can tell them anything.'

'Do you talk about your family with them? Troubles you may have at home?'

I started walking again and he fell in step beside me. It was funny he should ask that. I mean, I *can* tell my friends anything, but sometimes I choose not to. Like the Dad situation right now. I didn't want to talk to anyone about that. I wanted to fix it and make it better, *then* turn it into conversation. A conversation I could laugh in. That didn't mean I didn't think I could talk to the girls about stuff that was hurting me. I can. This just felt different. Private.

All this went through my head, but I didn't say anything to Ben. He was great to talk to, his eyes so soulful and understanding, but the way he looked at me made me feel ever so slightly like I was under the microscope too. *Silly*, I thought. I gave myself a mental headshake. This was how mature people dated. Meaningful conversation. Getting to know each other. *Before* kissing the night away.

'Talking with the girls? *We know every one of each other's darkest secrets*,' I said in a deep, melodramatic voice, like a narrator for one of those supernaturalist shows.

'Do you know your family's darkest secrets?' asked Ben, pulling me to a stop and smiling at me from under a streetlamp. (Note all the bright and efficient town lighting in this place. Not a single corner for romance anywhere from Albert Drive to Wellington Lane.)

'They have none,' I said lightly.

'Everyone's got secrets,' replied Ben, still smiling. 'I hope you feel you can trust me?'

'Sure . . .' I started, but he interrupted by touching his finger to my lips.

My heart stopped.

Literally, folks.

I could NOT breathe.

Then, 'Can I be really old fashioned?' he murmured into my ear as we turned the corner of the high street.

'Old fashioned? You want to walk me home?' I said hopefully when he lifted his finger, keeping it poised over my mouth.

'Of course I'm going to walk you home!' he said.

I grinned and he took my hand, pulling me close. Even though we were both wearing coats, I could feel the heat of him next to me and I wasn't sure I'd be able to get the whole way home without falling down in a faint.

Ben cleared his throat. 'Tallulah, can I ask you a question?'

'Yes,' I answered in a small voice.

'Can I kiss you?'

We were just coming into Hill Street now, under the tall trees that had dodged the moon on the night I'd been escorted home by Jack. My mouth was dry. I couldn't answer.

I coughed, then said, 'A kiss . . . would be . . . nice,' through a wide smile, and looked up at Ben.

His blue eyes sparkled at me in the moonlight. He laughed and said, 'Right, I hope there's a romantic spot on the way to your home.'

'Just past the crematorium,' I said decisively.

Ben burst out laughing. 'Sounds perfect,' he said drily, and squeezed my hand.

You know what the weird thing was? As we walked along, I felt completely safe. No prickling feeling at the back of my neck that someone was watching. No half-heard footfalls

267

behind me. No shadows merging with dark trees and hidden corners. I snuck a look at Ben, tall and confident, striding purposefully beside me, and a smile caught the corners of my mouth. *I'd found my knight in shining armour!* I may well be a girl that can kick a lurker in the groin harder than Jackie Chan, but it's still nice to feel safe around someone.

'Something funny?' asked Ben.

'Uh, just wondering how much further to the crematorium . . .' My smile crept out into a full-blown grin. *I was flirting!*

'It's just at the top of the rise.' Ben squeezed my hand again and smiled back. 'We'll need that quiet corner. Unusual amount of traffic tonight.'

I was still smiling when I put on an American accent and said, 'You come here often?' wiggling my eyebrows. 'How come you know all the traffic patterns?'

I was only joking, but he dropped my hand and said quickly, 'No. I've never been here, actually. Just seems busy for Hambledon.'

'Oh,' I said. I was still smiling, but must have looked a little uncertain because he kind of shook his head and said, 'Sorry, sweetie, cramp in my fingers,' and rubbed them hard.

'Oh,' I said again. Right, note to ridiculous self, too important to put in brackets: Do not flirt. Do not joke. This man means business. And I put the alarmed *Sweetie?*

He's calling me sweetie? thought out of my head.

I wondered how he remembered the crematorium was at the top of the hill if he never came here, but resolved not to ask. It was his turn to make conversation. I watched my feet stepping one in front of the other, reluctant to look up at Ben, and even more reluctant to check the night sky for dead-people smoke coming from the chimneys of Cluny's Crematorium.

If my first kiss had to have the taste of other people settling in hot ash on my tongue, then so be it. My birthday was tomorrow, dammit. Desperate times called for desperate measures.

'What the –' said Ben suddenly, stopping immediately so that I was a few steps ahead of him before I stopped too.

'What?' I asked, turning back to look up at his face.

He pointed wordlessly at the sky ahead of us, and I turned to see what he was staring at.

Oh, dear heaven, no. I'd tempted the fates. I had decided on a kissing place and Now Look.

Cluny's Crematorium was up in flames.

Chapter Twenty-one

'The body ovens are out of control!' I whispered.

'It's not the crematorium that's on fire,' said Ben urgently. 'It's somewhere further on.' And he began to jog forward.

I hurried after him, staring at the orange glow just ahead of us. Ben was right: Cluny's was quiet and dark – the glow was coming from much further down the road.

I suddenly remembered Mum's phone call in the restaurant, and Dad having to rush off.

'My God, it's my *house*!' I yelled, frozen in shock.

Yet another car came roaring by and I only just heard Ben say, 'No! It's the old people's home!'

How did he know about the Setting Sun? I pulled my little bag high on my shoulder and put my head down in a full-paced sprint.

I'd passed him after thirty paces and was still going at a hundred miles an hour when I at last caught sight of my home and the Setting Sun. My house was enough of a distance across the road to make me heave a panicked sigh of relief when I saw the blaze of the Sun on the other side. It was truly immense. Every part of it roared and racketed with a ferocious heat. I could see the framework of it, standing like stark black scaffolding within walls of red, gold and orange. The sound was incredible, like nothing I'd ever heard before – the noise of a monster busily consuming his feast, replete with cracks of bones and thumps and bangs of cutlery on a bowing wooden table. In the shadow of that the emergency services' flashing lights were puny and insignificant, the scurrying firemen with their thin jets of water completely ineffectual.

I didn't stop running, just pushed my way through my street, now packed with people pointing and oohing at parts of the fire that were truly momentous. Every one of Hambledon's sirened vehicles was there. I could see Mum and Dad ushering old people into our house, a lot of them in their night clothes, confused and bewildered, others really upset. Dad held one old lady close to his chest while she struggled and shouted something about her grandson's pictures. As I got closer I saw that even Blue was awake, standing in the doorway in her fabulous cloak, her hair rumpled from being just asleep. She ran from Great-aunt Phoebe's hug to clasp the fingers of the desperate old woman trying to do a mortal injury to Dad. Blue called something up to her, tugging relentlessly, and the white head turned to her, her rage disappearing. My little sister led her by the hand, and the old lady went into the house with her, like a child with her friend, and Great-aunt Phoebe followed them in.

I couldn't stop the thought that had first occurred to me

when I saw the blaze: *Where was Mr Kadinski?*

I remembered his earlier phone call. How it had broken off suddenly. I was now in a total panic. Grabbing a police officer I began to shout questions, but he shrugged and pointed me towards another officer with a clipboard who was calling out to the old people crossing the road to our house.

I was about to struggle over to her when someone in dark clothing caught at my sleeve. 'Tatty. You okay?'

'Sophie!' I said. 'Have you seen an old man with grey-white hair, thin, has a stick . . .' I stopped. 'Hey! This is serious!'

'Take a look at the evacuation,' said Sophie, still smiling. 'Who isn't old, thin, white-haired and carrying a stick? Some of the women could even pass as men. What's his name?'

'Mr Kadinski,' I said, rubbing my forehead where a dull pain was beginning to throb.

'I don't know him, but he'll have to head past Officer Clipboard sooner or later. Why don't you keep an eye out for him from up here?' and she hopped up on my huge tree-stump lookout.

I joined her up there for a better view, scanning the crowd for Mr Kadinski's beaky features. 'So,' I began abruptly, 'Mum said you were working late the night of the office invasion.' I kept my expression carefully controlled. A polite interest, a little concern.

'Uh, yeah,' said Sophie. 'Mabel's been keeping me

copying all the original land claims from the 1800s.' She glanced at me quickly, and I plastered a fake friendly smile on my face. She was encouraged. 'Quite interesting to see that some families have been here for generations.' I raised my eyebrows and she carried on babbling. 'Yeah, your dad's great-grandmother, your mum's great-grandmother, the Pilkingtons, the Clunys.'

'Wow,' I said. 'And did the Harrows build all their homes? They've been here forever too, haven't they?'

Sophie's face shut down. 'They're newbies,' she said in a hard voice. She turned to face me. 'I didn't take those documents, Tatty.'

I raised my eyebrows again. 'Are you still snogging Harrow Jr?' I asked mildly, examining the crowd for Ben and Mr Kadinski.

She snorted. 'Not likely. Little turd.'

'Pardon?'

'That guy . . .' She shook her head. 'He's really odd. Blows hot and cold.' Throwing me a sideways look, she said, 'I couldn't say whether those disks of your mum's got in his bag by accident or not, but getting off on the oldest desk in the library was definitely his idea.'

I looked at her face – the set firmness of it – and felt surely that she was telling the truth.

'Bum,' I said.

'Sorry to deprive you of a suspect.'

'I don't care about suspects – we need the papers!'

'Well, if I could offer a clue?' Sophie's studded brows were raised. 'That card of mine stank of garlic when I got it back. Just like stinky Mike Burdon. I know he made off with it. Him or Mabel. He's wrong – I never lose stuff. I'm very responsible.' She touched her tongue stud to her lips and I nearly laughed aloud, but then I thought, *Yes, actually. She is organised. And responsible.*

'Clue two,' Sophie continued. 'Vince's dad can't take him golfing tomorrow morning. He's got to pick up some "paperwork" instead. Vince is peed off. His dad's meeting is at nine a.m. I don't know where, but you could always follow him?'

'Could be nothing,' I said. 'Could be his tax return.'

'Dirty Harry wouldn't blow his precious son off for a tax return. This is something that can't wait.'

'Right,' I said, meeting her eye. Something was niggling away at the back of my mind. Something obvious. But I couldn't *think* with all this noise and chaos. Sophie gave me the Harrows' home address and hopped to the ground from the tree stump, her pupils going small in the bright light of the fire. Just then another huge crash came from the Sun. The crowd stepped back in a wave, oohing again at the sparks that flew, the flames that leapt higher still. I felt the rush of heat from the disintegrating building and watched glowing cinders land on our ancient picket fence.

I jumped down as the Sun's roof came down with a whoosh, and came face to well-formed chest with Ben.

'You run like a greyhound,' he said abruptly, and grabbed me by the elbows.

Does it make me a bad person that for that instant with his arms around me, Coven's Quarter and Mr Kadinski just kind of faded away? I think it does. It only lasted a second, and wasn't that comfortable, to be honest, because he had something really hard in his breast pocket that connected sharply with my collarbone, clicking and whirring. It hurt when he squeezed me, so in my defence there was no choice but to push away. I laughed. 'Ow! What is that in there? Your gun, Agent Latter?'

Not funny, I know. I must learn that not everyone is a *24* fan. That my interest in the secret service is not universal.

I had ruined the moment.

Ben rummaged in his pocket and pulled out a pen. 'Sorry,' he said.

I raised my eyebrows. A pen does not wound a collarbone. How intriguing! But worry for Mr Kadinski prodded away my curiosity. I glanced towards the policewoman with the clipboard.

'I'd better get going,' said Ben.

What? NO! What was happening here? My knight wanted to scarper. I grabbed at his arm in shock.

'I'm really busy this weekend,' Ben continued, 'so no can

do for another date' – he flashed a placatory smile – 'but would you mind dropping that questionnaire off at St Alban's for me tomorrow? It's really urgent.'

'Uh – wait,' I said, confused.

'In the morning?'

'Pardon?'

'The questionnaire,' he said impatiently. 'Could you drop it off in the morning?' I was too stunned to respond right away. He smiled encouragingly. 'I had a great time tonight, Tallulah. Pity about all this' – waving a hand at the pyre – 'maybe next time, hm?' and pecked me on the cheek before hurrying away.

'Wait!' I yelled, suddenly galvanised into action.

This was my last chance!

And with true love, no less!

He would not, COULD NOT, walk away from me now!

Then I felt someone grip my shoulder and I understood Ben's hasty retreat.

Dad.

I narrowed my eyes.

'Oh no you don't, Tallulah. Let him go. We need to have a conversation about that young man,' said Dad. I looked him in the eye. He met my gaze. 'I'm back,' he said grimly, holding my hand firmly.

I looked past him, my throat tight with anger and dismay.

Ben had vanished.

I tried to shake Dad off, but he looked at me warningly and dragged me with him to the nearest police officer.

He dropped my hand to explain to the officer about the troop of oldies in the house. I watched him for a minute, wondering at what he'd said. *I'm back*. What did that mean? Back from what? His affair? Was he telling me he was back in the family, committed again? Well, what if we didn't want him back?

My throat got even tighter. I was having trouble breathing and it had nothing to do with the smoke.

And then the west wing of the Sun came down with a roar. Dad grabbed hold of a tottery ancient and yelled at me to follow him back to the house.

Yeah, right.

With my dreams of being a normal kissed person now in ruins I had other fish to fry. I latched on to the officer.

'I'm looking for Mr Kadinski,' I yelled.

I could see she was about to brush me off, so I added, 'I'm his . . . step-granddaughter.'

'Miss Kadinski?' she said, her face suddenly concerned.

'Bird, Miss Bird,' I said. 'My mother's side.'

'Right. Where are your parents? Any adult next of kin here tonight?'

'Uh, in my house.' I gestured over the road. 'Anne and Spenser Bird.'

'Oh, okay. We didn't know they were related to Mr

Kadinski. They've already been informed that we received a distress call from the Setting Sun at around seven p.m. and came right over. There was no sign of any problem at the home, so we left, but twenty minutes later one of the carers called to say Mr Kadinski's room was on fire.'

I must have made some sort of sound then, because the police officer reached out to hold my arm. 'Would you like to sit down?' she asked.

I shook my head, nose prickling, eyes stinging with tears and smoke and flying ash.

'Look,' said the officer, 'the fire brigade got here as soon as possible, and there was no sign of any, uh, human remains in that room, and no sign of Mr Kadinski in any other part of the house during evacuation. We're hoping he was out at the time. You sure you're okay?'

I didn't feel okay. I felt *desperate*. But, 'Absolutely,' I said, and a random thought of Ben occurred as I stumbled towards my house.

What a night. Tallulah Bird now formally jinxed for life, a listed building burning before my eyes and one seriously senior citizen missing.

Chapter Twenty-two

It's still Friday night

You'd expect the air around a fire like that to be thick with smoke, but a breeze was blowing it all into the woods. It seemed less busy out on the street now; people were looking at their watches, shaking their heads and piling into cars to go home. They'd be back for sure tomorrow, I thought, just to see the full horror in the light of day.

If I'd been less fraught about Mr Kadinski I would have laughed at Boodle gently shepherding the last old people towards our gate with little nudges of her nose. She seemed to know who needed taking care of, and who needed to move out of the way. She turned and loped back over the road towards me just as a left-hand-drive Datsun '79 screeched to a halt an inch from my kneecaps. The car missed Boodle by a nose hair, but she was too far into her stride to stop. With a little spring from her back legs she simply leapt on to the bonnet, skittered over the paintwork and lolloped off the other side, forelegs on my shoulders.

The ground was cold and wet.

I hit it hard.

I could not breathe.

Boodle gave me a conciliatory slobber and headed

back inside our front garden with a carefree wave of her feathery tail.

The driver's window of the Datsun rolled down with a *clunk-eeee-clunk-eeee*, and Bludgeon yelled out, 'Geez! You okay, T?'

The air heaved back into my lungs with a nyheeeee of breath. I gasped and glared at Bludgeon's bulgy eyes. 'No,' I growled. 'No, I am *not* okay, you frikking frik frik.'

'Whazzat? 'Ang on. Can't get out this side. Gimme a mo.'

I heard the passenger door squeak open, some hurried footsteps and Bludgeon's face appeared an inch from my own. Twitching my fingers, I said, 'Space, space!' and Bludgeon backed away.

'Good thing I'm not, like, into this vehicle, T. Your dog's scratched the bonnet to shit.'

'Good thing you're nearly a relative,' I hissed back. 'Otherwise I'd get Pen on to the Legal Aid people to *sue* you to shit!'

'Geez! Whar I do?'

'You nearly killed my sister's dog, and my sister's dog nearly killed me.'

Bludgeon did not reply, just gave me a hand and pulled me up.

'You don't seem surprised by the fire,' I commented, brushing myself down and wincing at my sodden clothing and a tear on my coat from a Boodle claw.

'Saw it earlier,' said Bludgeon. 'Came round with the final identikit for Mr K to check, but all this was going on.'

'Identikit?'

Bludgeon's face lit up with a triumphant grin. 'Babe, I'm *soo* connected.'

'Yes,' I said, my face deadpan.

'I got ole whazzername down at the station to sit with Mr K while 'e described that lurker. 'E knows a thing or two, that old man.'

'Yes,' I said again, still unimpressed.

'An' thingummy just gets drawin' an' nex' thing y'know, Bob's yer uncle. She's drawn 'im, *an'* she recognises 'im too! I made a coupla calls, did a background check and mystery solved, babe. Mystery solved.'

'You know who's been hanging around me and my house?' I was surprised.

'Babe.' Bludgeon swaggered on the spot, his chest puffed out. 'I'm the man.'

I sighed. 'Who is it?'

'I've taken care of it.'

My eyes widened. 'Oh, God. What have you done?'

'Don't worry, don't worry. All fine. Caught up wif 'im jus' now. 'E was just a student. You wouldn't know 'im. 'E won't bovver you no more.'

'Bludgeon!' I could feel the tendons in my neck start to pop out. 'This is Hambledon. I know all the students! I *am* a student! Or do you mean like a university student? *What have you done?*'

'Geez. You are so wired, babe. If you just chilled out you'd be, like, really attractive.' I took a step towards him, my bag held at shoulder height, ready for a right hook. Bludgeon spoke fast. 'Alls I did is pulled 'im aside, like. Jus' tole 'im to leave y'alone. 'E said no probs, was jus' innerested in your dad more, y'know? Was jus' innerested in 'is problems, yeah?'

That stopped me in my tracks. 'What a frikking weirdo! Dad doesn't *have* problems!'

Bludgeon raised his eyebrows and was about to say something when the front gate slammed open so hard it caught me in the right hamstring.

'Ow!'

'Sorry, Lula!' It was Mum, red-faced and puffing. 'You have a good night? Could you go into the annexe and get out the blankets from the trunk in the eaves? The house is freezing and the Setting Suns are desperate for something to keep them warm.'

'A good curry, like,' suggested Bludgeon helpfully.

Mum regarded him for a second longer than was strictly polite.

'Jalfrezi,' he added.

Mum's head turned slowly towards me. 'This is not Len . . . er . . . Ken?' she said softly.

'It is not,' I said crisply.

Her face brightened. 'Hello,' she said to Bludgeon. 'Perhaps you could give Lu a hand with the blankets?' and she turned and scurried back to the main house, pulling the door closed behind her.

'C'mon,' I said to Bludgeon. 'Help me with the blankets and tell all about the stalker. What's his name?'

I led the way down the steps while he rattled off several versions of a name he'd forgotten.

'You're supposed to be a brilliant supersleuth, Bludgeon,' I said, rounding the corner of the house and rummaging in my bag for keys. 'How can you forget his name? What does he look like?'

'Identikit's in my car. I'll get it when we're done with the blankets.'

I sighed. 'Cool. Sounds like a loser anyway. I'm glad you dealt with it, actually.'

'Yeah, thought you would be. 'E paid me a lot of money to keep 'is identity secret, like.'

'Ah. So you *don't* have memory loss.'

'No, well, I do, but not really.'

I rolled my eyes, opened the door and stepped inside. Bludgeon came in with me and I fumbled with switches till I finally flicked on the lights.

'Eeeeeeeeeg!' I shrieked.

'Waargh!' shouted Bludgeon, and we cracked heads together, each jumping for the exit.

'Yoow!' I yelled.

'Sheeeeeyit!' yelled Bludgeon. 'Get a grip, woman! It's only Mr K!' He slammed the door behind us and headed for the kitchen area.

I rounded on Mr Kadinski sitting like a cadaver in the armchair, snacking on a bag of Maltesers. '*Mr K, what are you doing here?* The whole *world* is looking for you! There are people who think you are dead!' My voice cracked then, and my breath got shaky, rasping in and out like I'd been sprinting a ten-mile race.

'Good,' said Mr K, popping another chocolate ball into his mouth. His thick grey hair was still tidy, but it looked like he'd been running his fingers through it. There was a red welt on his forehead and I saw that his clothes were decidedly . . . sooty.

'Mate,' said Bludgeon, pouring himself a glass of water. 'You were never in that fire.'

'I certainly was,' said Mr Kadinski. 'Nearly didn't make it out.' One of his sleeves slipped down and I saw his wrist, raw and bloodied. 'I'm losing my touch.' He looked me in the eye and added, 'Perhaps I *am* getting old.'

I joined Bludgeon at the kitchen sink. 'Water?' I asked Mr K hoarsely.

He shook his head, and I poured myself the biggest mug I could find.

'I tried to call you, Tallulah,' said Mr Kadinski, through

honeycomb, 'but they got in through my window.'

'They? Who's they? What did they want? This is unbelievable. Unfrikkingbelievable. Where'd you get the chocolate? I thought I'd finished it all.'

Mr K pointed at his rear.

'No!' moaned Bludgeon. 'You got chocolate out your arse?'

I turned to stare him down. 'That's disgusting. You shouldn't be allowed out in public.'

He winked back at me. 'That's why you hired me, babe.'

I rolled my eyes. (They were starting to hurt.)

'I'd never seen *they* before,' mused Mr Kadinski, 'but both of them had construction worker's boots on, so I'm guessing they were from Harrow's crowd.'

'No!' I gaped at Mr K. 'What did they want?'

'My phone.'

'Phone? Why?' asked Bludgeon.

'I got a little video clip of a secret meeting on Monday.'

Bludgeon looked confused, but uninterested. He opened my little fridge and groaned. 'The cupboard is bare,' he muttered.

'Can you get the blankets out of the eaves cupboard in my room?' I asked him.

'Sure,' he said, and ambled out of the kitchen, jumping lightly up the steps to the bedroom. 'Nice,' came his voice from a long way away.

'They got the phone,' sighed Mr Kadinski.

'The police have the files,' I said.

'But the IT expert won't be in until Tuesday to analyse them.'

'Monday's the planning application deadline.'

'Exactly.' Mr Kadinski looked defeated.

'Come with me to the main house, Mr K,' I said. 'The whole Sun's in there, hunkering down for a night of comfort on the Birds' full quota of camping equipment.'

'You've got a lot of camp beds,' he replied, impressed.

'Probably supplemented by the best the fire brigade has to offer. Come on.' I put down my mug and walked towards him.

'I think I should keep a low profile,' he replied. 'I'm the reason for that bonfire over there, and I'm withdrawing my application to be chief Guy. Any chance I could stay in here?'

'Sure.' It took me a minute to process what he was saying. 'You take the bed and I'll make up a mattress here on the floor. Are you saying those construction guys set fire to your room *with you in it*?'

Mr Kadinski raised his eyebrows and grinned. Then Bludgeon appeared with armloads of blankets and I grabbed four of them for myself before packing him off to the main house. 'Can you give those to Mum and ask for the first-aid kit? Oh, and can you bring the identikit drawing back too?'

"Kay,' he said, and shouldered his way out of the door into the orange glow outside.

BONG!

My head jerked to look at my computer, open on my MSN page.

'*You did not,*' I shrieked, '*log on to my computer?*'

'Apologies,' said Mr Kadinski mildly. 'I wanted to check through picture files on the Hambledon University site. See if any matched the men I saw in the woods. Really I should have got the identikit woman to draw them up, but I know I've seen one of them before somewhere else . . . maybe on campus.'

'I hardly know you,' I muttered, and pushed off the pile of blankets to go over to my machine. 'And you've seen my desktop.'

I ignored the snort behind me.

Yep – I had a message.

Chapter Twenty-three

CARRIE: TALLULAH? ARE YOU THERE?

TATTY BIRD: Yep. What's with the caps lock? No need for any excitement. Newsflash: No damn kiss. There – I've admitted defeat. Tomorrow I am sweet sixteen and never been kissed.

CARRIE: Thank God!

TATTY BIRD: Are you out of your mind? The whole school is going to be laughing at me Monday morning! You guys should never have made your teasing so bliddy public. I'm ruined.

CARRIE: Rubbish – now just stay online so I can tell you some stuff, please. Ben Latter is not a science student!

TATTY BIRD: He so is. With a load of brainy friends. I've got to do some questionnaire for some research –

'You type really fast,' said Mr K, from behind me.

I turned to look at him. His head was back against the top of the chair, his eyes closed, his body relaxed.

'I do,' I replied. 'It's a special-agent skill.'

He smiled, eyes still closed. 'Don't be upset,' he said softly, 'when Bludgeon comes back with that drawing.'

My forehead wrinkled in confusion. 'What do you mean?' I asked.

But Mr K was silent. He looked like he'd fallen asleep.

I had a moment of angst: what was the risk of chocolate drool on the heirloom's antique satin?

With a sigh, I turned back to my screen and continued typing:

— that a friend of his needs for the Science Fair opener on Monday.
CARRIE: Have you looked at it yet? Go and get it. Tell me what it says.

I pushed away from my desk and stretched over to the kitchen counter for my bag as Bludgeon burst back in the door. I jumped; Mr K didn't move a muscle.

'What is wrong with you?' I hissed. 'He's old. Banging in like that could kill the man!'

Mr K laughed.

'Oh, so you're awake, are you?' I called over. 'Don't laugh at me, Mr Kadinski. You have the open wound – I have the neat Dettol. It would hurt. A lot.' I snatched the first-aid kit from Bludgeon and he closed the door, tossing a piece of paper on the counter. Closing in on Mr K with evil intent, I got out the antiseptic. 'Let's have those wrists,' I said with a nurse-ish smile.

'Oh no you don't,' he said firmly, and sat up to take all the paraphernalia from me. He pulled back his sleeves and I winced at the mess his skin was in.

'Mate,' squealed Bludgeon. 'That's nasty!'

'It'll scar,' agreed Mr K, coolly applying neat Dettol to cotton wool and swabbing carefully. I pulled the bin closer and he threw in the bloodied ball. Bludgeon made a small high-pitched noise and moved quickly to the bathroom.

'What did they tie you up with?' I asked.

'Those plastic rip-tie things that ratchet and hold automatically.'

'And you got out of those how?'

'Cut them off with the edge of the radiator.'

'Geez! Some radiator!'

'It's old and broken. Doesn't work. Been complaining about it for months.'

A familiar sound of retching came from the bathroom, followed by *BONG!* from the computer.

'He's not good with blood,' observed Mr K.

BONG!

Sighing, I walked to the counter and got the questionnaire out of my bag.

BONG! BONG! BONG!

I growled and sat back down at the computer.

TATTY BIRD: Are you insane? Hold your horses! What's the rush?

CARRIE: Why are you keeping me waiting?

TATTY BIRD: I'm really busy here right now! You have NO idea what's going on.

CARRIE: You're the one with no idea!

TATTY BIRD: What's that supposed to mean?

CARRIE: What does that questionnaire ask you about?

TATTY BIRD: Hang on.

I pressed the pages flat where they'd been bent to fit into my bag. It was at least twenty pages long. Hoo boy. This was going to take a while.

ANALYSIS OF PARENTAL ADDICTION EFFECTS ON THEIR CHILDREN
CASE STUDY BY FELIX KENNEDY

Hang on, wasn't that the journalist –? I carried on reading.

1. When did you first learn of your parent's alcohol dependency?

Pardon? What was all this about?

2. Do *you* have an addiction problem?

I wondered if Maltesers counted.

3. Do you feel your father's high profile has pushed you/him into narcotic-dependent behaviour?

What?

4. Do you feel your pastimes are attempts to escape the family environment, all being reclusive activities: intense friendships, dressmaking, motor mechanics?
5. If your home environment were a stable one, do you feel you'd be more outgoing and confident, interested in your friends' activities: singing, media, study groups, etc.?
6. Do you feel you relate to people differently because you have grown up witnessing a lack of strength in the paternal figure?

The hairs all over my body were standing on end. I felt a hot prickle on the back of my neck and my mouth was dry. I looked at the header of the questionnaire again and slowly typed a reply to Carrie:

TATTY BIRD: Did you know I was into motor mechanics?

CARRIE: Ha ha! Big and beefy or small and hairy?

She had no idea. One of my closest friends had no idea that I liked to fix cars. The only way a complete stranger could have any inkling about Oscar was if they had been spying on me.

I spun out of my chair and yelled to Bludgeon, 'That stalker! Was it Felix Kennedy?'

The toilet flushed and Bludgeon appeared in the doorway, looking bleary.

'That's the name I was given,' he said carefully.

Mr K shifted in his chair and I saw his brow furrow. He looked from the counter to me and back to the counter. I followed his gaze, got up and reached across the kitchen counter for the identikit I'd forgotten about.

I held the edges of the paper with the tips of my fingers as if it were something foul. Tears smarted the second I saw the beautiful eyes, the kissable lips, the perfect hair.

'But . . .' said Bludgeon slowly, 'I'll tell you for free that there's no such person as Felix Kennedy.'

'Yep,' I said bitterly.

'You know him?'

'Not well,' I said. 'Not well enough, at any rate.'

Bludgeon reached into his back pocket and pulled out a wad of £50 notes. 'Tatty, that guy is bad news. 'Ere's what 'e gave me to keep quiet. I'm not gonna keep it, cos I ain't kept my word to 'im, never intended to, y'know? Think you should 'ave it. Saves you suin' for mental scarrin' wif the stalkin' an all.' He shoved it towards me as I shook my head. 'Don't be a numpty. That's a lot o' fancy dinners an' tarty shoes.' He nodded at Mr Kadinski. 'See you later, Mr K. Gotta go.'

And he gave me a peck on the cheek and slammed out of the annexe.

BONG!

CARRIE: I'm dying here.

TATTY BIRD: Me too.

CARRIE: Oh no. Is it what I thought? Ben Latter has been researching you and your dad for his science presentation on Monday?

TATTY BIRD: I'm so embarrassed. I thought he liked me for *me*. He even *said* that.

CARRIE: Bastard. Listen, don't worry about it. We're on the first train out of here after Alex has said byedeebyes to her dad tomorrow. He's working so we can only leave at about 6.30 p.m. – we'll be in Hambledon about 8 p.m. Was supposed to be a birthday surprise, but we think you need to know there's something to look forward to.

TATTY BIRD: Thanks. I think I'm going to need to wallow, though. Things are not good on the Bird front. Text me when you get in, and I'll update you on my mental wellbeing.

CARRIE: Hey now! Remember you were born at 11 p.m. There's still tomorrow! Technically you're still 15 till 11 p.m., right?

TATTY BIRD: Small comfort, Carrie. I've got no boy options left.

CARRIE: I'm sure Alex will have more hot relatives.

TATTY BIRD: DON'T!

CARRIE: Sorry. Too soon for humour. Listen, forget about the faker. You've got to move on.

TATTY BIRD: I never thought I'd despise Ben Latter. I've loved him for *years*.

CARRIE: Forget him! No time for mourning! Call Bingley Clarendon for a pizza – he'll make you feel better, yes? No! Wait! He's seeing some PSG girl, Alex says. Hey! Billy Diggle for a DVD! Yes! Try Billy!

TATTY BIRD: Laters, Carrie.

I signed out and rubbed the back of my neck. It was rigid with stress, and another thought was niggling away at me, tautening tendons I never knew I had. If the stalker was right about my pastimes, was he right about Dad being a real live alcoholic?

I thought about the last year. All the drinking. How ill he'd been these last few days. I tried to remember some of the conversations I'd heard, and at last I turned to Mr K.

'I'm going to get you some PJs from the house,' I announced. 'You go and have a bath. I'll run it.'

I escaped into the tiny bathroom, ran a hot bath and set out clean towels, a new toothbrush I hadn't used yet and some toothpaste.

'Back in a minute,' I said to Mr K. He looked like a cadaver again, but was clearly alive, chomping on a fingernail with a brow so furrowed he suddenly seemed a hundred years old. A thought of the goons who'd tried to hurt him came to mind and anxiety rose so quickly I felt dizzy. I swallowed it back and legged it over to the main house.

*

The kitchen door was open and the house oddly quiet. Pen was sitting at the table staring into a cup of very black coffee.

'Where's Mum?' I asked.

'Settling wrinklies,' replied Pen.

'Where on earth are they all going to sleep?'

'Tallulah, we have probably the biggest house in Hambledon. Now that the *most* enormous just burned down.'

'Yeah, but most of this place is uninhabitable.'

'By your exacting standards.'

'By my *normal human being* standards.'

'You're a neat freak.' Pen took a sip of coffee and winced.

'You're too young to cope with that kind of caffeine intake, Pen,' I admonished, bending over her cup and sniffing. 'Frik! How many spoons did you put in there?'

'It's filter coffee. I got the machine out the box at last and it's really, really lovely. You can thank me later.'

I looked at a stainless steel and black machine skulking in the corner of the kitchen. It bubbled rudely at my stare and a red light began flashing aggressively.

'Great-aunt Phoebe was not thinking straight when she gave that to Mum and Dad for Christmas. I mean – filter coffee? In this household? Ha! Did you read the instructions?' I asked.

Pen swung back in her chair, threw an arm over the back of it and assumed an arrogant pose. 'It's coffee,' she said, with slitty eyes. 'How hard can it be?'

'Not very, but mayhap too much for a Pen with very little brain?' She spluttered as I continued, 'I hope you didn't serve this up to any of the pensioners. They'll be buzzed for weeks.'

'They're fine and they all loved it!'

A burst of song from a crowd of creaky voices lifted the roof with, 'New York, Neee-heeew YOOORK!'

'I hope there are medical staff at hand,' I muttered, and left the little horror chortling at the sink where she was draining her brew and searching for the coffee-machine instructions.

I didn't see Mum or Dad in the crowd, so I headed for the stairs, peering into Pen's room on the way up. Three beds in there. I didn't see the parentals till I got to the top of the first floor. They were hugging tightly in the hall outside their room, and then Dad kissed Mum like he was rehearsing for the final scene of *Casablanca*.

'Firstly,' I said loudly, 'ew!' They jumped and turned to squint at me in the gloom. 'Secondly, we need to talk.'

Dad was motionless, but Mum nodded. 'Dad was right,' she said. 'We should have had a proper sit-down last week. Let's go to the kitchen while the old folks are still partying in the lounge.'

I went down first. 'Where's everyone sleeping?' I asked.

'Eight arthritics on the ground floor, nine ables on the first in Pen's old room, six in the attic and two in the turret,' said Dad.

'You put old people in the turret? Are you out of your mind?'

'More on that in the kitchen,' said Mum grimly.

When we got to the heart of the home, Pen was very busy with a lot of black tar-like stuff that was mainly dribbling down the side of the bin.

'Oh geez, Pen,' said Dad. 'That machine should have been left for quieter days.'

'I see you're back to your usual self,' she replied snippily, and I squeaked when I saw she had dripped a lot of the coffee grounds on some jeans of mine. I'd spent hours sewing beads across the pockets of those! She held up a hand to me: 'Don't, Lula. A bit of soap powder, a cool handwash and they'll be right as rain.'

'But who'll be heading up the handwash team?' I shrilled. 'Me, Pen, that's who, ME!'

'Girls,' said Mum. 'Sit down.'

Pen and I glared at each other, she dropped the coffee jug into the sink and we both sulked into chairs on opposite sides of the table.

'Can I talk before you lay into me, T?' asked Dad. I looked him over. Despite the frantic night we'd all had –

him especially – his hands shook only slightly and he still smelled of Gio For Men instead of sewers. His eyes were red, but not watery, and he'd said more in the last ten minutes than he had in the last ten days.

'Yes, of course,' I said mildly. 'Let's hear all about your alcohol dependency. Or your extramarital affair.'

'A cross-examination! You sound like me,' said Pen admiringly. 'There's potential. Except that you're delusional.'

I stuck my tongue out at her and Mum said, 'Affair?' and burst out laughing. She got up to put on the kettle.

'Hey!' said Dad. 'I've still got all my hair!'

'I hate to break it to you,' I hissed in a barely audible whisper, leaning right across the table so that even Pen would be unable to hear, 'but *some* women find *balding* men attractive. They mistakenly associate it with maturity. Now, what does *Freya* find attractive? Let's talk about *Freya*, Dad!'

'Tea, anyone?' asked Mum, turning towards the table as she reached for the teabags. She stopped in mid-stretch. 'What's going on? Spenser? Lula?'

Dad grabbed my hand. 'No affair,' he said, leaning towards me and speaking firmly in a clear voice.

'What about your hot date tonight?' I said in a small voice, tears welling in my eyes.

'I may not look it, but I am hot,' said Mum.

'You are,' said Dad emphatically.

Pen and I burst out laughing, not unkindly, and the tears spilled on to my cheeks.

Mum looked from Dad to me, and asked, 'Why would you think your dad wasn't meeting me at the steakhouse?'

'Dad said he *shouldn't* be going on the hot date . . .' I said uncertainly. 'And I . . . I saw him with someone . . .'

'I said I shouldn't go because I still felt so sick! And that was Freya with me, my AA counsellor. I bumped into her as she was leaving.'

Okaaaay. My cheeks flared hot, hot, hot, and I felt myself reduce down to the size of a petit pois. Oh, frik.

So.

One sentence and it all becomes clear.

Dad grinned and patted my hand reassuringly. 'Freya wanted to meet Mum after our final session, but we couldn't find her in the restaurant.'

'Um, what's going on?' demanded Pen. 'What counsellor?'

'Three months ago,' said Dad, looking at Mum, 'your mother started on at me about how very little writing I've been doing. And I argued with her about that, but she got to documenting my movements, in that librarian way she has –'

'All numerically classified,' said Mum grimly. 'Bathroom visits, sleep time, telly time, eating time, what he ate –'

'What I drank, when I drank, when I remembered things and when I forgot them.'

'Dad realised he was drinking, um –'

'Too much alcohol,' I finished. 'Not exactly a breaking news item, but that doesn't make you an alcoholic, does it?' I asked Dad.

'Hell*ooo*? His name is Spenser and he is SO an alcoholic,' cried Pen, shaking her head at my stupidity.

'I'm sorry, love,' said Dad, dropping my hand and running it through his hair.

'Oh, Dad,' I said, and tears spilled down my cheeks.

'Now don't get upset, Lula,' said Mum, coming over to give me a hug. 'I can't quite believe it, but your father has tackled this AA detox with everything he has. Everything. He wanted to be sober by the time our anniversary rolled round.' She looked across at Dad with something like respect.

Dad looked up at us. 'Tomorrow I'm back in my office come hell or high water, to finish a song that's taken me forever to write.'

'That's why you've been so sick,' said Pen quietly. 'It was really cold turkey? All the shakes and vomiting?'

'Yes,' said Dad, fiddling with his thumbnail. 'Addiction is something I wouldn't wish on anyone.'

'Yes,' said Mum, looking at me hard.

I raised my index finger at Pen. 'Oh, you wicked sister. You put that record straight right now.'

Pen grinned. 'Sorry, Mum. I may have jumped to some conclusions.'

'Completely unfounded conclusions!' I yelped.

'Not!' cried Pen. 'What about you kicking the bathroom door down? Mrs Capone has just pinned up a pair of her big pants over the hole for privacy, and all the oldies think that's funny!'

'You shouldn't have got them high on caffeine!' I yelled back. 'And I was upset! Under duress! Not taking drugs!'

'Lu, you're always breaking things,' said Mum sadly. 'You may not have an addiction, but you do have issues. Maybe you should see someone.'

I was speechless at the unfairness of it all.

'Well, hang on a minute. I'm not sure I agree,' said Dad. 'Tallulah thought I was having an affair. She was angry.'

'All the late nights out . . .' I said lamely, not wanting to mention the eavesdropping I'd become so good at.

'I was going to an AA group.'

'His leader there, Freya, has been brilliant,' said Mum. 'Really understanding and so discreet. It's hard going to sessions like that in a place as small as Hambledon. But Freya went to a lot of trouble to keep Dad's identity . . . if not secret, then downplayed. He went into a group of much younger people who have probably never read a poem in their lives –'

'And that's where I met Ben,' said Dad suddenly.

'Who's Ben?' asked Mum.

Dad raised his eyebrows at Mum.

'Not Ben Latter? *He's an alcoholic?*' gasped Pen.

'Ben Latter – your first love, Tallulah?' said Mum. 'But I thought his name was Len, sorry, Sven.'

'What hope have I got,' Pen muttered, 'with this gene pool?'

'What was he doing there . . .?' I asked. The answer hit me with full force.

'He's an alcoholic, T. We actually spent a lot of time together, talking about everything. It was nearly as helpful as my one-to-one sessions with Freya, feeling that someone else was in the same situation. But, that said, I just don't want you seeing him, T-Bird. There's something about him . . .'

'Like that he's a lying, scheming, self-serving piece of sh–'

'Tallulah!' said Mum.

'He is!' I burst out. 'Worse than! He's been following me around, lurking outside the workshop, *pretending* to be an alcoholic, gaining Dad's confidence – all to present a poxy paper at the Science Fair!'

'Hang on,' said Dad. 'Ben is not an alcoholic?'

'He's doing psychology at St Alban's,' I said. 'And he probably found out about what a big poet/songwriter you are while he was trying to get Lily Allen on board with his research.'

'That kid!' exclaimed Dad. 'I'll – I'll – Ben used you?'

I swallowed until my nose stopped prickling. 'He was working on an analysis of the impact of parents' alcoholism on their children. He even gave me a questionnaire – with such obviously personal questions in it, I mean, I don't know how he thought he'd get away with just putting a false name on it.'

'So no first kiss?' asked Pen, appalled.

'Pen!' said Mum and I together.

Pen's face brightened. 'Sweet sixteen and never been kissed! Yes!' She punched the air with her fist.

'That's kind,' I said. 'Thanks, Pen.'

'Rubbish,' she said. 'We can halve the winnings. Thirty quid each off a puny two-pound bet – not bad, eh?' She wiggled her eyebrows.

'Lovely.' I turned to Mum. 'Clearly Penelope has a gambling addiction. Let *that* be cause for concern!'

'Just a savvy boyfriend,' said Pen, tapping the side of her nose like someone three generations older. 'I'm glad we've got this all sorted out, though. Lula's going to withhold information to scupper Slimeball Ben's little project, Dad can call Freya to expose Slimeball completely, Dad is back on track with his writing, and I'm in the monaaay!' She punched the air with her fist again.

'There's just me with my smashed office, missing Coven's Quarter documents and reputation in ruins to bring us all down,' moaned Mum.

'Oh, Mum,' I said. 'I'd so hoped we'd have got the papers back by now.' I brightened. 'But, hey, Mr Kadinski has video evidence of a meeting at Coven's Quarter –'

'Even if I could believe something so very Bond,' said Mum, 'Mr Kadinski's disappeared. That's our real problem.' She rubbed her forehead with both hands and squeezed her eyes shut. 'Oh dear, I shouldn't be so selfish.' And then she screamed so loudly that the singing voices in the lounge broke off, with just old Mrs Bugos warbling the last stanza. We all nearly had heart attacks, especially Dad in his fragile state, and followed Mum's shaking finger to stare out into the night at a pale face looking in at us from the kitchen window.

Being fearless, I was the first to the back door. Also because I recognised Mr Kadinski for a real person immediately, but it's my courage that must be remembered.

'Dear heaven!' gasped Mum, standing up from the table shakily. 'I thought you were a ghost!'

Then she shrieked again when Mr K came round the door in just his towel.

'Sorry, was waiting for pyjamas,' he said, looking at me hard. I rushed off to get him a dressing gown and heard him fess up as I ran out: 'I booted up your computer again, Tallulah.'

I was back down in seconds with the warmest things I could find, and noticed Mum looking flushed and excited.

(Fear not, it wasn't the sight of Mr K's naked torso and surprisingly toned legs.)

'Lu!' she burst out. 'Mr Kadinski thinks one of the men he saw in the woods was Mike! Mike Burdon!'

'No way! Stinky Mike? He's your *friend*, Mum! You think he's really involved?' I came to an abrupt halt. Then, 'Police! Let's tell the police – there's still time!'

'I don't know,' said Mum, still looking shocked and uncertain. 'Will they believe us? He's such a well-connected man.'

'Hardly, Mum,' I said, hands on my hips, my back to Mr K as he struggled into Dad's gown.

'He is!' insisted Mum. 'Day before yesterday he was hobnobbing with the mayor!'

'The mayor? With Mike? Day before yesterday?'

'Yes!' said Mum. 'Sleezeballs, the pair of them. My PA saw them in the car park being all close and matey. Probably arranging a golf game. I should do golf,' she mused.

'Oh, man!' I said. 'I need to call Arns!'

It took a few minutes to wake Arnold from his deep-sleep cycle, but he confirmed what he'd been trying to tell me this afternoon: the conversation he'd overheard was definitely between Stinky Mike and the mayor, about handing over The Stuff tomorrow morning. I hung up and let him go back to sleep.

'Mum!' I babbled. 'Arns must be referring to the same

conversation your PA saw!'

'Exciting,' said Pen in a monotone.

'It is!' I squeaked.

'Michael Burdon, the mayor and the developer all connected,' said Mr K.

I turned round, relieved to see that all of his special-agent body was clothed. 'And we know they're meeting tomorrow at nine a.m.! Maybe Arns can remember if they said where. Shall I call hi–?'

'Mike has booked the rare-documents room for a private meeting tomorrow at nine!' interrupted Mum. 'Claudia Hautsenfurg told me!'

'Could that be it?' I whirled back to Mr Kadinski.

'I wonder if the police could be convinced,' he said thoughtfully.

'Why don't I go in there and put a camera in the room?' suggested Mum.

'The rare-documents room is huge, Mum,' I objected. 'Book stacks everywhere.'

'But they'd probably go to the central area, with the reading table,' said Mum. 'It's the only place with chairs.'

'That's still a massive area, though,' I said, not wanting to sound pessimistic. 'There's too much space to cover.'

'Who's brave enough to hide out in there?' piped Pen. 'They could take a camera and zoom in. Problem solved.'

'I'll do it!' I cried. Mum was already shaking her head at

me, and Dad had his *over my dead body* face on.

'Firstly, I don't *think* so!' said Dad in a withering tone. 'And, secondly, with what camera, T-Bird? Pen smashed ours, remember?'

'C'mon, Dad! Please! Alex asked me to keep covering the Coven's Quarter issue for the *Hambledon Herald*. I could have a published story to submit for my term paper. Think of my English results! For once you wouldn't be shamed!'

'Lula *does* need to improve her terrible averages, which have deteriorated so dramatically due to family problems,' intoned Pen from behind.

Dad reddened and blinked.

My mind raced. 'I know someone with a camera. And expertise . . .' I said. My pride would take a beating, but Coven's Quarter was at stake.

'Yes?' said Mr Kadinski, pulling up a chair at the table and lowering himself into it. I was pleased Dad's gown covered his wrists and that Mum and Dad hadn't noticed their mangledness earlier. If they'd seen what Harrow's people could do to a person, there'd be no chance of me being involved in this, and something made me, *me*, want to stop the development in its tracks. Forever. Something . . . I glanced at Grandma Bird's chicken claw hanging from the rafters and I swear it was waving gently at me.

I cleared my throat. It was time for parental manipulation. '*Arnold Trenchard*'s [with heavy emphasis and wide eyes at

Mum] girlfriend's brother is an investigative journalist . . .'

'He's such a lovely boy – Arnold, I mean,' said Mum mistily to Dad.

I gave her a look and continued: 'Well, *Arnold Trenchard*'s girlfriend's brother is studying at uni to be an investigative journalist – and he's got loads of equipment, and I'm sure he'd *love* to be involved in a scoop! He's – he's really *big*!'

'He's really big?' Pen leaned forward, her eyes wide in disbelief. '*Really big?* Like, how is that relevant?'

I was about to say that he could handle goons with his height and strength, but then I remembered that any mention of violence would have my parents locking me in my room all weekend.

'Uh, he can reach up really high to hide his listening devices!'

'Does he have that kind of equipment?' asked Mr K.

I thought back to Alex's ravings about Cousin Jack, and rattled off some specs.

'Let's give him a call,' said Mr Kadinski.

'It's two in the morning!' said Pen. 'Does no one but me think that this is a very, very bad idea?'

Mum sat back down at the table. 'Pen, ordinarily I'd also be pooh-poohing all these outrageous suggestions, but the police have done nothing to help and this is Grandma Bird's magical place. A place that has been in existence probably for thousands of years. Those stolen documents that might be handed over to a shredding machine tomorrow morning could save a place that not only is a part of our family story, but means more than any of us could imagine to this country's spiritual heritage too.'

Dad nodded. He picked up the handset and held it out to me. 'Let's call this guy.'

Prostrating myself with apologies to Jack in front of everyone else would be horrible. I coughed. 'Thanks, Dad. I'll just call him from the annexe, if that's okay?'

Mr Kadinksi blinked when I grabbed the chicken claw for luck on the way out, but the rest of the family didn't turn a hair.

Chapter Twenty-four

I had to wake up Alex to get Jack's number.

'Tatty,' she said sleepily, 'you know I support every effort of yours for a romantic encounter, but Jack is not your man. You've burned boats, bridges and, um . . .'

'Bras?' I suggested.

'No.'

'It's not for romance, Alex. It's to save Coven's Quarter. We need Jack's help. If you don't give me his number now, I'll just have to phone Arns, who'll phone Mona, who'll then have to phone me. That's twice as many people again to inconvenience.'

'Two.'

'Y'have the number?'

Alex sighed and rattled it off to me and I wrote it down. 'Good thing I can sleep on the train tomorrow,' she grumbled.

'Can't wait to see you!' I said.

Alex grunted and hung up. I pressed the hang-up button too, and dialled the number in front of me. It rang for a while before a very groggy person answered.

'H'lo?'

'Hi, Jack, it's Tallulah.'

Silence.

'I want to apologise for thinking you may be the person following me around.'

'You've figured out it was Ben Latter,' stated Jack, sounding a little more awake.

My face flushed. 'You know?'

He sighed. 'I'm sorry. I know you liked him.'

'No, I'm sorry,' I said, my face going even hotter. 'I don't know what I saw in him. Or why I thought it was you lurking around the place.'

'Not many people dislike me as intensely as you do,' said Jack. 'I reckon it's because I was chivalrous walking you home, and you're one of those bra-burners who wants to be independent, so I stepped on your toes.'

'No!' I said. 'Though I burn bridges and boats, I've been reliably informed that I am not a bra-burner.'

Jack snorted, unimpressed.

'Look,' I said, digging my nails into my palm, 'I am really sorry, and I hope you can take that into account when I ask you for a very big favour.'

'You're not serious.'

A thought occurred to me. 'Actually, *I'm* going to be doing *you* a favour. Consider it my balm for your wounded soul.'

'I'm listening.'

'We've figured out who's involved in the disappearance of the Coven's Quarter documents.'

'Oh?'

'But the police aren't interested. They've got video footage implicating Michael Burdon from the library and another man, probably from Harrow Construction, but they can only analyse it on Tuesday.'

'So?'

'So, Monday afternoon, after the final hearing at the civic offices, the bulldozers move in. Really Coven's Quarter is all about the stones, isn't it? It'll take an hour at most to rip up thousands of years of history.'

'Okay. What do you want me to do?'

'Well, there's a meeting tomorrow morning in the uni library's rare-documents room. Mike Burdon will be handing the papers over to someone – I'd bet anything it's Harry Harrow himself. We need you to tape the whole thing, with sound, for evidence. Nine o'clock. Please?'

'I think the police should be involved.'

'They *won't* be involved.'

'Do you think that's the mayor's influence?'

'Dunno, could be. A bit weird that they can't get a wiggle on to analyse the tapes until Tuesday.'

'My sister's mother-in-law-to-be wouldn't be implicated in that, surely?'

'Sergeant Trenchard! Brilliant!' I cried. 'I'll call Arns right now! Why didn't I think of that before?'

'D'you still need me?' asked Jack. 'The police will probably –'

'Please!' I said, then gritted my teeth. 'Can you be there at, say, seven a.m.?'

'I'd better get some sleep.'

'Great. Thank you, Jack.'

Back in the kitchen we laid plans, Mr Kadinski offering ideas too, and by the time three a.m. rolled round, Arns and his mum had been called and another camera sourced.

We'd be ready if we could just wake up in time.

Chapter Twenty-five

Saturday morning. Yep, you guessed it: my birthday
Waking up was not a problem.

My eyes batted open through a blur of sleepiness to see a walking stick gently tapping my shoulder.

'It's six thirty,' said Mr Kadinski, fully dressed. 'You ready to rumble?' I groaned and rolled out of bed. 'See you in the car,' said Mr K, and he let himself out quietly.

I checked the end of my bed, then looked around the room. Uh-*huh*! So. No presents. Right. Well. Okay, I couldn't help observing that it was my sixteenth birthday, I was still jinxed and unkissed and there was not a gift in sight to ease the pain.

With true secret-agent superspy grit and determination I put this from my mind, threw a toothbrush round my mouth, and scrambled into stretchy clothes and rubber-soled shoes. I found Mum at the wheel of the Renault outside, engine running, with Mr K in the back seat. A small dark rectangular object lay in a clump of weeds on the edge of the drive. What was it? I scooped it up before diving into the car.

We took off with a roar, and ate miles. (Of which there are few in Hambledon.)

'We'll have to park at the sports complex,' yelled Mr Kadinski to Mum.

'Good idea!' she called back.

The sports complex was a pain to get to because you had to drive all the way round the edge of campus to find the entrance, but on foot it was a two-minute walk through to the library.

Sinking back into the seat, I looked closely at the object I'd picked up.

'Ah,' said Mr Kadinski, looking over his shoulder. 'A Dictaphone.'

'Right,' I said, wondering if it were Dad's or Pen's. I pressed PLAY and there was a click and whirr that was instantly recognisable. I switched it off quickly as the memory slotted into place – it was the sound from Ben's chest when we'd hugged. The sound, too, of that silhouette speaking into his machine in the workshop. He must have dropped it last night. This could be his, with all his invasive comments on my life carefully recorded for scientific analysis.

I knew if I swallowed, if I blinked, if I breathed, I would cry. Last night had been such a rollercoaster that I'd not had a chance to think properly about Ben Latter. The evening with him had been so wonderful and – without the moments of Mum and Dadness at the restaurant, oh, and that Skinny Sue waitress – I knew that in one short-lived evening I had moved from a nostalgic *I've always loved you* to a *Wow, I'm really crazy about you*. It had been an amazing feeling. Even though it had lasted a few hours only, now that it was gone it felt like it had left a big hole in my chest.

A hole in my sixteen-year-old chest.

Listening to whatever was on that tape wouldn't be news, but it could hurt, and it would make a badly bad birthday an irretrievably bad *bad* day. Taking a shaky breath, I dropped the Dictaphone out of the car window as we roared into Albert Avenue, letting the cold, noisy air blast my flushed face.

Mum drove fast, and I'd barely got it together as we pulled into the sports-complex car park.

We hurried down the path to the library – well, Mum and I did, but Mr Kadinski just seemed to lengthen his stride. When we got to the front door, Jack was talking in a low voice with Arns, Mona and Sergeant Trenchard. There were bags at his feet that he was pointing to, while the others nodded, looking impressed.

Arns and Mona grinned a dozy hello, while Jack gave me a curt nod, and Mum a polite smile.

'Thanks for coming, everyone,' whispered Mum.

'It *is* two hours till they get here, right?' asked Sergeant Trenchard, looking suddenly alarmed at Mum's skulking behaviour.

'Yes, nine a.m.,' whispered Mum. 'Don't know why I'm whispering.'

She unlocked the door to let us into the main foyer. I introduced everyone, and Mum led the way up the stairs to her department, explaining that it was quickest to take the fire-escape route from here to the rare-documents room. Her office door had been repaired, all the desks neatly straightened, the police tape taken down and fingerprint powder gone.

'Wow,' I said. 'Back to normal, Mum.'

'Nearly,' she said, and pointed at her door.

I squinted.

'Is that a fen raft spider?' gasped Jack, lowering a bag on to one of the desks and unzipping frantically.

'Oooh, he's back,' I said, catching sight of a dark circle of arachnid on the bottom panel of Mum's office door. 'How're we going to catch him again, Mum?'

'You caught him before?' Jack's voice sounded strangled.

'Let's not get distracted,' cautioned Sergeant Trenchard.

'Let's not,' agreed Mr Kadinski. 'But we do have a little time. A fen raft spider is very rare. You know about them, Jack?'

'Oh, yes. Year ten biology project. It *is* very rare. The zoo department would pay a lot for this guy, and I'd love to get a few shots of him before we catch him. Won't take a minute – if no one minds?'

Jack pulled out a small camera from the bag and unclipped a lens cap from a big zoom. He put his eye to the eyepiece and pressed a few buttons. 'Our shadows are on the glass of the door. Could everyone hunker down a little? And if you could keep absolutely quiet, so I've got less sound to edit out later.'

We did what we were told and I watched Jack move at a crouching prowl towards the office door. Everything he did had a liquid ease about it and all of us were mesmerised. You could have heard a pin drop. Which is why the sound of the library front door opening was perfectly audible, even though it was quietly done. The *click click* of a woman's heels followed, hurrying across the foyer, up the stairs. I looked at Sergeant Trenchard in a panic and saw that everyone else was too. She put a finger to her lips and bounced both palms close to the floor, mouthing, *stay down.*

Someone walked over to a desk and opened a few drawers. Papers were flipped and riffled. Then came the sound of a phone receiver being lifted and the keypad tapped.

'Hello?' It was Tweedy Mabel.

I looked at Mum incredulously. She looked bemused. Jack turned in the direction of Mabel's position and rested his camera on the desk he was hiding behind. I watched in amazement as he angled the little view screen down and sank to his knees, eyes on the image of Mabel.

'Well, I've just come in, but it's obvious there's no one

here.' Mabel sounded a little snippy. 'That's not necessary, Michael. There are no cars in the campus car park or the library car park, and the front door was locked.' Mabel stopped speaking and I could hear that she was fidgeting with papers on her desk. 'I don't want to wait down there! I can see everything from the balcony up here. If I wait down there, Campus Security might see me sitting at the front desk through the glass! That makes no sense.'

Another pause.

'Sit still. You want me to sit still for two hours.'

Quiet again. I was terrified Jack's machine would beep or something, and this whole exercise would prove fruitless.

'Fine, fine,' said Mabel. 'I'll wait down there. Will you call on the mobile or main line? . . . Okay, I'll take it off night service . . . Are you sure the Coven's Quarter documents are still there? I wouldn't want to get on the wrong side of Harry Harrow, Michael. You know the Setting Sun fire last night was all about poor old Mr Kadinski, don't you?'

Goosebumps crawled out all over my body. I glanced at Mr K and saw his face was still completely expressionless.

Then Mabel tittered. 'Yes, I'm looking forward to a *special* thank you, Michael. From you personally, big boy.' She giggled again and I closed my eyes. The image of Stinky Mike thanking Tweedy Mabel in his own sweaty way was truly nauseating.

When Tweedy Mabel had scurried downstairs, Mr K

turned to Mum with a question in his eyes. She nodded and, bent over, made her way to the fire-exit doors at the back of the office. Arns and Mona followed, hand in hand. I brought up the rear, leaving Jack to retrieve his camera and bags. When we were halfway down the stairs I realised Jack still wasn't behind me, so I stopped and listened. Just the barest whisper of footfalls from the five people ahead of me. I turned, made my way back up the stairs and looked through the fire-exit doors to see Jack easing the huge spider into a clear document filing box. It scurried up the side at incredible speed, but he dropped the lid on top and clipped it closed, totally in control. He saw me looking through the door and nodded coolly.

Minutes later we'd caught up with everyone else, me carrying the biggest spider on the planet in the plastic box. Mum was letting us into the hermetically controlled basement safe that was the library's rare-documents room.

The door closed behind us with a hiss and the silence was disturbed only by a quiet *tick tick tick* of a barometer-type instrument mounted in a glass case on the wall. Mum looked at it nervously. 'We're probably going to upset the temperature,' she said softly. 'Seven bodies under stress.'

'Why are you and Mona here?' I asked Arns suddenly.

'Same reason you are,' said Arns. 'Mum can't trust her police officers – someone has kept Mr K's video clip very quiet and she thinks the files have probably been deleted. It's up to us trustworthy civilians. She'll only call for back-up when we have the evidence we need.'

'Jack phoned me last night,' said Mona. 'This morning, I mean. Asked me if I could hold a camera for him.'

Hn. So much for me not disturbing everyone.

Arns leaned over to ask me something. I knew he'd want to know whether there'd been romance with Ben Latter, so I moved quickly to where Mr Kadinski was examining the central area. He was pointing to the book stacks looming up on either side and discussing where best to position microphones and cameras with Jack. It was chilly in there and I was glad to have my fleecy top.

'I wonder where Mike hid the documents,' I said. 'If he starts hunting around the book stacks, we'll all be seen straight away.'

'Good point, Tallulah,' said Mr Kadinski.

Jack groaned. 'Is this all pointless?'

Everyone stopped what they were doing, and Sergeant Trenchard said, 'I need to make a few calls.' She headed towards the stairs where she'd have more hope of reception.

'Course it's not pointless,' said Mum. 'It's a bit of a gamble but . . .' She scurried down the central area, and fetched a long ladder on wheels from the far end. 'Mike's been tracing the Duchess of Cornwall's family tree,' she called back to us, 'and we were lucky enough to have letters from Camilla's great-aunt to the Cathedral office to work from.' The ladder glided soundlessly across the floor in front of her. She stopped and checked a list of numbers and keywords stuck to a vertical strut of the book stack. 'Now where is it . . .' She started climbing. I checked my watch. 7.42. No rush. Mum stopped, and I could see by the way her arm jerked up to the shelf that she was suddenly stressed. 'It's not here!'

Mr Kadinski came over to the base of the ladder. 'Maybe he moved it to a place where it would be more accessible. With another person in the room, he may have thought he'd be vulnerable climbing all the way up there.'

'What does the file look like?' asked Mona, joining Mr Kadinski. 'We can help you find it while Jack sets up the cameras.'

'Er,' said Arns, looking around him at row upon row, stack upon stack, of identical brown document boxes with neatly typed labels at the base of their spines.

'Frik,' I said.

Mum was looking anxiously across at other boxes. 'It's definitely not anywhere near here,' she concluded eventually.

'I'm sure I'm right,' said Mr Kadinski. 'He'd want the file somewhere accessible. What does the label say?'

Mum gave us the details and suggested shelves to search first. We'd start at eye-level, first stack, and work our way down, me and Mum on the right-hand side and Arns and Mona on the left.

We got going straight away and didn't stop, our eyes and fingers moving anxiously from box to box. I was on the very bottom row, Arns and Mona still had more to go, when Jack called me over to him. I pulled a file out slightly to mark the spot where I'd need to start my checking from again, and ran over to him.

'This is where we're going to sit,' he explained.

'We?'

His eyes flipped dismissively to me and I saw his jaw clench. 'I need someone to hold this sound boom,' he said tightly. 'That okay?'

'Sure,' I said hastily.

'Arnold and Mona will be on the opposite side. Mona with the camera, Arnold with the sound. Mr K said better to have girl-boy combinations in case things go wrong. We don't know how many Harrow will bring to the meeting.' My heart started to patter. 'Mr K and your mum down the far end, and Sergeant Trenchard near the door. Here's how you need to position the boom.'

I listened carefully, then got back to my checking while Jack ran through things with his sister and Arnold. Mum and I met halfway down the bottom row. We looked at each other in despair. 'It's not on this side,' called Mum to the others.

Feeling hot and panicky, I pulled off my fleece, leaving a stretchy black camisole top on underneath, and checked my watch. 8.44. 'Omigod,' I whispered to Mum.

'Not here either,' said Arns, coming over.

'We're just going to have to take our chances,' said Sergeant Trenchard. 'There's nothing to worry about. I'll call for back-up at nine ten when the men are safely in the building for their meeting. Everyone in their positions, please.'

My hands shook as I held the boom beside Jack. The space between us was charged and I just couldn't look at him. He was in an awkward position, his body bent a little to shoot the camera at shoulder height. That way he could focus on faces and then angle down to the top of the desk around which we hoped the men would sit. I peered through the gap between the top of the boxes and the next shelf to see from roughly Jack's viewpoint, and that's when I noticed that I hadn't pushed the file I'd pulled out as a marker back in. It stood proud from the others by five centimetres at least, a clear indicator that someone had been fossicking about in the room Mike had been the last to vacate.

Frikly frik frik!

Chapter Twenty-six

Jack followed my frozen stare. He shifted closer to see what I was looking at, and leaned into my exact line of vision. I could feel his breath on my cheek, ever so slightly, and a small movement sent the hairs of his forearms whispering across my skin.

I swallowed.

I felt hotter than ever.

Focus, Tallulah! I scolded.

'Was that file like that before?' whispered Jack.

I shook my head.

'Will he notice it?'

I nodded my head.

'This could be bad.'

For once I agreed with him. Should I dash out and fix it? Would there be time? As if sensing my thoughts, Jack mouthed *no* at me. Not worth the risk.

I was about to argue when there was a sound from the door, then the hiss of it opening.

'. . . cost millions to build. Regulated temperatures, the lot,' Mike was saying to someone.

Jack swivelled his camera slowly and carefully and lowered his eye to the viewer. Lifting the boom, I leaned into the stack to get the best possible view. Stinky Mike Burdon and Harry Harrow, big cahuna of Harrow Construction, were in the room. The door swung shut behind them.

'I know all that,' growled Harrow. 'I built it ten years ago, remember?'

Even though Mike was the taller man, Harrow's pit-bull stature, his thatch of sandy hair, those little *miss-nothing* eyes rendered him somehow more malevolently powerful.

Mike laughed nervously. 'You've had some interesting projects, Mr Harrow.' He walked over to the table in the central area, and I felt relief wash over me. It was all going to be fine. They were perfectly positioned for us to catch every word.

'Nothing as interesting as Coven's Quarter.'

Mike was walking over to the book stack opposite us, but he stopped and turned to face Harrow. 'Coven's Quarter is just going to be turned into townhouses, though.'

'Luxury townhouses. And once Cluny's Crematorium sells out to me, I'll have the whole of that wasted forest space to build on. It's gonna be the biggest development outside the university.'

'Ah. Yes. Mabel mentioned that Cluny owned the north-west area.'

Harrow laughed. 'She told me first. Did you think you'd use that info to squeeze even more out of me? That's what got me into this tidy little project – her telling me that historical documents show that Cluny owns the mountain from the crematorium all the way to the west side.'

Mike went red. 'She should be reporting directly to me.'

Harrow laughed again, and pulled out a chair. 'Handy, innit? Having a little historical mole like her around. Cluny doesn't know what he's got, obviously. There was once a deed for the Coven's patch too, but that's been missing for so many centuries it's presumed common land now.'

Clearing his throat, Mike said, 'You won't get planning for a development that size. It would change all of Hambledon.'

'Hambledon *needs* to change. Once the new rail line is in, thirty minutes to the city, this will be just another happening place on the commuter belt.'

'New rail line?'

'Yes, Mr Burdon. I have a reliable source – the mayor got a tidy payment from me for that titbit. Not even the councillors know about the new rail line yet.'

'I –' Mike took a step towards the developer, but Harrow wagged his forefinger and leaned back in his chair.

'Nuh-uh uh-uh, Mr Burdon. You've done well here too. Ten grand is a handsome price for the Coven's Quarter documents.'

'Not in the light of all you're talking about.'

'Now don't get greedy. Remember that even if the documents were presented on Monday, my *friends* in the council would refute their significance. But I don't like to rely on others too much. I'd rather they just weren't an issue to begin with. Now, hand them over, please.'

My eyes slid to Jack's, widening in panic. No! That couldn't be true! I thought about Mr Kadinski's video evidence. The attack on him. They wouldn't have gone to so much trouble to shut him up if that were true, surely.

'Why do you want the documents if you have contacts in the council you can trust?' Mike's voice was whiny now. 'Why didn't you just have me shred them?'

'Well now. I like to control such, uh, *vital* information myself. I wouldn't want certain destroyed documents suddenly turning up on Monday. It could cause delays when my bulldozers are ready to move in. Expensive delays.'

'But –'

'Besides, I think I'm going to hang on to these papers. A miraculous reappearance of them once the complex is built will add something priceless to the townhouses. I can see the fancy brochures now: a truly magical home, sited on Britain's earliest . . . I can't remember it all exactly; it's in those documents *you're just not handing over*.' Harrow suddenly stood and Mike took a step back, turning abruptly to the stack he'd been moving towards earlier.

'They're right he– Oh! Tha–'

'What is it?' Harrow's fists bunched.

'It looks like one of the files has been moved.' Mike rubbed at his forehead, perplexed.

'What does that mean? Is there a problem?' Harrow began walking over to Mike. '*I want that paperwork!*' he hissed.

I felt myself stop breathing.

'It certainly is a problem.' Mike put his hands on his hips and looked around as if expecting to see a hoard of file-tamperers with his x-ray eyes.

My heart stopped and I took a tiny step towards Jack, though every cell in my brain was screaming at me to stay very, very still. The silence was so absolute that for a moment I felt claustrophobic, felt how far under the ground we were, how windowless the space was. Everything seemed to be rushing in towards me. All the walls and shelves and even the great height of the ceiling seemed to close in. I thought my legs were about to give way when Jack, eyes still forward behind the camera, reached out and held on to my wrist for a second. It brought me back to earth, but my limbs were still a pile of scaredy-ass jelly.

Mike stooped and ran his finger along the files.

'Oh, that's fine,' he said. 'Must've been me. This is the box the documents are in.'

What?

How typical! I was a total cretin. I'd pulled the file to mark the spot to start checking from again, and had gone on to the next without checking it and pushing it back – it *had* to be that one, didn't it?

Mike opened the box file and removed a very old leather folder, which he placed carefully on the table. He opened it reverently and pointed out the text on the first page. 'It's quite hard to read. Written with a quill around AD 800, and roughly translated from Old English it means: *Keep this place, for it is sacred. Have respect for all its energy.*' He turned another page. 'There's weight to the argument for "energy" meaning "magic", but that's the fanciful interpretation.'

Harrow stepped towards Mike, and though Mike was one of my least-liked people in the world I winced at the twinge of menace I felt in the air.

'*Just give me the damn folder*,' Harrow hissed, all the conviviality of his previous patter gone. 'I should have had this a week ago!' He reached over and snatched it up, pressing it close to his chest.

Stinky Mike frowned. 'I've not caused the delay,' he said, sounding put out. 'There was the problem with payment . . . and I told the mayor to explain to you that there was a history tour last week. Campus Security was here. I couldn't just walk out with some of the most valuable documents this institution holds. And everything's been on high alert since then. The best I could do was hide them here till it was safe to get them out.'

Harrow shifted uneasily. 'And you're sure there's no security today?'

'Very,' replied Mike. 'Everyone has assumed the documents are elsewhere now, and the library is closed for the weekend. Anne trusts me in here on my own.'

My arms, holding the boom at shoulder height, were starting to hurt. I rested my clenched hands ever so carefully on the files in front of me, making sure the boom still stood proud, picking up all the incriminating conversation.

As I took the weight off, a loud *crrrcrrcccrr* noise crackled into the air. Aghast, I lifted my hands back up. The sound came again. It hadn't been my clumsiness, but Sergeant Trenchard's radio, I realised, as yet another burst of transmission echoed across the room.

Mike and Harrow froze to the spot, staring in panic at each other, and then Harrow pulled out a gun and backed into the stack Jack and I were hiding behind. Suddenly we were faced with the rear of his head, thirty centimetres from our noses on the other side of the box files, as he scanned the room in front of him. I could see every shiny black detail of that gun and my skin prickled with a fear so cold I couldn't move. Then adrenalin flooded into every vein and suddenly I saw that it wasn't me that was shaking.

It was Harry Harrow.

With that gleaming barrel pointing this way and that, at

last he cried, 'I can see you, whoever you are, behind those shelves! Come out or I'll shoot!'

As Sergeant Hilda Trenchard came into view slowly, her hands up in the air, I held my breath. 'A police team outside are coming down, Harrow,' she said, still walking towards him. 'And you'd do well to turn yourself in with dignity. You're not going to gain anything by doing something stupid to me.'

'We'll see about that!' hissed Harrow, and he cocked his gun.

Mum says only someone with scant regard for the value of historical documents could do what I did then, but I disagree. I go with Mr Kadinski's verdict that I am a brave and wonderful human being. Though privately I know it was the look in Sergeant T's eyes, changing from confidence to sudden uncertainty, that triggered the tae kwon do kick Carrie taught me last year – lightning fast at knee level – perfect for the job. I smashed the document boxes from my side right through to the next stack and caught Harrow just behind both knees, sending him thudding to the ground.

Sergeant T was on him in an instant. In the same moment, the door to the room hissed open and six more officers flooded in, guns up and ready to shoot.

I was about to jump up and down with wild excitement now that Harrow and Mike were on the ground with revolvers up their nostrils, but Jack hissed, 'Stay with me, keep the sound at shoulder height,' and started moving in on the action, camera still running.

He got everything on tape. The handcuffing, Mum retrieving the documents, Sergeant T authorising the arrest of the mayor of Hambledon and his stick-insect sister, Tweedy Mabel. Even Harrow hissing 'No comment' between gritted teeth to Jack's questions.

When the fingerprint guys arrived, Sergeant T asked everyone to reconvene in the staffroom upstairs for a debrief. Mum started ushering everyone up the stairs, and at last Jack lowered the camera.

'Thanks,' he said with a grin. He took the sound boom from me, checked all his settings and began packing equipment into bags.

'You need a hand with anything?' I asked awkwardly.

He glanced up at me and flashed a quick smile, politely. 'No thank you, Tallulah,' and shouldered all of the bags in one go, moving out of the room in front of me.

The stairwell that had been so silent on the way down was filled with laughter and joking as we headed upstairs. I glanced up at everyone ahead of me as natural light flooded in at the first ground-floor window and, seeing Mona and Arnold squashed side by side in the narrow space, had to swallow a mega lump in my throat. They looked so *in love*. Mum was on her mobile talking to Dad, and Mr K was discussing combat drills with Jack. I felt absolutely exhausted, and awfully . . . alone.

In the staffroom, Mona and Arns got the couch. They were well behaved (I'm guessing they had to be with Arns's mum fully armed) but the long lustful looks at each other left me more nauseous than ever. I flopped into an armchair to the right of them, figuring if I were just at their side I wouldn't have to look at them. I kicked my feet up on a low table, stretched my arms out on the armrests and closed my eyes. A minute later I felt the table shift under my feet, and peeked out under my heavy eyelids. Mr K had settled in a matching chair opposite me, his feet right next to my own. I gave him a little finger wave and he winked back. Someone turned a radio on and a soppy song crooned over the airwaves. Mona giggled and I heard Arns's low tones, making her laugh a little louder.

Oh, geez.

Please. Let this day end.

One by one we had to go into the next room for a debrief with Sergeant T's boss, who didn't look too happy to be called out on a Saturday.

Jack was the first to be summoned, and when eventually he sauntered back to the staffroom he threw himself into a chintz-covered armchair, pulled a laptop from one of the bags and began tapping away at the keyboard like a demented person, his dark hair falling forward, even darker stubble shadowing his jaw.

I was the last to be called. I gave my account of events to Sergeant Trenchard, her boss and another officer whom I recognised from the fire last night.

'Well done, Tallulah,' said Sergeant Trenchard. 'It looks like you played a big part in saving this town's heritage site.'

I shrugged. 'It was Mr Kadinski, really,' I said. 'He filled in all the gaps.'

'His video footage will prove useful in his assault charge against Harrow Construction, and in the public case too,' said Sergeant T. 'I just wonder why it wasn't prioritised immediately.' Her eyes drifted to her boss and then back to me. 'Also, young lady . . .'

Uh-oh, I thought. *What have I done now?*

'. . . I want to say how grateful I am for your superagent moves in the book stacks.' Her eyes twinkled and I grinned. 'Harry Harrow was about to do something stupid and you saved my bacon.'

'Oh . . . u-um,' I stammered.

'Thank you, Tallulah,' said Sergeant T, and she held out her hand, though I could tell she would have hugged me if her colleagues hadn't been there.

I shook it solemnly.

'Well, we're all finished up here now,' she said. 'Would you let everyone know they're free to go?'

'Sure,' I said, turning to leave.

'Oh, and happy birthday, Tallulah,' she concluded, glancing at the information I'd given her. 'I'm sorry I can't be there for any celebrations. Got to get back to the station.' She stood suddenly and patted me on the shoulder with another big softy grin.

Trudging back to the staffroom, I soon felt deflated and very sorry for myself. My first birthday greeting of the day and it comes from a police officer taking down my particulars. Any celebrations would be strictly lonesome ones, though I suspected Dad might have remembered.

Maybe not: twenty-five old people at home and an impaired memory, like thinking he and Mum had been married for an extra year.

I grinned. Maybe I could tell him I was eighteen and able to drive Oscar on my own. So what if everyone knew I was strangely jinxed, with a no-boy perimeter a mile long around me. It would all be negligible in the light of racing Oscar up Port Albert Road all the way to the ocean. With my savings and half of Pen's winnings I could afford to buy a new head gasket, then I just had to put the engine block back in and *voilà*!

I was still smiling at my ridiculous fantasy when I pushed open the staffroom door.

Yowzer!

Instinctively, I dropped to my knees, shielding my head from a chaotic bombardment.

A gazillion party poppers, blow-out tooters and people yelling *SURPRISE!* was absolutely the very best birthday party I could have hoped for. Dad was presiding at the coffee table, holding a very pink heart-shaped balloon with 16! on it (damn – finally it's official) and wielding a massive knife over a tower of cake. And a good thing there *was* a tower of a cake because the entire octogenarian refugee camp had come along to wish me happy birthday too.

'Rent a wrinkly crowd,' declared Pen, gesturing at the room. 'Because you have no friends in Hambledon –'

'At the moment,' I interjected.

She ignored me. 'Don't think the ancients want to pat you on the back or anything – they're only here for the sugar high.'

'Must be hard coming down from the caffeine,' I noted.

Dad came and tied the 16! balloon round my wrist. 'I'm so proud of my girls,' he said, and pulled us to him in a painful hug. We both groaned. 'I *am*!' he insisted.

He wandered off muttering about song lyrics and I said, 'Give me some space, Pen, or I'll spill the beans on why you wanted my bedroom. Seducing Fat Angus! Ew!'

'Don't start on that again, Tallulah,' muttered Pen. 'Don't you get it? I don't believe in sex before marriage!' Mrs Capone burst out laughing as she passed by, and clapped my sister on the back.

Pen threw me a huffy stare and flounced off to cut herself another slice of cake.

I didn't have much time to look around because the lovely oldies made sure I was bombarded with talk and chatter, but, glancing over at the chintz armchair by the coffee machine early in proceedings, I noticed it was empty, and all the camera bags gone.

'I see your brother escaped the mayhem,' I said to Mona a little later through a mouthful of cake. She was holding a saucer with a minuscule wedge on it, carefully cutting off the icing and eating the sponge slowly with a teaspoon.

'Mm,' she replied, perhaps reluctant to talk with her mouth not quite empty.

'Jack took the fen raft spider to some guy in the zoo department. A couple of professors are meeting there right now.' Arns took a sip from a small cup. I noticed with alarm that he was back on the espresso. 'Nobody can believe you found it behind your bathtub. It's supposed to live near water, you know.'

'Yeah, my bathtub's very far from H_2O,' I said, then in a stage whisper to Mona, '*I don't like to wash.*'

Arns rolled his eyes. 'Funny ha ha. Keep that up and you'll be a Lonely Only for a loooong time.'

I stuffed the rest of the cake on my serviette into my mouth to stop myself from ranting a reply. My mouth was so full I could barely chew.

'Ignore her,' said Arns to Mona. 'She's trying to shock us with her heathen ways.'

Mona smiled at me. 'Futile, Tatty. No one's more heathen than Jack. I've endured a lifetime of barbaric behaviour from my brother. Ask him about what he did in the tooth mug when you see him tonight.'

'Tonight?' I looked confused.

Mona nibbled at her cake, and looked to Arns.

'Your mum volunteered your services at Coven's Quarter tonight,' explained Arns.

'My services?'

'Yep. Jack's going up there to finish off the story. Film a tidy conclusion to it all.'

'So what's that got to do with me?'

'Well, he was saying goodbye to your mum and asked if she had any other historical material on the place that he could read up on. She said it was all under lock and key, and would be till the whole planning permission mess is sorted, but that you were the most knowledgeable in town.'

'I don't like where this is going.'

'She said she was sure you wouldn't mind going up to Coven's Quarter to explain everything about it.'

'No way.'

'Completely yes way. Your mum – she likes the guy!' He grinned at my morose expression. 'She's a trusting soul, eh?'

'She just knows there's no chance of hanky panky if I'm in the equation.' I looked at Mona pleadingly. 'Don't get me wrong, Mona – I'm sure your brother is just lovely, but we haven't got off to the best start and I'm just not in the mood to be tour guide tonight. My friends are all back from the city and I'm probably not even going to see them – I'm so tired I think I'm just going to chill out with my family and go to bed. Maybe another time. Can you tell him for me, please?'

Arns looked outraged. 'Don't use Mona as some kind of go-between, Lula! *You* call him and tell him. Your mum won't be impressed, though, cos Jack really wants to shoot tonight.'

'Why?'

'Full moon, and Channel Four wants his story for Monday night's news, once the planning is well and truly refuted at the council's ten a.m. meeting.'

'Mum can go,' I said stoutly. 'She knows more than me.'

'I do not, dear,' came Mum's voice at my shoulder. 'You were Grandma Bird's protégé, no one else. She told you all the stories. You've read everything there is to read on the place. You're *always* up there. Jack seems like a nice boy. Help him out. This is a big deal, you know, Lula. Channel Four!'

I growled grumpily. 'Frik! Okay, *fine*. Fine fine fine.' And stomped over to join Pen for more cake.

'That Jack guy is seriously hot,' said Pen. 'Why don't you snog him as a kind of Plan B?'

'He loathes me,' I muttered. 'I'd need metal restraints to hold him down. What did he say when Mum suggested my services?'

'He –' Pen burst out laughing, covering her crumbly mouth with her forearm, her other arm crooked round one of *my* handbags – 'he was very polite.'

I sighed. 'I hate you, Pen,' I said, and stabbed at a lump of frosting with my cake fork.

Tonight was going to be agony.

Chapter Twenty-seven

Still my frikking birthday

You'd be amazed by how unruly old people can be. Mum tried getting everyone to shift their bones out to the Setting Sun bus at about noon, but it seemed the cake had filled a lot of stomachs and no one wanted to move. They hung around for ages nattering, and nattered on the bus all the way home, and nattered around our living room right up until supper time. I guess there's a lot to talk over when you've got at least eighty years of life experience under your belt.

I will say that although having twenty-five ancients staying with us put a strain on the bathroom facilities, when Madame Polanikov started dancing the Charleston with Mr Kadinski, followed immediately thereafter by a trio of ladies singing a raunchy stage-stomper about men and sizeable organs, I really wanted to stay put. Going out in the cold and dark with Jack de Souza had absolutely no appeal. I begged Mum till I was teary eyed to take my place, but she was having none of it.

'No, Lula. Dad and I have not had a chance to celebrate our wedding anniversary. Once we've had dinner, we're outta here to the cinema and a late-night coffee at Big Mama's.'

'But it's my *birthday*, Mum!' It was the first time I'd really played this one, and I knew I was being unfair. I mean, there'd been so much going on with all of us that I hardly thought there'd be time to pop out and choose me some *stunning* shoes, or a thoughtful range of shifting spanners, but still. No gifts, *and* parents absconding for their own celebration meal?

Mum looked me in the eye, refusing to feel bad.

'Tallulah, I have a feeling you'd spend your special evening in your room mooning over that halfwit Ben Latter, instead of celebrating properly. So . . . this is for your own good.'

'How, Mum, *how*? Jack de Souza –'

'Is wonderful, *wonderful*!' interjected Pen, passing by with a tray of empty teacups.

I was dumbstruck for a second by the sight of my sister being helpful, then: 'Pen! YOU go! You, you, you! You'd love it!'

'You, you yourself,' she said shortly. 'Angus would –'

'Forget Fat Angus,' I said firmly. 'Jack is –'

'Hairy,' finished Pen, pushing the kitchen door open with her back like an experienced waitress, and disappearing from sight with a wink.

Mum laughed at my face creased in disbelief. 'You'll have a lovely time, dear,' she said, patting my arm. 'Hairy is attractive.'

'He's not hairy,' I muttered. Mum laughed again. I

narrowed my eyes at her. 'Who's going to look after Blue?' I asked suddenly. 'You can't rely on Great-aunt Phoebe with all her boozy cronies around.'

Mum hesitated. Then, 'I'm going to tell her you said that,' she said, with a wicked gleam in her eye, before heading for Dad's desk to find the takeaway pizza menus.

'Knowing there are doubts about her capabilities is not going to stop her being irresponsible,' I called after Mum, but there was no reply, just a lot of cheering from the elderly. Mrs Capone had started pole dancing, using Mum's brass floor-lamp as a prop. It could hardly hold a lampshade, let alone a large and voluptuous octogenarian.

'Myyy God!' Dad breathed, staring intently at Mrs Capone's juddering bottom, as Mum shoved the menu in his hand.

I had decided to share my large pizza with Pen, and we were both salivating at the thought of olives, extra cheeeese and artichokes, ready with Bludgeon's blood money to pay for it all, when Pen checked her watch. 'It's been over an hour since Dad put the order in,' she said. 'Do you think Bing lost it on the other end?'

Bingley Clarendon ran the takeaway pizza place on the high street for his dad on a Saturday night. He was an expert in his field, and his only fault as far as anyone could see was that he would shut up shop early if there was a party on anywhere that evening. He had a scary girlfriend. Kitty Manfred made demands and when a social engagement called, Bing obliged. Or else.

'More likely Bing is in the kitchen helping to put together the biggest takeaway order this town has ever had,' I replied. I spoke softly. You wouldn't think this many people were here. It was eerily quiet. We could hear Mum's black plastic alarm clock ticking efficiently away on the mantelpiece along with the scritch of several pencils and the shuffling sounds of cards being organised and handed out – games night had commenced.

'Right!' called Jeremiah Coldstock (ninety-six, folks, and still going strong), standing up near the telly. 'Everyone ready?'

There were murmurs of assent and he drew breath to start calling numbers when there was a loud thud on the door.

'Food!' squeaked Pen, and bolted up the hall.

'Don't get excited,' I called after her. 'That's got to be Boodle wanting to come in. If it were one of Bing's guys, they would have rung from the road. No way they'd risk mutilation by your hound.'

Pen ignored me and flung the door open. I got up to help her get Boodle into her room so the dog didn't go bouncing around a crowded house of fragile people with her wayward tail.

'I knew I had feelings for you,' I heard Pen say to someone

on the front veranda. 'I can tell you I *love* you right now. You want to come in?'

'I'd better,' was the wry response. 'No way you girls are going to get this truckload in without help.'

As he came into view, I stared at Arnold's red shirt. It said PIZZA PERSON on it in big white letters. 'Let it go,' he said, handing me more pizza boxes than I thought I could carry. 'Tonight's my first night.'

'Are you quitting the library?' I asked over my shoulder, going down the hall and into the kitchen to dump the pizza on the table.

'No way! Tallulah, do you have any idea how high maintenance a PSG girl is?' he asked proudly. 'Mona expects, like, *flowers* and stuff.'

'Hn,' I said, returning to the front door, Arns trailing behind. 'You going up to Frey's Dam tonight? Or will you be out buying caviar and Veuve Clicquot?'

'Frey's,' said Arns firmly. 'Straight after this order. Ben Latter's going to be there.' He gave me an odd look, and began to say something, then stopped.

'What?' I asked.

'That guy,' he said, shifting from his left foot to his right, then back again. 'You sure you like him?'

'I . . . I've seen the error of my ways,' I said uncomfortably, and flushed red when Arns went, 'Yessss!' with both his thumbs in the air.

'Why don't you like him?' I asked.

'He's too smooth. Why don't you?'

I sighed. 'Turns out he was just using my small talk as background info on my dad.'

Arns looked appalled. 'Gosh,' he said. 'That's terrible, Lula. I'm sorry. I never got that angle on the whole *I have a famous father* scenario.'

'It's usually not an issue,' I said shortly.

Arns's pager beeped. 'I've got a pager,' he explained unnecessarily. 'Bing says he's closing the shop.'

'Change your shirt,' I advised, and Arns saluted before heading up the hall to leave, calling goodbye to my parents before he went. I watched him pull the door closed behind him, new jeans if I wasn't mistaken – very tasty on his butt, and the pizza shirt was a small one. Arns was getting to grips with his makeover. Definitely safe for him to go solo. I felt all warm and fuzzy with pride.

I went to click the latch when there was another knock and, lo, before us was the gorgeous boy next-door, Dan. We'd all thought he was away for the holidays.

'Whoa,' said Pen. I shot her a look and she went a suitable scarlet. 'I mean, helloa, Dan,' she said.

'Hey, Pen,' he replied, his hugeness filling the doorway, green eyes winking out at her from under his thick browny-blond fringe. He winked at me too. 'Got something for you, babe,' he said to me, unzipping his jacket.

'A strippogram!' squealed Pen, clapping her hands and doing a load of little jumps.

I couldn't shoot her another look, because I too was totally gobsmacked. He really was stripping! Off came the jacket. Underneath was a snug fleece that showed a very acceptable V shape tapering to hips that many a girl probably had smutty thoughts of.

'Come in, Dan!' called Mum from behind us in the hall. 'Did you get it?'

Dan smiled and began unzipping his fleece too.

'Oh, boy,' breathed Pen.

I just *didn't* breathe.

Mum came scurrying up. 'You clever, clever lad! Thank you, Dan!' she sang.

Dan grinned a cheeky grin. He unzzzzipped the fleece with a flourish to reveal . . . a large manila envelope.

'Aw!' whimpered Pen.

'Frik!' I shrieked, noting the label top right. 'Mum! Dad! It's a gasket for Oscar, isn't it?'

'It is,' said Mum smugly. She beamed at me. 'Happy birthday, Lula.'

'Thank you so much!' I said, and enveloped her in an excited squeeze.

Dad laughed and came up the hall for a group hug. 'Glad you like your present, T-Bird,' he said. 'Took a while to get it, but seems like Dan's the man with a gasket plan.' He paused. 'Ooh, good lyric. Better write that down. Cheers, Dan,' he called as he bolted back down the hall.

'Gasket. Huh,' muttered Pen, and disappeared.

'Wow, Dan,' I said, 'thank you! Where'd you get it?'

Dan tapped the side of his nose and raised his eyebrows mysteriously as he slunk out of the house. 'Just let me know if you need a hand lifting the engine block in. Maybe when Darcy's back?'

'Darcy. Sure,' I said, and I was so happy I didn't even eyeroll his lovestruckness.

My phone buzzed in my back pocket as I shut the door. I fished it out. New message from Carrie:

Just crossed the county border! C u at Frey's 9pm? C x

I sighed and thumbed back:

Got to help JdS with poxy film. Grr. T x

Carrie:

Nooooo! We have b'day surprises!

Hmm. Gifts would have to wait. After a frosty session with 'This is Jack de Souza reporting from Coven's Quarter' all I'd want was recovery time back at home, nursing my damaged ego.

My phone beeped again. Carrie:

And Tam's got a new song. Be there.

I sighed. Would I be a bad, bad friend if I didn't turn up to Frey's at all? The thought of going on my own, when slimy Ben was going to be there, was a total downer. I clicked out of the message menu and my wallpaper flipped up: the four of us girls – me, Carrie, Alex and Tam in the spring sunshine, cherry blossoms in the background. I looked at our laughing faces, the way we were hanging all over each other, relaxed and easy and having a great time.

It occurred to me that I wouldn't be alone at Frey's at all. I got a nervous flutter in my chest. Maybe a showdown with Ben Latter was just what I needed.

Chapter Twenty-eight

Saturday night fever

I checked my watch. 7.15. Just a quarter of an hour to brush teeth and lash on mascara before Grumpy Jack arrived.

'What're you gonna wear?' called Pen as I squeezed past the pizza boxes to retreat to the annexe.

'Don't know, don't care,' I said glumly.

But standing in front of my drawers, and the tiny cupboard under the eaves, I realised I did. Not in an *I wanna seduce you* kind of way, but in an *I'm a fabulous girl so put that in your pipe and smoke it* kind of way. 'Nothing wrong with wanting to make a good impression,' I murmured to myself, bath water pounding into the tub in the background as I pulled out my favourite dark blue jeans with the sparkly ribbon on the pocket edges. Fossicking around, I found a plain fitted lilac T-shirt and a soft black cardigan that was so old the cotton trim at the bottom was starting to come off. I didn't care; I loved the drapy sleeves and I loved the small round buttons that shone like oyster shells all the way down the front.

As I jumped in the bath, though, I had a sudden pang. Would I feel okay facing up to Ben in this outfit? I had the fastest scrub ever, threw myself into pretty unders and swapped the lilac T for a sparkly silver mesh top that clung, cough, becomingly to my slim and athletic form. Cough.

I was just brushing out my hair – no time to put it up – and slapping on some lip gloss when I heard Boodle harassing someone at the front gate. 'Jack de Souza is no Arns,' I muttered, and found a bag for my phone, purse and pepper spray. I threw my keys in too once I'd locked the annexe door, then had a thought when I glimpsed my phone. Hm. I got it out while I walked round the house and typed in 999 to speed dial just in case Jack was a mass murderer before putting it back in my bag. I flung the front door open, yelling to Mum and Dad that I was off. Boodle thankfully did not cover me in slobber and drool because she was too busy harassing Jack. Madame Polanikov and Mr K caught the tail-end of my 'I'm gooOOOIIING! SEE YOU LATER!' as they came up the hall, and Madame Polanikov winced. (I think I heard her hearing aid squeal.)

'See you later! Have a nice time!' Mum called back.

I hesitated at the bottom of the steps to the front gate. Boodle gave a final wrooarrf and turned back to the house, leaving a tall, dark silhouette at the gate.

Mr Kadinski patted my shoulder.

'Mum and Dad won't even know if I'm back before eleven,' I grumbled. 'I could be dead by then and they'd still be strolling about the streets of Hambledon declaring undying love for each other.' I sighed heavily.

'I had this Jack boy checked out,' was Mr K's reply, 'and I assured your mother he was fine.'

There was no time to give him a piece of my mind because Jack was already holding the gate open for us, and Madame Polanikov was tottering up, oozing charm.

Jack bowed with a flourish, even with two camera bags hanging from his shoulders and a fluffy sound thingy slung across his back.

'You look . . . sparkly,' he said to me when the romantic couple had started downhill for their evening stroll.

'You look . . . laden,' I said. 'Want me to carry anything?'

'It's okay, thanks,' he replied. 'Listen, Tallulah, this film could be a big breakthrough for me. Thank you for volunteering your services.'

'Um, volunteering?' I asked. 'I think if you hit playback you'll find my *mum* volunteered my services. Which she should not have done.'

'Right,' said Jack. 'Well, I'm pleased to be with the most shimmering girl on the mountain tonight.' He might have been smiling, but he was a step ahead of me, so I couldn't know for sure.

I snorted. 'There'll be a lot of bling up there this evening.'

'What's that supposed to mean?' asked Jack. 'You got buried treasure to show me?'

'Just a party at Frey's Dam. It's not far from Coven's

Quarter. Lots of girls in sequins. No treasure. Seems to me you're going to be disappointed by this guided tour.'

'I think not,' replied Jack, and this time he was definitely smiling because he turned and looked at me.

I stopped and glared at him suspiciously. 'What's with the friendliness all of a sudden?' I sniped.

Jack turned and carried on walking up the road. I fell into step beside him. 'I've always been friendly,' he said to me, pulling a camera-bag strap into a more comfortable position. 'Even when you accused me of being a stalker. It's you who keeps acting like a crazy weirdo.'

I opened my mouth to deny all of the above, but shut it again. It was so not worth arguing with this guy. I just had to get through the next little while and then I'd be fine.

'How long do you need to film?' I asked.

'Not long, if I get the right shots,' replied Jack. 'I'm relying on you to tell me the fascinating stuff. How about we start now?'

'But we're not there yet.'

'Doesn't matter. I need some personal background here. What was your grandmother's name? What did she do for a living? How did she come to be linked with Coven's Quarter? Do you mind talking into this?'

Jack held out a Dictaphone, and I recoiled immediately.

'What's wrong?' asked Jack. 'A technophobe?'

'No . . . uh . . . I've had bad experiences with recorded

conversations.' But I took the little recorder from him and explained about my grandmother. How people adored her and how she helped them. How she was an incredible healer. A warm and funny woman who loved to laugh and sing and dance. I missed her.

'Sounds like she was quite a grandma,' said Jack, taking the Dictaphone from me and turning it off.

'We should have come on bikes,' I mused. 'This road seems a long way by foot.'

'Quite a person too,' continued Jack. 'But not very witchy. So the whole Coven's Quarter thing – just an urban myth?'

'Hardly,' I said, irritated.

'What's that supposed to mean?'

'Clearly you don't believe in magic,' I said, lengthening my stride. I wanted to finish this and get over to Frey's asap. 'And, sure, sometimes *I'm* not completely convinced by it all, but Grandma Bird had a lot of uncanny abilities. There's got to be more to it than just knowing the right herbs for the right ills, you know?'

'Okay,' said Jack doubtfully.

I began speaking faster, then tried to slow down. 'Grandma said she wasn't a powerful sort of witch, because she got too wrapped up in people and healing and stuff to practise all she should, but she looked after Coven's Quarter. That was her responsibility.' I paused, thinking about what Harry Harrow had said at the library. 'Do you think Dirty

Harry was just bragging about connections in the council? That the documents are just a fly in the ointment?'

Jack shrugged. 'I don't think so, but the other councillors wouldn't dare allow planning permission, now that Harrow has been arrested. Sounds like the Quarter means a lot to everyone, not just your family.'

'Mm,' I agreed. 'It's a special place, apparently, because it's a node at which a lot of energy planes converge. Every once in a while other witches would come to meet Grandma Bird there.'

'Other witches?'

'Yep. Not a lot, six at the most, sometimes less. Grandma Bird was always really buzzed after sessions with her cronies.'

'You ever go up there with them?'

'Never. The jinx rumour is bad enough without adding me being a witch to the story.'

'So you're not a witch?'

Something in Jack's voice made me feel suddenly vengeful because of all his recent coldness towards me, even though I knew I deserved it.

'Me, a witch?' I smiled. 'Maybe, maybe not.'

'Huh,' said Jack. He didn't look at all afraid like I'd hoped. 'Well, you certainly can't read minds,' he said, only half joking. 'The whole Ben Latter thing . . .'

I kept quiet, my cheeks aflame.

'What made you fall for him?'

'He got my fairy wings back from Eamonn Higgs before they got bent into jet-engine propellers.' I sighed. 'He was my hero.'

Jack cleared his throat. 'Erm, I take it this wasn't a recent event?'

I ankle-tapped Jack with the toe of a fabulous French pump as he was about to take another step. He stumbled with a curse.

'*When I was six*,' I explained, as if to a non-English speaker. Then I shook my head. 'He was probably in cahoots with the little bully. Let's not talk about him.'

'Let's not. How much further?'

'See the clearing up ahead?' Jack nodded, and pulled at the camera-bag strap again. 'That's where the road ends, and we cut into the woods at that point. From there, about ten minutes' walk. I'd feel much better if I were helping with something.'

Jack stopped. 'Okay. Fine. I admit defeat. Not because I'm lacking in muscle power, okay?' I nodded solemnly. 'Only because I want you to feel part of the team. And because this bag' – he pulled off the smaller of the two – 'is very manageable for someone who can do tae kwon do.' I sniffed haughtily. 'And because this little thing' – off came the furry microphone – 'is just making it hard for me to carry the big bag.'

I loaded up and noted that Jack was right. Neither was

heavy. Both were inconvenient to carry. We speeded up, and stopped again only for Jack to shoot a few views over Hambledon from the clearing. The cloud hung back from the moon till he was done, and then drifted quickly across it, plunging us into near darkness.

'Have you got a torch?' I asked.

'Yes,' said Jack, and he pulled out his keys to show me a mini-mini Maglite on the keyring. He twisted the head of it and a small beam shone out, enough to light up the path just ahead. 'You can take it,' he said, holding it out to me.

'No, no. You take it and go ahead. I'll step where you step. I wouldn't want you to hit the ground with that bag.'

'Me neither,' he said, that smile back on his face.

'Not overly chivalrous, are you?' I said. 'You're supposed to argue with me till I give in and take the torch.'

'If you take the torch, I'm going to hold on to the back of your jeans so I don't get lost in the dark, dark woods.'

'Just teasing,' I said hastily. 'You take the torch.'

'And you hold on to my jeans.'

'That won't be necessary,' I said, more hastily still. 'Turns out I *do* have second sight.'

'Ha ha,' said Jack, and he set off, holding the torch down by his side, so I could see where to step too. It was slow going and I had to grab on to branches once or twice where I lost my footing in the bracken and mulchy earth, but at last the ground began to slope and I could feel that familiar stillness.

'Are we here?' asked Jack in a whisper.

'Just about. Can you feel it?'

He didn't say anything for a minute, just stood still for a while. 'Is it warmer?' he asked then.

'*I* think it is. Alex and Carrie say I'm crazy, but Tam agrees with me. We should measure one day. Prove the presence of energies.'

We started off again, but the slope made it difficult to keep my footing, so I swallowed my pride and held on to Jack's forearm. 'Your damn bags,' I said crossly. 'They keep unbalancing me.'

'Sure,' said Jack, that smile in his voice again. 'Blame the bags.'

'Oh, sorry,' I replied. 'You're right. It is your animal magnetism that's unsettling me. *Yeeep!*' I slipped then and would have fallen hard on a knobbly tree root, but Jack's reflexes were good and he yanked me up before I even went down.

'Thanks,' I said. Then, 'Look,' and I pointed downhill. The trees had thinned out ahead of us and the moon was glowing brightly again so that Coven's Quarter looked like it was spotlit.

'Beautiful,' said Jack.

I let go of his forearm and reached for the camera in the

bag on my chest and Jack took it from me along with the sound device, which he plugged in and held in his other hand. He kept the camera at his eye all the way down.

When we entered the circle of stone chairs, I walked over to my throne and dropped my hand to stroke the back of it. My fingers tingled and I sat down while Jack stood in the centre of the circle, filming each of the other stone chairs in turn. He came to mine and began walking towards me slowly. I stared at the camera lens as he got closer, keeping quiet in case he needed the background noise, or lack of it, for the final mix of his film. He stopped three metres from where I sat, and kept the camera on me. My eyes moved from it to the dark face behind, the thick straight hair falling over his forehead on to the camera itself, just touching the top of his collar. He seemed backlit in the moonlight, his wide shoulders and lean legs forming a strong silhouette in the silver glow. I wondered what his face looked like behind the lens. Serious? Smiling?

His dark eyes came to mind, his craggy nose, the way he always looked unshaven. I thought of his lips, soft and full, his teeth white and even.

My mouth went dry.

Jack lowered the camera, standing in the same spot.

He lowered the sound boom.

Then he placed them carefully on the ground, took off the heavy bag and walked slowly over to where I sat.

Our eyes met. (I know. But they really did, so I'm telling you.) He crouched down in front of me and put his hands on my knees.

I noticed that his face was very serious. I could not speak.

One hand left my knee and touched my lips. Suddenly he was sitting beside me, turning my face to his, his mouth an inch from mine.

'You look like a princess,' he breathed.

'Careful,' I said, and he drew back to look me in the eyes. 'I'm actually a witch.'

He smiled a little. 'Mm,' he said. 'Flirting.'

And then he tasted my lips, and I tasted his and we were kissing.

Kissing.

Chapter Twenty-nine

Blood rushed. Hearts pounded. Moonlight shone. A button may have popped on my sparkly top, but there was no apology and none demanded.

When our eyes finally opened and Jack drew a little away, I saw he was still looking at my mouth with heavy eyes.

'Are you hungry?' he asked in a gravelly voice.

Omigod, I thought. Pen was right. *We're going to go from first kiss to getting laid in ten minutes.*

I think he must have read my thoughts because he grinned suddenly and said, 'It's just that I heard you liked chocolate.' He pulled me up from my throne and over to the centre of the clearing, then bent to unzip the big bag. Folded carefully on top was a bright pink picnic blanket. Jack pulled it out and threw it down on the ground. My jaw dropped. He laughed and rummaged in the bag. In minutes a banquet of my favourite things lay before me.

Tall spindly glasses rapidly filling with something sparkly, salty tortilla crisps, a tiny saucer of chocolate and two bowls of strawberries that Jack was pouring a rich chocolate sauce over.

'Sit down,' said Jack, still smiling.

I sat down, speechless. 'Y-you planned all this?'

He touched my lips with his finger again and whispered, 'Not the kiss.'

'W-w—' I started to stammer.

'I just wanted to say thank you for coming up here with me tonight. I know it was a big ask on your birthday, and I had a feeling your mum was blurring the truth when she said you'd be happy to help me.'

I gestured at the food, and Jack put a fizzing glass quickly into my hand. 'All this to say thank you?'

Jack smiled uncertainly. 'Uh, if I'm honest, probably also to ask if we could start again. I-I . . . I like you . . . a lot.'

I smiled back. 'I think I like you too,' I confessed.

We kissed again, laughing, and ate strawberries and laughed some more and clinked glasses to toast the rescue of a magical place from evil capitalist pigs.

'And the final toast,' I said, touching my glass to Jack's, 'to my first kiss. At last.'

I took a sip and Jack looked at me, confused.

'Hey,' he said, pulling me close. 'I didn't know this was your first kiss.'

I stiffened. 'Uh . . .'

'You're so good at it!' he teased, a glint in his eye. 'I'm amazed that Alex person didn't let me know.'

'Me too,' I said, grinning. 'What's the time?'

Jack angled his watch to the moonlight. 'About ten

to nine. Do you need to get to that party?' His face was suddenly serious.

'Nope,' I said. 'Just checking the timing of things. In just over two hours I really will be sixteen.'

Jack lowered his watch, a slow smile starting up. 'Aha!' he said. 'You were so very nearly sweet sixteen and never been kissed or whatever that saying is.'

'Can I just make sure . . .' I said, moving in.

'More flirting!' he muttered, before I threw myself at him.

At 9.30 I pulled away, with a quick gulp of the last of my drink. 'The girls will begin to worry about me,' I said.

Jack sighed. 'The princess shall go to the ball.' He looked at me and sat up straight. 'Can I come too?'

The Frey's Dam guest list sparked through my mind, and I smiled. 'I would *love* that,' I said.

'Uh-oh,' said Jack. 'Will Ben Latter be there?'

I nodded.

'You want to flaunt your conquest in front of him? Make him writhe with jealousy?'

'Hardly!' I tried to laugh, but it sounded strained. 'He was never interested in me in the first place. Just my dad. I don't think the sight of us in a passionate embrace would make him feel anything at all. I just want to see the girls.'

We loaded up and, with the moon still out, I picked a path through the sparsest parts of the woods, up north

365

towards Frey's Dam, talking and nattering without pause. When we got high enough, reception obviously kicked in. My phone buzzed with a load of text messages, and I pulled it out reluctantly. The first was from Ben:

Hey, Tatty – where's that questionnaire?

I hit delete so hard my thumb hurt, but it felt good. The next message was from Pen:

Just snogged Angus! How does it feel to be pipped at the post?

'Sorry,' I said to Jack, and thumbed out a reply:

I've been kissing since 8.15, little sister. And you were right: HE'S PERFECT!

I hit SEND and turned the phone off. The only distraction I wanted was just ahead – tall, dark and fanfrikkingtastically handsome. He was standing at the top of the rise, his hands jammed into his back pockets, laughing softly.

I leapt up the last few paces towards him and laced my fingers into his. 'What's so funny?'

'This whole town is under your spell, Lula,' he replied, and gestured down below. The still surface of Frey's Dam glimmered with dancing light. It was dark and quiet, but . . .

'What the –' I stared, blinked and began to smile. Below me were a myriad tiny tealights flickering out HAPPY BIRTHDAY TATTY, with three decisive kisses beneath.

X X X

'She's here,' came a voice from near the water's edge.

'Carrie?' I murmured, walking forward a little, now grinning widely. Then I heard Tam strum her guitar and a motley horde of voices sang out:

Happy birthday to you
We promise not to sue
When you kiss us and we get hurt
Cos of your craaaaaa-zy voodooooo.

I burst out laughing and clapped my hands.

'Thank you!' I called. There were shouts and whistles and then the tealights shifted around as groups of people hunkered down to start a Frey's party in earnest. I could see Arns and Mona talking to girls from PSG, Jessica Hartley making moves on a boy I didn't recognise and even Sophie Wenger, who raised a flickering flame in salute before turning to some guys from Hambledon Boys' High.

Suddenly Carrie was at my side. 'Enjoy your b'day surprise, Lula?' she asked, a big grin plastered all over her face.

'Don't take those lyrics too seriously, though,' said Tam, breathless from the climb up to us.

'Yeah,' said Alex, joining her. 'None of 'em will touch you with a bargepole.'

'Great,' said Jack. The girls started. They hadn't seen him in the shadows. He came up behind me and murmured in my ear. 'Means I don't need to get heavy with anyone.'

My friends' jaws dropped. They looked from me to Jack, to me again.

'No way!' said Alex.

'Look!' said Tam.

'Her lipgloss is smudged!' said Carrie.

Jack laughed out loud as I got peppered with their jubilant kisses. Then my best friends in the world scrambled back down the hill with breaking news for the rest of Hambledon.

'Oh boy,' I murmured. 'What are they going to be saying about me now?'

'There's plenty to talk about,' said Jack, pulling me close. 'But for now it's my turn for kisses.'

Acknowledgements

Huge thank yous to my friends, from way back and from right now, in particular (fanfare, please) Pippa le Quesne, editor extraordinaire, who wouldn't let me give up; Leah Thaxton (more fanfare!), publisher extraordinaire, who made this book a reality; Karen Bugos, Jacqueline Thompson, Tamlyn Stewart Strong, Fiona Bell, Shirley Stewart, Kavitha Surana, Emma Gunner and Carrie Pascoe who read early drafts and inspired many words within; Bradley Mackintosh who wouldn't read a word, but is a good kisser (eee! too much information!); and Angeli Söderberg, vital food supplementer and chief advisor in ALL things.

Enormous gratitude to the lovelies who keep me in my day job – I can't write a word without you: Sarah Hulbert, Jennie Morris, Nikki Sinclair, Ellie Smith, Fliss Stevens, Keith Taylor and Wendy Tse.

Thank you to Charlie Viney of the Viney Agency and everyone at Egmont who has taken such care: the wondrous Ali Dougal, boy's-eye view Tim Deakin, Philippa Donovan, Emma Eldridge and Alistair Spalding.

Squeezy hugs to Tam and Fi for sisterly wonderfulness and terribleness, and thank you always to Mom, for giving me the love of words, and to Dad for laughing at them.

Dad, how I wish I'd been more like Lula for you.

An interview with Samantha Mackintosh

(and, err, Lula as it turns out)

Ali from Egmont: Hi, Samantha, do you mind if I ask you a few questions so readers can get to know the mastermind behind *Kisses for Lula*?

Samantha: I will tell you terrible lies.

Ali: Nope, you're not wriggling out of it that easily. Here's an easy one to start off with: where were you born, and where do you live now?

Samantha: I was born in Chingola, Zambia, where it gets seriously hot, and now I live in a village close to London, where it gets seriously cold.

Ali: And if you could live anywhere in the world, where would you choose?

Samantha: I love where I am (it's not always freezing!), but I wouldn't say no to a New York apartment . . . a villa in Greece . . . a cottage in St Ives . . . a farm in the Lake District . . . Y'know. A diddy little property portfolio.

Ali: Is it true you learned to read from watching *Sesame Street*?

Samantha: Yes. And my mum made flashcards too. Things like

HEAD and HAND and HAIRY ASS. Okay, not the last one, but you get the picture.

Ali: Who were your favourite authors as a child, and what books are you into now?

Samantha: I remember crying with disappointment when there were no more Sue Barton books (written by Helen Dore Boylston) to read from our local public library, but I devoured plenty of other stuff, from Blyton to Blume to Boon (Mills and). As a teen I fell in love with poetry: Wilfred Owen, Dylan Thomas, Lord Byron, Sylvia Plath, Ted Hughes, but always had to rely on the antiquated local library. We had two university booksellers with teeny fiction sections, and no money to buy books, so I'm a total book glutton now.

My recent favourites are *City of Thieves* by David Benioff, *The Book Thief* by Marcus Zusak, *This Charming Man* (I love Marian Keyes) and Janet Evanovich's Stephanie Plum series. Also the crime club: Patricia Cornwell, Kathy Reichs, Tess Gerritsen. And literary fiction from the likes of Anne Tyler, Barbara Kingsolver, Penelope Lively and Margaret Atwood. Lordy, are there any books I *don't* like?

Ali: What did you do before you wrote *Kisses for Lula*?

Samantha: I've worked for book publishers, magazine publishers and legal publishers. I've also waitressed, slaved behind bars, sold sausage rolls and worked in a bookshop (heaven!).

Ali: Wow! So what made you decide you wanted to become a writer?

Samantha: When I was nine I got cross about the fact that there were no books for nine-year-olds and decided then I'd write them myself when I grew up. Then I grew up and realised how impossible it is to become a real-life, all-day long, I-get-paid-for-this-lark writer. So that idea fell by the wayside for a long time – but now look! Wahey!

Ali: Hurray! Now you're a real-life, bona fide, published author! So, where do you like to write?

Samantha: I like to write at my desk in the attic, with the heater on underneath and my feet in cosy slippers right on top of it. Sometimes real life gets in the way, though, and I end up writing on the train, at the gym, in the bathroom (don't ask), upstairs in my sister's house, early in the morning, late at night, any chance I get.

Ali: Is there much of you in Lula? Or in any of the other characters in the story? Please say Boodle!

Samantha: I'm afraid, like Lula, I have been known to put on clothes that were left in a crumpled heap beside the bed from the day before. (Always clean unders, though!) And like Lula, I eat way too much chocolate, and –

Lula: Now just hang on one frikking minute . . .

Samantha: Oh no you don't. Back in the head! Back in the head!

Lula: No can do, writer lady. Hey, Ali?

Ali: Uh . . .

Lula: I'd like to state for the record that Samantha's implication that I wear dirty unders –

Samantha: I did not imply! I expressly said –

Lula: Uh-huh, sure. Please note, I absolutely never wear unders more than a day, and I eat chocolate for *medicinal purposes only*! Do you have any idea how much iron there is in choc–

Samantha: That is a total lie. You eat chocolate because you love it and you're a greedy pig. What normal person stashes chocolate everywhere? Sharing is caring, Tallulah Bird.

Lula: Hey! You see the people I live with! You INVENTED the people I live with! Ali!

Ali: I'm staying out of this. Perhaps this is a good point to close the interview –

Lula: Nonononono! It's just getting interesting! To answer your question, Ali: Samantha is exactly like Boodle. Big, hairy, always knocking people over. Especially boys. She's nervous around boys. She only has sisters, you see, so no experience of boys whatsoever. Maybe a teeeensy bit like me there.

Samantha: LULA!

Lula: But she's quite sweet too. You know – she cares about people. Makes sure they get a decent kiss in, even though it's not with the guy you –

Ali: Yes, we know about your first kiss, Lula.

Samantha: Yeah. Put that grin away. I'm in control here. You could end up doing the hula and never getting another snog EVER AGAIN.

[Ed: *Lula Does the Hula*, the second book starring Lula and friends, is coming soon, in case you were wondering.]

Lula: You wouldn't!

Samantha: That depends. Will you be quiet? Will you behave?

Lula: [Obedient silence]

Ali: [Cough] Okaaaay. So, Samantha, tell us about *your* first kiss.

Samantha: Oh *nooooo*!

Ali: Oh yes, or we're not gonna print this book.

Samantha: Okay! Okay! But this is just between you and me, right? It won't go in the book?

Ali: Yeah, sure. [Evil glint in her eye]

Samantha: Right, well, if you must know, I was sweet sixteen and never been kissed, and had *zero* clue about boys. So that's why I welcomed Stephen Measey into my life.

Ali: Stephen Measey? Seriously?

Samantha: No. His real name is much, much worse. Anyway, at first glance he was all right, I guess, but on closer inspection he laughed like a horse, had teeth like a horse, but I suspect a horse would be a much better kisser.

Ali: Huh?

Samantha: One word: HOOVER.

Ali: Oh no.

Samantha: Oh yes! I swear, I thought I was going to lose my tongue. When he finally broke away I was speechless. Well, how *could* a person speak after that kind of action? I just stood there blinking in the sunlight thinking, *Was that normal? IS THIS WHAT A KISS IS?*

Ali: Ew! Enough! Right, any wise words for all those aspiring writers out there?

Samantha: Start and don't stop. Don't ever say you don't have time. If you say you don't have time, I'll come round and wallop you.

Ali: Lula ends up in all sorts of sticky situations in the book. What's been your most embarrassing moment? Go on, spill!

Samantha: Grggnn, fine, but only cos I trust you.

Ali: Oh dear . . . are you sure about that?

Samantha: It was a bright and gorgeous day, the kind of weather you always forget is actually possible, and I was loping happily across Waterloo Bridge in central London, in my gorgeous, swingy, silk dress, bag slung confidently over the shoulder, mad grin on my face. An Australian woman drew up alongside me:

'G'day,' she said.

'Uh, hi,' I said.

'I can see ya knickers,' she said.

Wh-what? Is my dress see-through? I thought.

'Ya bag,' she said, 'it's pulled ya dress right up.'

I looked down in horror, and she was aaabsoluuutely right.